The Long Journey Home

by

Ed Londergan

While *The Long Journey Home* is based on historical characters and events, the book is a work of fiction. Most of the events are real, while the depictions of those types of events common to the period of the story, the characters, and dialogue are products of the author's imagination.

Cover graphics by Belinda Mazur

ISBN 978-0-9893049-1-7

www.edlondergan.com
www.facebook.com/EdLondergan
www.twitter.com/EdLondergan
Published by Indian Rock Publishing

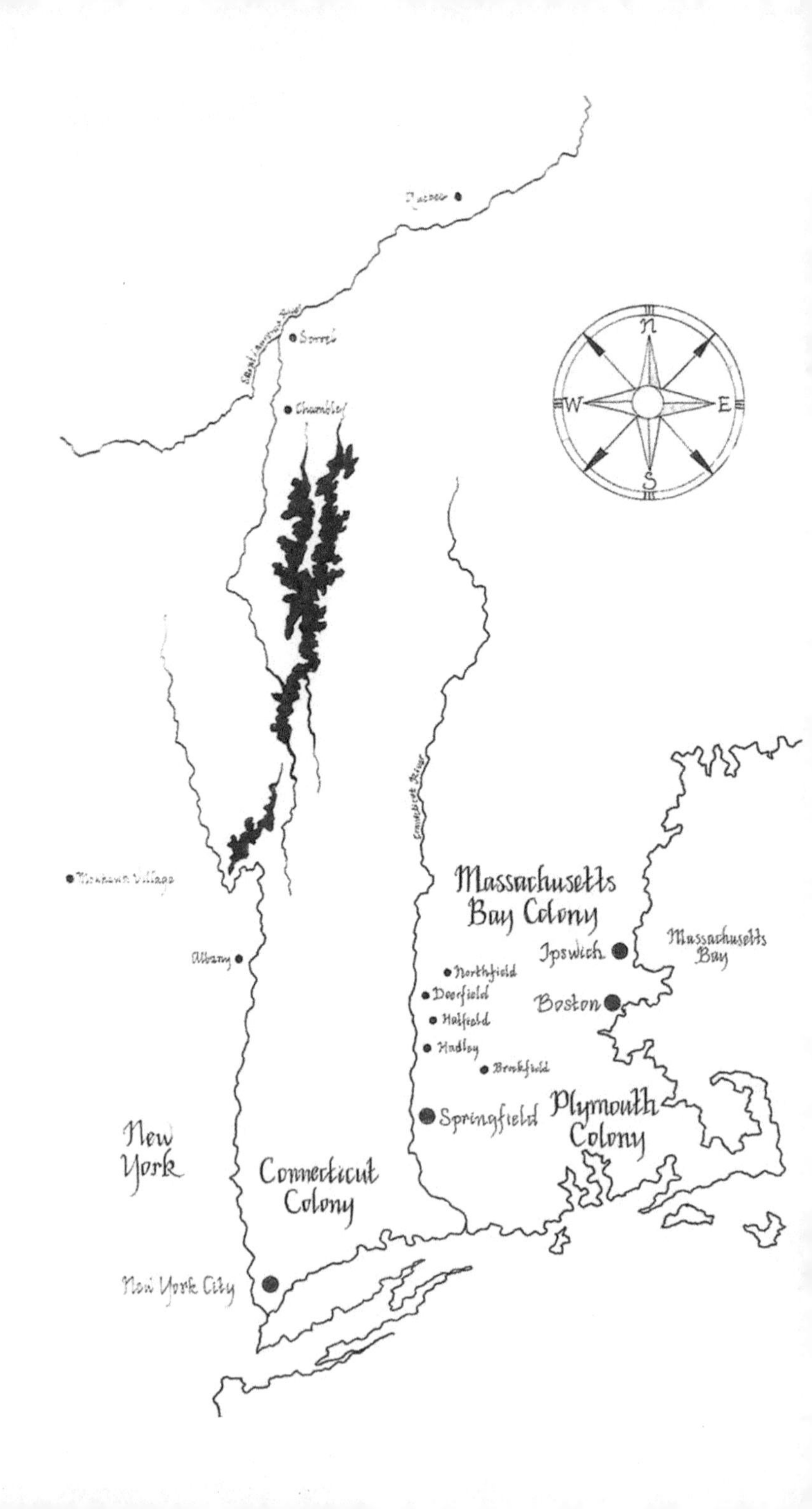

N
E
S
W
Sorrel
Chambley
Albany
Massachusetts Bay Colony
Massachusetts Bay
Ipswich
Boston
Northfield
Deerfield
Hatfield
Hadley
Brookfield
Springfield
Plymouth Colony
New York
Connecticut Colony
New York City

This book is dedicated to my mother, who taught me about life; to my wife and best friend Barbara, who taught me about love; to my grandfather, Bumpy, for telling me all his stories; and to you dear reader…this story is for you.

May 29, 1721

This jotting down of words has become a habit. It began years ago when I was a young man as a way to record the happenings of the day, but now in my old age, it's a way to pass the long winter evenings and lonely afternoons. I now find myself telling this story, a second story for you, seemingly without any conscious thought.

My father told me two things in the few years I knew him: If you have something to say, say it without thought of anything but the truth, and that the measure of a man is how he deals with life's difficulties.

I think of these more often as I get older and I know both to be true. Much of my life has been in turmoil and it has had a great effect in making me the man I am. Through all of it, I never wavered from what I had to do, no matter how good or bad it was. I stood by my family, ready and willing to sacrifice my life if necessary. Through the years, I have come to believe that hope and perseverance are the two greatest values a person can have, for they will get you through the greatest difficulties and most trying times you will ever face.

The older you get, the more important certain people and things become. Through the years, there is a process of weeding out the unimportant things. When I consider those things, I find myself sitting in front of the fire, feeling the soft warmth, staring hypnotically at the flames dancing over the logs. My mind falls back to particular times or moments, some good, some not. We all do this at one time or another but I seem to do it more often now than in days past. As we go through life, our view of the world changes and most of these changes are unexpected. That is what happened to us.

CHAPTER 1

We were alive and that is all that mattered.

When we arrived, it was early evening, with the western horizon showing shades of orange clouds above a band of light blue sky. Becky and I reached Springfield after escaping a brutal three-day siege in Brookfield, twenty-five miles to the east, along with ninety-seven others. It was one of the first attacks at the start of what came to be known as King Philip's War.

We were trapped in a four-room fortified house for the first three days of a very hot and humid August. We survived only because a sudden, tremendous thunderstorm doused the flames that were leaping up the side of the house as 400 Indians stood, yelling in joy that we were about to burn to death. Soldiers came riding into the tiny village soon after and the Indians scattered.

The town of Springfield lies in the western part of the Massachusetts Bay Colony, west of Brookfield and south of Northampton and Deerfield. It is not a large town by any means and, for almost a year after we arrived, I thought it might have been a mistake to go there instead of back to Ipswich with the other survivors.

I found, as I hope you have, that throughout life, the power of a dream can sustain a person through the most difficult of times and circumstances. For my wife and me, married less than two years and her pregnant with our first child, we had to survive a brutal and bloody war before we could start on our dream.

Now, I need to make it clear that I was somewhat unusual because I had a dream unlike many people of the day. Most people would do what their fathers did: farm, or become small-town merchants or tradesmen. I was an orphan farm boy, raised in Ipswich by my Aunt Charity and Uncle Josiah after my mother's death when I was fourteen years old. I was apprenticed to a greedy and brutal Boston merchant, but was rescued by my uncle who bought out my apprenticeship. I returned to Ipswich and then moved to Brookfield with Charity and Josiah, where I would make a life, marry the girl I loved since we were children growing up in Ipswich, and start a family.

Mr. John Pynchon, one of the most important men in the Bay Colony, was pleased to see us but concerned about our welfare. I had first met him when I was an apprentice in Boston and he took a liking to me. When I first came to Brookfield, I began working for him as a messenger, taking his letters to many of the towns in the colony. Among his other civic and military duties, Mr. Pynchon was also a magistrate and he married Becky and me in a small ceremony at his home and was kind enough to give us a small feast at the tavern.

He was obviously worried that the attacks would continue and there was the possibility that other villages could be destroyed and more people would be killed. The ambush and siege in Brookfield really shook him; the extraordinary violence from supposedly friendly Indian neighbors shocked all of us, but him the most.

It only took us a couple of weeks to find that out and when the Indian attacks began again, they were savage and swift.

We had only three weeks to be settled before the troubles intensified all across the Bay Colony. The week after we reached Springfield, the Great Council ordered all Christian Indians to be confined to praying towns. Shortly after that, a group of unknown Indians killed seven colonists at Lancaster, seventy miles from Springfield. Towards the end of August, Captain Samuel Moseley arrested fifteen Hassanemesit Indians near Marlborough for the Lancaster assault and marched them to Boston.

Tom Cooper, a friend and business associate of Mr. Pynchon, told several of us the afternoon after we arrived that there were reports of over a thousand Indians at Wachusett, only sixty miles from Springfield, waiting to attack. When I heard that, my stomach tightened and a light sweat broke out on my face. Some people said they heard it was almost 2,000 Indians. With that many, they could kill everyone in town, and any other place, even Boston, with ease. There would be no survivors and nothing left standing. Nothing but total destruction. The Massachusetts Bay Colony would cease to exist.

As with all rumors, there was a bit of truth in what he heard. We found out that there was a large number of Indians at Wachusett and they would attack. Besides that, nothing I heard was true.

It all started on the night of August 31. It was a warm, humid evening with what seemed like thousands of mosquitoes biting every living thing they could find. Two riders came in—one from Boston, the other from Connecticut Colony—with reports that the Indians were moving in our direction. The tension was high in every corner of the colony so people were seeking every scrap of information that might help us prepare for an attack. The fort was as prepared as it could be with every man having at least two pounds of powder and four pounds of lead, enough for each of us to shoot for a long time. As the night wore on, riders kept coming into the fort with more news about how the enemy was now fifty, then forty, then only thirty miles away and moving fast. No one slept that night. We all waited and checked over and over again to make sure there was nothing we left undone. We expected an attack around dawn, but were surprised and relieved when nothing happened.

At about eleven o'clock on the morning of Sunday, September 1, a boy came galloping into the fort on a horse almost dead on its feet with news that Deerfield was under attack. Everyone except a few of the soldiers was at Sabbath meeting.

Two hundred Nipmucks and Wampanoags attacked before dawn, the boy explained. His father told him to take the horse and spread the alarm. The boy managed to get away but he said that as he rode off, he looked back and saw one of the attackers shoot his father.

Since Deerfield is thirty miles up the Connecticut River from Springfield, it would take six hours to get there. It couldn't be done any sooner as the road ran through some swampy areas and dangerously close to several Indian villages and fishing sites. Mr. Pynchon, as colonel of the First Hampshire Regiment, ordered half the militia to stay behind to guard the fort and the other half to ride with him to Deerfield.

Becky did not want me to go to Deerfield. After all that she had been through in the last month, I couldn't blame her for wanting me to stay with her. She was six months pregnant and getting bigger every day. She was due in December, which was only three months away. Her greatest fear was that something would happen to me and the baby.

"Jack, I'm tired of this … so tired. We came within a hair's breadth of getting slaughtered three weeks ago and now this. I don't want this. I want to go home, back to Ipswich," she said, her exhaustion apparent in the dark circles under her eyes. The constant fear was taking a toll on her.

"Becky, I don't know if we can go home," I told her. "It is too dangerous to be out traveling now with the Indians attacking everywhere. I know this is not what we expected and maybe we made the wrong decision, at least for right now, but I know it will work out, I know it will."

"Yes, if we don't get killed first," she snapped.

"I wouldn't dare take you on a 125-mile trip across the colony."

When I told Becky that Mr. Pynchon wanted me to go with him, she was very upset. I couldn't very well let the other men face the prospect of a fight while I stayed at the fort like an old man who couldn't fight anymore. I was torn between going and asking Mr. Pynchon if I could stay on account of Becky being pregnant and her not feeling well, but I decided to go with the militia. There were many other men who were staying behind and there were women to take care of Becky should something happen while I was gone. I wasn't concerned about my safety. From what the boy said, the attack was over and we would be getting to Deerfield after the Indians had left the village.

When we got to Deerfield, the dead were scattered everywhere. Most of those killed were men, but there were quite a few women and children, too. It was a gruesome, grisly scene. Some of the dead were scalped and others were mutilated in unimaginable ways. I saw two dead children lying next to each other, face down in a pigsty, the backs of their heads split open by a war club. The only sounds were those of our horses, our leather saddles squeaking as we rode, and the buzz and hum of millions of flies feasting on the bodies. The village was destroyed; there was nothing left except the smoldering ashes of houses and barns.

It took us two days to bury the dead. We worked from sunrise to sunset trying to lay the poor souls to rest as the days were warm and the bodies were beginning to decay. The smell of death stayed with us, a sweet, sickening smell that seeps into your clothes and combines with the dirt on your hands. On the way back to Springfield, we stopped a few miles south of Deerfield to wash in the river. No matter how much water I used on my hands, arms and face, I could not get rid of the smell.

We were a quiet, sorrowful group as we made our way back into Springfield. When we arrived in town, people were waiting for us since Mr. Pynchon had sent a messenger on ahead.

When Becky saw me, she began to cry, whether from happiness or relief I could not tell, though it didn't matter.

We related what we'd found and all that happened. Everyone worried that we would be attacked in the next few days and some began to panic. A guard was mounted with ten men watching at all times, each man taking his turn. Food was brought into the fort and most people worked in the fields during the day as several men always kept guard over each group with everyone coming back into the fort at night.

Things seemed to quiet down for a couple of weeks until September 18, when a large load of threshed wheat needed to be taken from the fields at Deerfield to the gristmill north of Hadley. Captain Thomas Lathrop, who I'd met six weeks prior in Brookfield, took eighty militia to guard the seventeen wagons of grain. They were on watch for bands of warriors roaming the river valley. The carts started from Deerfield in the early morning.

When the men realized that it would take a while for the carts to cross a narrow, swampy thicket that they had come to, they decided to take a rest. Some put their guns down, while others picked grapes growing near the brook.

Suddenly, hundreds of Indians jumped out of the bushes and thickets and opened fire on the men. Bullets and arrows were coming from every direction and without their guns handy and being too far from the other militia; they were cut down in an instant. Captain Lathrop was one of the first of seventy-two men killed, none of the teamsters survived, and only eight escaped. Captain Moseley and his band of sixty soldiers were on patrol in the area and heard the attack. They rushed to the scene and for nearly six hours, fought a desperate battle with the attackers. Moseley sent word back of what happened. Over 100 Connecticut soldiers along with a large group of Mohegan Indians who were allied with us were on their way to patrol toward Brookfield. When word came in of the attack, they hurried to the place and joined the fight. Once the enemy saw the greater number of our men, they quickly vanished into the forest. Moseley and the rest of the men made their way to what was left of Deerfield for the night. They were taunted all night by the Indians who waved clothing and other items that they had taken from the dead. The soldiers went back the next day to bury the dead in a large grave, just as we had done at Deerfield. They then trudged back to Springfield to relay their grim experience. Moseley told us that one of the Indian leaders was Muttawmp, a Quaboag sachem and once my friend, before he led the attack on Brookfield.

Almost 300 people had been killed in three weeks. With the large number of enemy roaming at will, we were trapped and could only fight for our lives, our families, and our neighbors. I was afraid we would all die in the next few days. I didn't see how we in Springfield, the largest town west of Marlborough, could not be attacked. I expected hundreds of Indians to swoop down on us like a ravaging wind and destroy everything in their path. When I looked at my wife, her hands resting on her belly, cradling our unborn child, I vowed that I would do everything in my power to the last moment of my life, to keep them safe from harm.

A few weeks after the attack on Deerfield, I went to see Mr. Pynchon about a place for Becky and me to live. We were staying in the small, crowded back room at the tavern, helping the owners, Jeremiah and Mary; however we could to pay for our room and board. They were very kind to us, always treating us well since our wedding night that we spent at the tavern. It was a special place for us, but it was time to find a place of our own.

He was coming out of his house when I caught up to him.

"Mr. Pynchon?"

"Jack," he said without breaking stride. "How are you and Becky making out? I haven't seen you."

He looked as if he aged ten years in three weeks time. "That's what I wanted to talk to you about, Sir. We need a new place to live. We can't stay at the tavern too much longer, even though Jeremiah and Mary have been more than gracious."

He stopped and turned around.

"I will do what I can for you but the only homes available now are down the river. They are isolated and unsafe so it's best you stay at the tavern. There aren't any travelers so you are not taking a room from anyone else. Now, I have to go."

I stood for a moment, watching him walk away. Feeling discouraged and not knowing what to do with myself, I wandered back to the tavern.

Becky was helping Mary in the kitchen, trying to be as useful as she could under the circumstances. I leaned against the doorframe and watched her as she moved with a grace that only pregnant women possessed. There was a radiant beauty about her, almost as if she had a special secret that she couldn't possibly share. Mary was talking to her. Although I was too far away to hear what they were saying, I could tell Mary was giving her advice. Becky listened intently as she worked, taking it all in, and nodding now and then. At moments like that, I fell in love with her all over again.

CHAPTER 2

Shortly after sunrise on October 4, a cold and rainy day, the type of day that whispered winter was on its way, with dark gray, low hanging clouds filling a gloomy sky, a rider came to Mr. Pynchon with word that an attack on Hadley was to happen that day. He promptly gathered 200 men, all members of the militia, and had set off for Hadley by mid-morning. Mr. Pynchon allowed me to stay behind as part of the guard because Becky was feeling unwell, having frequent sudden sharp pains and vomiting, and then, for more than a week, she had not felt the baby move at all. We were afraid something was wrong and she might lose the baby. We prayed that everything was well with our first child and that we would be spared any suffering and heartache. With almost all of the men gone, the town felt eerily empty. Besides me, there were no more than fifteen other men, most of them older, including my friend Tom Cooper, a lieutenant in the militia, along with Deacon Chapin, Constable Tom Miller, Reverend Glover, and several others.

It was once common to see many Indians walking the streets of Springfield, visiting their English friends, buying things at the shops, and bringing grain to the gristmill. In 1670, the townspeople had built a fort several miles down the river for the safety and protection of the local Indians. The good relations we had were severely strained when, shortly after Mr. Pynchon left for Hadley, we learned that two men on the other side of the river took several Agawam Indian children hostage in hopes of preventing an attack on themselves. This caused a stir in the town as people expressed their disbelief in the stupidity of these men.

A few hours after sunset, a rider came galloping in with word that a friendly Indian named Toto, who lived in Windsor in the Connecticut Colony, warned that King Philip and many other hostile Indians were at the Indian fort and planning to attack the next morning. Another rider was given the task of heading to Hadley to get word to Mr. Pynchon. He took one of the fastest horses in town and galloped off on his mission.

We were immediately on alert. We scrambled to get our guns ready and hung pouches full of ball and horns of powder around our necks. The women and children were tucked away inside the houses. Every bucket in town was filled with water in case of fire. None of us slept that night, listening for the slightest sound of an attack. The only thing I heard was the pounding of my own heartbeat.

When sunrise came with no sign of an attack, we began to question the message from Toto. Tom Cooper and Constable Miller, both of whom traded with the Indians for years and knew them well, didn't believe the warning and set out on horseback for the Indian fort. I watched them ride away with a bad feeling fluttering in my stomach. They were gone about an hour when we heard horses galloping toward us. I ran out onto the street and saw Tom Cooper slumped over his horse, blood running from his upper body onto the horse's neck. I tried to stop the horse but it ran past me, stopping in front of Mr. Pynchon's house. Tom attempted to get off but fell heavily to the ground.

I ran over to him and knelt down. His eyelids fluttered and he grabbed my hand. I put my arm around his back to support him. I felt an arrow buried deep in his body, the shaft sticking out his back. He was shot in the chest, too, and blood flowed freely from the wound.

"Tom, Tom, listen to me," I said as I tried to lift him. "I'll get you inside. Just hold on." I tried to drag him but he slid out of my grasp. I knelt beside him again and as I turned him on his side, he took my hand again. He looked at me with a clear, knowing look before taking his last ragged breath.

I turned and saw everyone standing behind me, staring at Tom's lifeless body in silence. I looked down and saw my shirt and pants covered in his blood. I looked down at the body of my friend thinking that if some of us had gone with him and the constable, he might still be alive. A sob escaped me when I saw Tom's wife running through the crowd.

"I'm sorry," I said "I am so sorry. I couldn't save him." She stood frozen for a moment, looking down at me, before she dropped to her knees beside me, cradled her husband's head in shaking hands, and cried. With the sticky blood drying on my hands and clothes, I gathered enough strength to stand and went to look for Becky.

I found her in the tavern. When she turned and saw me standing in the doorway covered in blood, she almost dropped the pie that she was carrying.

"Jack! What happened to you? Are you hurt?"

I shook my head. "No. It was Tom. They got Tom. He's dead." I saw the careworn look that had come over her in the last two months. I saw her round belly carrying our child. I took her hands and held them in mine. I felt her slender, delicate fingers and looked into her eyes. "I will protect you, Becky. Until I take my last dying breath, I will protect you."

She wrapped her arms around me and put her head on my shoulder. “I love you, Jack.”

Becky and I awoke to the sounds of piercing screams. Mary and Jeremiah rushed into our room. “They’re coming!” Jeremiah yelled. The battle cries were getting louder as the Indians got closer and closer. I told Becky and Mary to get to Pynchon’s. I began to move away but Becky grabbed my arm.

“Jack,” she sobbed. “No, not again. I can’t go through this again. I can’t—”

I gave her a quick kiss on the forehead and took her chin in my hand. “Becky, you have to be strong. They are attacking and I need you to be safe. Go and help the woman with children.”

“What about my child?” she demanded.

“Our child. I protect you and you protect our child. Now go and be safe, please!”

She didn’t move. For the first time since we met, I yelled at her. “Move! Now!” I grabbed her by the arm and shoved her towards Mary. “Take her to Pynchon’s!” I ran to the door and looked back at Jeremiah. “Jeremiah, get your gun and follow me.”

It did not take long to realize that we would not be able to hold them off. Hundreds of Indians charged at the town about two hours after the sun rose. The acrid smell of smoke filled the air as the red glow from the flames illuminated the town. We could hear the screams from the settlers as they ran from their burning homes to the blockhouse. Flaming arrows flew over the palisade, burning whatever building they landed in. The thatched roofs of many buildings caught fire quickly. Soon, a hot, choking haze of smoke was all around us. I looked up and saw thousands of embers rising into the sky.

Jeremiah, several others, and I got to the palisade and saw hundreds of Indians descending upon us. I debated whether to fire or not, for sending a few balls of lead into such a large group would have almost no effect. I thought of Tom and a flaming anger rose up inside of me. I picked up my gun and began shooting at a torrid pace. I was unstoppable, hitting every Indian I took aim at, one after another. I had eight balls in my pouch and that matched the number of dead Indians lying nearby. I used the last ball on an Indian who got into someone's house and stole a pewter platter. He held it up in front of him as a shield but it served only to attract our attention. I aimed at this large, bright target and squeezed the trigger. He let out a shriek as the bullet hit him and fell to the ground. We realized we could do no more and ran to shelter.

There was yelling and confusion as men, women, and children rushed about trying to save their homes and belongings. Others made a mad dash for the three blockhouses. Each was only slightly larger than the Ayres' tavern in Brookfield where ninety-nine of us had stood off 400 Indians. There were far more people in Springfield than in Brookfield, perhaps four times as many, so no matter what we did, it was going to be crowded in the fortified buildings. I sent Becky and Mary to Pynchon's because it was the largest and strongest of all the houses as it was made of brick.

One of the young boys cried out that the sawmill was on fire. It was located down by the river, about two hundred yards away. The flames began on the side away from us and grew until they were shooting out of the roof. It burned quickly, with the roof and one side collapsing with a loud bang.

Captain Miles Morgan, the commander of the fort, was running around trying to restore some order. I ran to him. "What can I do?" I asked.

"Get the women and children to the blockhouses and then come back here."

With that, I ran around the fort directing all the women and children to the blockhouses. I went back to Captain Morgan who was ordering men to various positions where they could shoot to slow down the attack. I got to the palisade and was just about to begin shooting, when I looked to my right. Five Indians were running hard, coming on fast. One of the Indians raised his rifle and fired. I took some balls from the pouch of the man next to me. As I loaded, several other shots rang out. I looked up and saw three Indians fall. I threw my gun up and, just as I was about to pull the trigger, an Indian threw his tomahawk with all his might, grunting as he let it go. It slammed into the stake in front of me, landing no more than four inches from my head.

I raised my gun to my shoulder but before I could pull the trigger, I heard a bullet whistle by my head, then felt an arrow slice my sleeve. I looked out and saw well over a hundred attackers charging toward us. I took aim at the Indian that threw the tomahawk and put a bullet in his chest.

CHAPTER 3

By late afternoon, most of the town was a smoldering ruin. Surprisingly, only a few other people besides Tom and Constable Miller were killed. Pentecost Mathews was one of them. She was the wife of John Mathews, a well-respected man who was with Mr. Pynchon. She was fleeing from her house in the southern end of town when the attackers smashed her in the head with a club and threw her into the burning house.

Despite our best efforts, there was nothing left except the three blockhouses, Mr. Pynchon's large brick home, the tavern, eight other houses, and a few barns. Everything else was gone. Thirty-three houses and twenty-five barns were destroyed.

Mr. Pynchon and the soldiers made it back to Springfield soon after the Indians abandoned their efforts. They found it a wasteland. In a less than a day, everything they knew was gone. I will never forget the look on their faces when they saw the destruction.

The first thing we did was set a guard around what was left of the town, for we had no idea where the Indians were hiding. Then we gathered all the food we could find and brought it to Captain Morgan's blockhouse. There were over 300 people that needed to be fed and housed. Luckily, there were a dozen pigs and several cows, so we did have meat, but there was no flour for bread. Even those animals would not feed that many people for more than a couple of days. Most of the harvest was in, so our winter stores were destroyed in the fire, except for those few lucky farmers whose barns were spared. Even so, they didn't have enough to feed such a large number of hungry people.

Mr. Pynchon sent letters off to several people in authority looking for their assistance. He asked the governors of both the Bay Colony and the Connecticut Colony for food supplies. He asked if I would ride as a messenger for him to get his letter to Governor Leverett in Boston, but told me he would understand if I refused. It was too dangerous for me to go with Becky only a few weeks from having the baby. With the attacks happening all over the colony, there was a good chance that whoever went to Boston might never make it there or back.

Many people began talk of leaving but did not know if they could travel in safety with the Indians whereabouts unknown. There really wasn't much we could do except wait.

Several ideas were proposed, including sending small groups of men to go out and try to locate the Indians. Since the danger was still too great, we did nothing.

People crammed into the remaining houses and barns located closest to the center of town. No one wanted to be more than a couple of minutes away from safety. Since Pynchon's was the largest house, we went there as a precaution at Mrs. Pynchon's urging. She wanted Becky and the baby to be where it was safest. We hoped to have a little more space than if we went to any of the other buildings, but it did not turn out that way. We shared a first floor room with twenty other people.

I took Becky by the hand and we sat in a corner.

"This is all my fault," I said, looking at the floor between my crossed legs. "If I hadn't been so set on coming here we would be back in Ipswich with our families."

She didn't say anything but moved so that her legs were straight out in front of her, resting her back against the wall, trying to get into a comfortable position.

"If we get through this, we will go wherever you want. If it's back to Ipswich then that's where we will go."

She turned to look at me. "Jack, listen to me. I hope this war won't last long. Some women at the tavern said they heard it could be over soon. If it is, then I want to stay right here with you. This is where we want to make our life and our family, where we want to work as hard as we can to make our dream come true." She wrapped her arms around her belly as if to shield our unborn child from harm.

I took her hand and began idly playing with her fingers. "Well, let's get through this first. Our need is to stay alive, find food to eat and be somewhere safe when the baby comes."

She sighed and put her head on my shoulder. I held her hand and we sat lost in our own thoughts for a long time.

Sleeping in a crowded room is almost impossible. No one could get comfortable trying to sleep on a hard floor. The fireplace threw off a good amount of heat, and along with all of the people crammed inside, the room was soon hot. There was mumbling and grumbling for an hour or more as mothers tried to get their children to sleep. When everyone finally fell asleep, the snoring started. Three men and two women made such frightful noises you would have thought they were in a contest to see who could be the loudest. Becky slept but I only dozed, half listening for sounds of an attack. I jumped at the slightest noises, at least those I could hear between the bouts of snoring.

It was early morning when we made our way outside. Mrs. Pynchon's servant made a large pot of mush out of the last bushel of dried corn. We all ate out of the pot, passing spoons around. It wasn't much, but it was better than not having anything.

I went on watch and spent the morning looking up and down the river for the slightest sign of trouble. Twice I spotted small groups of Indians on the other side of the river, but they left after watching us for a few minutes. Besides that, there was none of the enemy to be seen.

Since we would run out of food in a couple of days, I suggested that we hunt for any game we could find. Groups could go in four different directions, not too far from the fort so we could make it back quickly if we were ambushed. Not only would it help us get more food, it would also give us something to do. I have always been someone who likes to get things done and not wait for things to happen. Captain Morgan and Major Pynchon agreed to the idea but would only allow two groups to go out hunting at one time.

My group went out first thing the next morning. Ten of us were armed with our guns and knives and some carried tomahawks. We went down toward the river, keeping a watchful eye for the slightest sign of trouble. We killed several geese with only three shots. We wanted to keep the number of shots to a minimum so as not to give away our position. We grabbed the geese and ran back to the fort. A short time after we got back, two sentries saw a dozen Indians come out of the trees a few hundred yards away trying to find the source of the shots. After a while, they disappeared back into the woods.

Things continued this way for a few days. Every time a group would go out, they would see a small band of the enemy who left the area after a few minutes. It was enough to know that they were still around. It was a cloudy day with a light rain falling when I led the next hunting party. I wanted to see how far we could go before the Indians appeared, so we headed north away from most of the destruction. We moved slowly, trying to make as little noise as possible, and we were alert for anything. A loud shot rang out and we all jumped at the noise. It turns out, John Stuart, the town blacksmith, had shot a large deer. The sound of the shot seemed to hang in the air for a long time. We waited to see if a group of Indians would come charging out of the woods upon hearing the noise, but to our relief, no one did. John and another hunter retrieved the deer to drag it back with us. We were halfway back when we heard a shot coming from our right, ripping through the air above our heads. We stopped in our tracks. They did hear our shots and were coming for us. We got out of there as fast as possible and made it back to the fort safely, but not by much. We didn't go out again for the next two days.

The weather turned cold in early November and the town had its first coating of snow by the middle of the month. The wind picked up and gusted for a week. It was difficult for many of the townspeople because they lost their clothes when their houses burned. Becky and I were lucky because we still had some thick, wool clothes. Others were wearing thin linen blankets in place of coats. Those of us with extra clothes shared with those without. The lack of good clothing would be an even bigger problem since the winter would be upon us soon. People came to enjoy sharing the cramped quarters because it was the only time during the day that they were warm.

Since the threat of being attacked seemed to quiet down, Becky and I decided to move back to the tavern since the room at Pynchon's was too crowded and noisy.

The food supply dwindled quickly. No matter how much game the hunters brought in, which some days was a lot and other days was nothing, there wasn't enough to feed everyone. The men made sure the children and women had food before they would take any for themselves. I gladly gave most of mine to Becky because she needed extra for the baby. My thoughts turned dark as I wondered what would happen when we ran out of food.

CHAPTER 4

One day I was working with a few others to build a shelter for the few remaining animals. Since most of our sawn wood was destroyed in the fire, we were pulling pieces from what was left of Dan Thornton's barn. It was a bright, sunny, but cold early December day. We had been working for a couple of hours and decided to stop for a short rest. I had just sat down when I heard my name. I stood and saw young Sue Prescott running towards me, waving her arms. From the look on her face I sensed something was wrong.

"Jack!"

I started to run to her. "What?" I asked. "What is it?"

"Becky," she said, trying to catch her breath. "She's gone into labor. Mary told me to come get you."

I took off at a run, leaving her behind me. I made it to the tavern in less than a minute, bursting through the door, looking for anyone to tell me what was happening. Jeremiah came out from the kitchen.

"Where?" I asked.

"In the back room. The baby is coming fast."

I turned and almost ran into two women outside the door. I tried to enter the room but one of them put her hand on my arm. "The midwife and her assistant are with her. There's no need for you to be here," she said as if dismissing me from attending the birth of my own child.

When I didn't move away, she stood between me and the door, folded her arms and glared at me. "There's no need for you to be here so go … now."

The other woman, a small, mousy looking creature, tittered at the statement before adding her own thoughts. "It's no place for a man," she said with a hint of a giggle.

A memory of the day my mother died during childbirth flashed before my eyes. I saw her grimacing in pain, clutching her belly with both hands as the midwife lay her down on the bed. It was the last time I ever saw her. I heard my uncle Josiah telling me that there was nothing anyone could do, that she was hurt bad inside. A fear crept up inside me. The thought that it could happen to Becky too knocked me backward. The sound of her crying out brought me back.

I looked at the two women standing before me and with one great sweep of my arm, moved them out of my way. When I opened the door, I saw Mary on her knees supporting Becky's head, talking to her softly to comfort her. Becky was lying on a blanket, clenching her teeth and hands, legs spread with her feet on the floor. When she turned and saw me, she smiled. I looked into her eyes and saw both happiness and pain. The midwife came in and gave Becky a round piece of wood wrapped in cloth to bite on to ease the pain. She grasped it in her teeth just as a new wave of pain came upon her. It hurt me to see my wife in agony and I knew that it was only just beginning and would get worse as the day went on. Not knowing what to do, I knelt beside Becky and took her hand.

Sweat was pouring down her face. She opened her eyes for a moment to look at me, and then screamed in pain.

"It's time you should go," Mary said to me. "No need of you being here." I nodded and kissed Becky on the head and squeezed her hand before I left.

The rest of the afternoon wore on. Each minute seemed liked an hour. I paced the length of the entire fort, but always circled back to be near the tavern. I went inside once to get a glass of rum to soothe my nerves, but Jeremiah wouldn't give it to me and ushered me outside so I wouldn't hear Becky's screams. The image of my mother kept coming back to me over and over again, worrying me more and more that the same thing might happen to Becky. I was so lost in my thoughts I didn't even notice that the sun had set and I was standing outside in the dark.

Not having anything else to do, I went in to tell Jeremiah I was going back to Pynchon's for a while. I don't know why I thought of going there, because there was nothing there for me to do either.

When I entered, there was a small group of men at a table near the front to the right of the door. They were talking low, trying to get as far away from the room where Becky was as possible. When Jeremiah looked at me, I saw a look of concern on his face. He waved me over.

"Sit down and I'll give you the mug you asked for before," he said. He brought me a small mug and placed it in front of me then sat in the chair next to me. "Jack, I know what you are feeling right now. It is a difficult thing to know your wife is going through something so painful and you cannot do anything to help her. I was in your place when Mary had our three girls. I didn't know what to do with myself. We have seen enough problems with our animals giving birth so we worry for our women." He patted my arm twice. "Well, let me get you something to eat."

I could hear him but I wasn't really listening. When I didn't respond, he came and stood in front of me, adjusting his breeches. "You have to eat, Jack. I have some beef and parsnip stew."

I shook myself out of my daze. “Yes, thank you, Jeremiah. That would be good.”

When he brought my stew, a bit of a smile came to his face. “I bet you never thought that you would be having your first child in the same place you spent your wedding night.”

That had not occurred to me. I sat sipping my cider with an ear cocked for the slightest sound of a baby crying, but all I heard was mumbled talk and sounds that I could not make out. I picked up a spoon and my stew was gone before I knew it. I was too nervous to concentrate on anything. It was as if I was living in a dream. Hours went by without any word from Mary or the midwife. I couldn’t take it any longer and made my way to Becky’s room. As I approached the door, I heard Becky sobbing and seconds later the loud cry of a baby. I opened the door and saw the midwife holding our baby, wiping the blood off with a linen cloth. I went to Becky and looked down at her. She was drenched in sweat. There was blood on the mattress and floor. When Becky looked up at me, I saw not just my wife but also the mother of my child. I knelt beside her as the midwife handed her the baby.

“You’re a father,” Becky told me in a weak but happy voice with tears streaming down her beautiful face. “We have a son. What should we name him?”

"Samuel … after my father," I said, trying to hold back tears.

She smiled and looked down at him. "This is your father, Samuel," she whispered to him. "His name is Jack and he is a good man and will be a good father to you, I know he will."

The midwife and her assistant were cleaning up. I felt a hand on my shoulder and looked up to see Mary, her face drawn and tired. She smiled. "She needs to rest now," she said, "Let her sleep for a few hours."

I leaned over and kissed Becky on the forehead, and then kissed my newborn son for the first time. I followed Mary out into the big room where several people were waiting.

"It's a boy," I told them. "A boy named Samuel, after my father." I realized how tired I was and made my way to the fireplace, moved a bench in front of it, lay down and slept until Jeremiah woke me in the morning.

When word of Samuel's birth got out, everyone I met congratulated me. Most of the women and a few of the men had a look in their eye, one that showed their fear of the situation. I admit there was a strong disquiet and worry in my heart. At times, the fear almost got the best of me until I thought that the war couldn't possibly last much longer. If I was wrong and it continued, the winter would be very hard for us all. The thought of Becky not getting enough to eat, and how Samuel would suffer for it made my stomach burn.

I went to see my wife and son early the next morning. Becky was awake, sitting in a chair holding Samuel on her stomach. I went and knelt next to her and patted his head. The hair was so fine, like feathers of a baby bird.

She looked from me to the baby a few times, the smile on her face widening. "I can't believe it," she whispered so not to wake Sam. "This is our son, our child, our little boy." The glow of being a new mother radiated from her. She moved slightly and winced. "It hurts," she said.

"Let me hold him," I said.

She gently lifted him into my arms. He stirred and made a face but did not wake up. "Come here my boy," I said. I rocked him slowly, feeling his small, warm body against me. I kissed his forehead.

At that moment, I was very happy. My wife, the girl I knew from so long ago when we were children, and our newborn son were together in a quiet, joyful moment that I have never forgotten. I can still conjure the feeling up whenever I think about it.

I looked at Becky, her green eyes shining with happiness and wonder. I handed Sam back to her.

"I love you," I told her.

"I love you too, Jack." Just then, the door opened and Mary came in with a mug and small trencher with last night's stew on it.

"I thought you'd be hungry," she said to Becky and then turned to me. "Mr. Pynchon is asking for you."

"I'll go see what he wants," I said. "I'll be back in a while." I turned before going out the door, taking another look at my son. I vowed to protect them with my life, if that was what it would take to ensure that my family would survive and prosper. I had not gone through everything I had in my years to see it fall apart.

I found Mr. Pynchon at Captain Morgan's fortified house. They were standing outside talking and gesturing as I came up to them.

"Jack," Mr. Pynchon said, shaking my hand. "Congratulations. Praise to God for the safety and health of Becky and your son. What name have you given to him?"

"Samuel. That was my father's name."

"How is Becky?" he asked. "Amy will see her this afternoon."

"She is fine. Tired and sore but happy." I realized I was smiling.

“It’s quite an experience being a father isn’t it?” Captain Morgan asked.

“Yes, it is,” I replied.

“You’ll get used to it. We all did.”

CHAPTER 5

Almost two months had passed and the war was still dragging on. We were limited as to where and how far we could go. Captain Morgan gathered 100 men, of which I was one, to try to drive the Indians away. We could not believe that there were hundreds of Indians remaining in the area because it didn't make sense that they would leave such a large group just to harass us when they could be attacking somewhere else. My own guess was that it was no more than a couple dozen attackers watching us. Captain Morgan wanted to find out once and for all.

A small group of Indians ambushed us as we went along the edge of the woods north of the fort. After a brief skirmish, I found myself surrounded by two dozen Indians. I had nowhere to go; they had me trapped. The others from the fort made it back safely but I was not so lucky.

From behind my band of captors came an Indian I recognized as Muttawmp, one of the Quaboag sachems. With him was Sagamore John from the Packachoag tribe. Muttawmp had been a friend but turned on us a couple of weeks before the attack on Brookfield. Since then he had been a hated enemy.

A Narragansett Indian with a stocky build and a wide scar from his right eye to his chin and a flattened nose that was broken and never healed, rushed up to me and grabbed my gun. I knew I couldn't say anything because if I did, he would not hesitate to bury his tomahawk in my head. He reached out, yanked my powder flask, and shot pouch from around my neck. He held them up and gave a yell. Other Indians turned to see what he was yelling about and then yelled at his success. He looked at me with a smirk. I stared back at him, anger growing within me.

Another Indian of moderate height with a broad chest and wide face, narrow eyes and a long thin nose, came to me and looked me up and down. He wore a red wool cape over his shoulders, deerskin leggings and a shirt decorated with colored porcupine quills, a red beaded sash around his waist, moccasins that came up over his ankles, and bone earrings. A blue beaded band around his head held back his long, thick, black hair. Around his neck hung a shot pouch, decorated horn powder flask, and a braided cord from which hung a large yellow five-pointed star. In his sash, he carried a large war club, the handle decorated with white and purple shells.

"Let us go," he said as he moved behind me and began talking with Muttawmp and a couple of others. I stopped in my tracks and turned to him.

“Metacomet.” I used his Indian name instead of King Philip, the name the English used for him. He came up to my side and stood looking at me, no more than a foot away.

“Please. Let me go. My wife had a baby, my first son, just two days ago. You can go on your way. I will not tell anyone you have been here until tomorrow. By then you will be safely away. I do not know where you are headed so I can’t tell anyone anything. Let me just see my son again.”

He looked me in the eye, considering my request. “No,” was all he said before moving quickly to the front of the long line of warriors.

Indians have an ability to move through the forest and fields unlike any of us English can. They move quickly but are never in a hurry. Their stride is not overly long but is at such a pace that they can walk all day and into the night without stopping. They are as silent as shadows, their moccasins make no sound and the leaves and branches glide off their deerskin leggings and shirts without so much as a whisper.

I looked around, trying to get my bearings and searching for a way to escape. If I was going to try to get away, I would need to do it soon, because the farther from the fort we got, the less chance of success I had. All of the Indians around me, most my age or younger, threw sidelong glances my way from time to time. We were coming to the top of a small hill and I recognized the trail running off to my left, down the side of the hill. It went into a swamp and was a mile, maybe more, from the fort. I looked around me quickly and was about to run when I felt a hand on my right shoulder.

"Don't."

I turned and saw Ahanu, the son of Conkganasco, sachem of the Quaboag tribe. I first met Ahanu the day we came to Brookfield. He and his father, along with Muttawmp, were introduced to us by John Ayres, Sr. as friends who helped them through the first two difficult years at the new settlement. Ahanu had grown and filled out. He was a handsome young man about my age, with deerskin leggings, moccasins, and a turkey feather in his braided hair that hung down over his left shoulder. He carried a new musket and had a pouch for musket balls and a plain horn flask for powder slung across his chest.

"You will not get far, Jack." He said nodded towards the others around him, "They will kill you within a minute if you try to run. Do you really want your wife to be a widow today?"

I knew that was true. "No," I said. "Of course not." I looked at this man, once a good friend of the people in our small village, and wondered about all that had happened in the last few months, how the world turned upside down. One day things were good between us and our Indian neighbors, and the next they were attacking us with a ferocity that was beyond belief. He moved close to me.

"We will talk later," he said before moving up towards the front of the line.

I walked many miles during my time, as we had no other means of getting around than our feet and a horse, but I never walked for a longer time or at such a ground-eating pace than I did that day and the two that followed. We had to walk at least fifty miles each day, never slowing, never stopping, and always moving in the same direction. I had spent much time in the woods around Brookfield, hunting every chance I got and thought I was able to see the trails that animals, mostly deer, used during their daily movements, but the trails we were following were imperceptible to me. There were no marks on the trees and no piles of stones to mark the way.

Before we stopped shortly after dark, another group joined us at the top of a hill under large elm and chestnut trees. With them were several other captives: two men, three women, and three children. Two of the children were five or six years old, the other was an infant. My heart sank as I looked at the baby. Thoughts of Sam and Becky crowded my thoughts. The mother put the baby to her breast and fed him. All of them had a look of bone-shaking fear on their faces.

I went to sit by myself because I did not want to talk to anyone. The feeling of loss overtook me completely, dragging my soul down to one of the darkest places I had ever known. I was filled with the certainty that I would never see my family again. As I sat on a rock, shivering with the deepening cold, I heard my father's voice from his deathbed telling me that the measure of a man is how he deals with the difficulties he encounters and that I had an inner strength that no one could take away unless I let them. His words had brought me comfort during the three harrowing days we were surrounded by Indians in Brookfield, and they now made me determined that I would get back to Becky and Sam no matter what I had to do. Nothing would keep me from them.

Two fires were burning, one at each end of the campsite. Several of the Indians made lean-to's of strong saplings and spruce boughs while all of us captives were herded together and bound with a thick cord. It was made clear to us that we would be bound like this every night. Even though we could not go anywhere, our captors never let us out of their sight. They gave each of us a small amount of meal made from bear fat, berries, and corn. It was hard, dry, and took some getting used to, but it filled you up. It was cold and getting colder as the wind began to blow, not much but just enough to cut you to the bone. I knew I would not sleep. All we had were the clothes we wore and they were not enough.

All of a sudden, an Indian came charging toward me, a knife in his hand and hate in his eye. He caught me by surprise, so I didn't react fast enough. The knife sliced through the air missing my chest by inches. The other captives cried out in fear. I glanced up and saw Wematin, the brother of an Indian I had killed during the siege at Brookfield. He came at me again, slashing the knife back and forth in front of me before trying to get behind me. I moved to the right and, when he came at me, I tried to grab him but couldn't move my arms more than a foot or two. When he slashed at me, I caught his wrist and yanked it backwards as hard and far as I could. I put my foot out and tripped him. The knife lay on the ground at my feet.

"What is this?" Philip asked.

"He killed my brother," Wematin hissed. He got on his knees struggling to get up. "You killed my brother!" he screamed.

"Yes, I did!" I shot back at him. "He tried to kill me four times! The last time he tried he missed, so I killed him."

Philip put his hand out to command me to stop talking. “What is this about?” he asked again. Wematin stood and grabbed his own arm, grimacing as he turned toward Philip.

“He killed my brother Matchithew at Brookfield.” He thrust his arm at me.

Philip turned to me, looking me up and down.

“You were at Brookfield?”

“Yes, I was.”

“What is your name?”

“Jack Parker.”

Philip went and sat on a rock and appraised me for a few minute before he stood suddenly and walked away.

Once things quieted down, all of us captives sat on the ground and began talking about the war and where we might be going. The men told me they were taken outside of Marlborough while one of the women and her infant were taken near Lancaster while her husband was working in the field.

After a while, Ahanu came to me.

“That was a brave but foolish thing you did. Wematin will try to kill you every chance he gets.”

I shook my head. “If I didn’t do anything, he would have killed me then and there.”

He turned to look at the other Indians, making sure they were not in hearing range. "I will try to get word to Becky that you are safe. I should not be telling you this but I have no hard feelings against you, Jack," he whispered.

I saw several of the Indians sitting around the fires while others kept watch.

"Where are we going?" I asked.

"To the Mohawk." He nodded towards Philip. "He intends to ask them to join us."

"What will happen to us?" I waved my arm towards the group of captives.

"You will probably be given to the Mohawk as a gift so they will join with us."

"And if they don't want to join you?"

"You may be ransomed but I am not sure that is what he will do."

I sat there, trying to figure out what, if anything, I could do to get me us all out of this mess. Nothing came to mind.

"Maybe I will ask him what his intentions are," I said more to myself than Ahanu. He gave no response.

I decided to change the subject to something hopefully more pleasant. "What do you know of Kanti, Oota, and William?" They were three of my close friends from the

Wekapauge clan, part of the Quaboag tribe. Kanti was the mother of William and aunt of Oota-dabun.

Ahanu looked around before he spoke. “Oota and Kanti are safe. They are five days walk from here.” He pointed north, away from the fighting. “We sent all the women and children there.”

That news filled me with a sense of relief. To know they were safe put one of the fears to rest. He looked glum and hesitated to tell me about William.

“What about William? Is he fighting, too?”

He shook his head. “No, he isn’t. He was captured by soldiers near Natick three months ago. He is in prison in Boston.”

From the stories I’d heard, the conditions were horrible, with prisoners getting almost nothing to eat and no blankets or clothing of any type. They were just stuck in a cell, a cage really, with other men all in the same condition. Women and children had it no better. Many prisoners died in those deplorable conditions. The thought of William trying to survive like that made me angry and filled me with disgust for the authorities who would treat other people like that. I shook my head at this news. “Thank you for telling me, Ahanu.”

I watched him walk away, seeing something of the boy I once knew.

We were gathered up and brought to a lean-to. Through gestures, we were made to understand that we would sleep there. It wasn't very large, so we squeezed in as best we could. I lay on the other side of the women and children trying to block the wind, hoping to help keep them keep as warm as possible.

Just after we started out the next morning, after being given nothing to eat, Philip, Ahanu, and a few others went on ahead, leaving us captives with the worst of the lot of captors. One of them proved how cruel they could be.

The infant, hungry and cold, had been crying since well before dawn. No matter what the mother did, she could not get the baby to stop. We came down a slight slope that was covered in large rocks and moss. To the left, the hill dropped off steeply. To the right was a swamp with large bushes growing in it so you saw pockets of water between the bushes. The baby was wailing uncontrollably. The scar-faced Indian, the one who had taken my gun, came stomping back toward us, a naturally murderous expression on his face, grabbed the baby by the ankles out of the mother's arms, and threw it into the swamp. He turned and walked away. We were stunned and did not respond for a few seconds. The mother began screaming and ran into the swamp to save her child. The other captives yelled curses at the Indian. I began to follow her but was hit on the head and fell hard onto the rocks. I looked up to see that bastard dragging the mother kicking and screaming back to the path. I stood, pain throbbing through my head. I knew the baby was dead and there was not a thing any of us could do about it.

The mother, who was no more than twenty years old, was inconsolable. She cried and whimpered for days and only slept from cold and exhaustion. Whenever I looked at her, all I could think about was Sam, his round, fat face with the wisp of downy soft hair, and double chin. I remembered holding his tiny hand in mine, his fingers shorter than the fingernail of my little finger.

There have been three men in my life that I truly hated. One was Quimby, the bastard who ran the coastal schooner I was on during my apprenticeship, the second was Wematin's brother Matchitehew, and now the third was this horrible Indian. I vowed that I would somehow make him pay for what he had done.

We were up well before dawn and heading northwest. I did not speak with Ahanu or any of the other Indians until we stopped late in the day. One of them killed a small deer. It was butchered and roasting on the fire in a matter of minutes. The smell that came from the meat was one of the best things I have ever smelled. The children were shivering from the cold, so the other men and I collected some wood and started our own fire. I took one of the pine branches I found and went to the cooking fire. All talk stopped when I approached and stuck the branch in the fire. The Indians looked at me, eating pieces of deer meat with their hands. When the branch was burning, I turned and went back to where we captives were, all the while feeling their eyes boring into me. Once I had our fire going, small conversation started again. I sat and warmed my hands, warning the children not to get too close. When I looked up, I saw Philip watching me. He motioned for me to join him.

Philip had a look of natural authority, a commanding presence and was intelligent and articulate. His English was remarkable; he spoke better than many of the people I knew, and could write, which was something unheard of for an Indian at that time.

I sat on a pile of spruce boughs across from him. He did not say anything for a few minutes but sat looking down, rolling a small, smooth stone in his fingers, rubbing it now and then with his thumb.

"This," he said, "is a stone from the place where I live next to the ocean. It was on a small bit of land that stuck out into the water, and was there a long time before I picked it up. I keep it to remind me of my home and family."

“Will I see my family again?” I asked.

“Perhaps. I understand what it is like to be a father so I know that you want to be back with them. As long as you do not anger the Narragansett, you should survive. I have difficulty controlling them.”

We sat for a minute before he resumed. “I was not at Brookfield.”

“I was,” I shot back.

“I was also not at Swansea or Taunton,” he said, ignoring me, referring to the first two battles of the war. “I did not want this war. I wanted the governor and others in authority from both the Plymouth and Bay Colonies to listen to me and my people, to help us, as my father Massasoit helped them. We had simple requests but they poisoned my brother Wamsutta, they captured twenty-three of my people and executed them without any reason. That made my people angry, and they didn’t listen to me but to the ones who urged them on, to strike back at the English.”

“So why are you leading them now?” I asked.

He rolled the stone in his hands again, before tossing it from hand to hand.

“If I don’t lead them, they will be slaughtered. In the last few months, I have come to understand that this war is now necessary for our people, for all the tribes in New England. It is now the only way we can gain a position to negotiate with your leaders." He waved his arm at those around the large fire. "Some of these men don't understand this. They want to kill all of you, believing that will drive you back to England, but it will not. The number of our people is getting less as the number of your people is growing all the time. It is only a matter of time before we are enslaved."

"I don't understand. If you know that is inevitable, why fight like this? Why kill so many who don't mean you harm? We had good relations with the Nipmuck, Quaboag, and Wekapauge for ten years. Then it all changed almost overnight."

A bittersweet smile came to his face and he sighed. "I thought everything changed at once, too, but looking back, I see that was not true. We have been moving towards this result for years, ever since my father died. More and more land was taken from us, your religion was forced upon us, no attempt was made to understand our beliefs, except for Roger Williams in the Providence Plantation, and our customs and way of life were outlawed by the authorities. We have been ill-treated for a long time and this is the result – death and destruction."

I didn't know how to respond so I sat there quietly, thinking about what he'd said.

He got up, walked toward a small group of his men, and spoke to them. When he came back, he sighed. “I told them not to harm any of you.”

I jumped up and began yelling at him. “Why didn’t you tell them that before? Maybe that would have saved the baby!”

He looked confused. “What are you talking about? What baby?” he asked.

I turned and pointed at the mother.

“Her baby,” I said nodding toward the distraught young mother. “He,” I said pointing at the Narragansett, “threw it into a swamp because it wouldn’t stop crying … he killed an infant!”

“What?”

“He killed a baby!”

Philip jumped up and stormed over to the Narragansett, grabbed him by the hair and threw him to the ground. He stood over him, yelling at him in their language. The Narragansett yelled back. Philip grabbed his war club and beat him with five blows. While not fluent in the Indian language, I knew enough to understand what was being said.

“We are not fighting against infants! Do you not understand what this will do to the English if they learn about your stupid act? It will give them greater strength to fight against us. You idiot!” Philip yelled pacing back and forth in front of the man who cowered before the Indian leader. The Narragansett expected more blows, and held his hands in front of him to ward off another attack. Philip grabbed him by the front of the shirt and lifted him up off the ground.

"Go! Away from here! Go back to where you came from. You are of no help here."

The Indian stood, angry now, glaring at Philip. "Do not try to join me again or I will kill you." Philip dismissed the Narragansett with a wave of his hand. Two other Narragansett left with him, looking at Philip's group with disdain. Philip came to me, shaking his head. "We'll finish our conversation another time perhaps." He quietly walked away.

We began our trek on the third day under cloudy skies with a sharp, biting northwest wind that chilled you to the bone in a couple of minutes. The Indians did not seem to feel the cold for they all wore deerskin moccasins, leggings and a shirt. The children were crying from the cold. The other men and I gave them what little food we had gotten the night before. I couldn't eat when they were hungry. I had been hungry before and hoped to live long enough to be hungry again.

At mid-day, Philip sent a runner ahead with a belt of wampum, the formal way the Indian tribes had of asking to meet about something important. I watched as the runner headed south, making me wonder where he was going since we were headed west.

I couldn't think of anything other than Becky and Sam. As we marched along, grueling mile after mile, I could see Becky, her green eyes sparkling, the golden freckles across her nose, her heartwarming smile. I could smell her special smell and feel her body against me. I thought of holding her and the comfort it brought me. Being with my wife in that way was one of the most special moments I could ever hope for.

CHAPTER 6

We headed west all day and reached the river before sunset. It was the widest river I had ever seen, even wider than the Connecticut. The current looked slow and lazy. The clouds were breaking up, promising a cold night and a sunny day tomorrow. The fading sunlight illuminated the trees around us, turning the trunks a golden gray.

I watched Philip and a dozen others sit around a small fire. I ate three bites of my food before giving it to the always-hungry children. Ahanu got up and began walking away from Philip so I hurried to catch him.

"Ahanu," I said.

He stopped and turned to face me.

"Where are we going? How many more days will we travel?"

"You and the others will go on for two more days. A dozen men and I are leaving tomorrow. You will go with Philip and some of the others."

"Are you going back, Ahanu? If you are, please get word to Becky if you can. Let her know that I am alright."

"If I can, I will," he said. He put his hand on my shoulder before walking away.

A few of the Indians left the fire, so I walked over to Philip and asked if we could continue our conversation. He replied by motioning for me to sit next to him.

"So what happens now?" I asked.

"The runner came back with a belt of wampum from the Mohawk. They agreed to meet with me. We will be there tomorrow. I will talk to them. It may take several days, perhaps more, for me to convince them to join us. You and the others will be taken care of by the women. While the men are always warlike, the women will treat you well."

"What happens to us if they agree to join you?"

He looked at me for a moment. "They will want you to remain with them."

"And if they don't agree to join you? Will we go with you everywhere? Do you really want to drag us around with you?"

He looked at me. "I haven't decided what I will do with you. Maybe send you to another place with other captives. You know, you are smarter than the others."

"Well, I don't know about being smarter. I don't want to die and will do anything to get back to my wife and son. If that's what makes me smarter, than I guess I am."

He chuckled at this remark. Then I asked a question I had debated asking, not sure of the response I would get.

"Do you think you will win?"

"We may not win," he told me, "but we will do all we can to make them see we are a people to be dealt with and not punished for no reason and humiliated." He did not say anything for a minute but sat playing with his stone. "I am sure that I will die a violent death. There really is no other way for my life to end."

When we got to the river, the Indians found the canoes hidden among the brush, ready and waiting for them.

We crossed the river at dawn the next day in several large canoes. I was in the one with three other captives, Philip, and another of his men as well as the two paddlers. Philip stood the whole time balancing on his feet, moving with the motion of the canoe as it sliced through the water. I was on my knees towards the stern watching the woods and fields on each side of the river. The day was very nice, with a light wind from the southwest. The water was calm and we made the crossing quickly.

We were still moving northwest, as we had for the last three days. We had gone a good ways when we came to the top of a large hill and looking to the southwest, I saw mountains that showed dark blue against the sky. They were the largest hills I'd ever seen and a good way to mark the position and direction. After a minute's rest, we began walking again, the children and women having difficulty keeping pace. When I asked, Philip was good enough to slow down the pace although I could tell he was anxious to get to the Mohawk village.

We camped before sunset on the edge of a field surrounded by several large chestnut and elm trees. We ate the meal we were given, though, as I had done since being captured, I took only a few bites and gave the rest to the children. I knew I was losing weight but the children needed the food to survive. I had every intention of getting back to my family, but I was not going to see young children die from lack of enough food. I think it was the fact that they wanted to get to the Mohawk country as soon as they could. Philip did not want to be away from the war any longer than he had to be.

I sat with him again in front of a small fire.

"Do you need the Mohawk to fight with you?" I asked.

"I do not need them, but it would be a good thing if they did. Bringing in another nation would make us that much more powerful."

"Do you think they will join you?"

"I don't know. I will make the best argument I can. The decision is theirs to make."

I sat watching the flames, thinking of home, and wishing I were there instead of where I was.

"If the Mohawks take me, I will not stay with them. I will escape and get home. Nothing will keep me from my wife and son."

He regarded me for a moment, tossing the stone in his right hand.

"I admire your courage but it will be difficult for you to escape. They like to keep the captives they get, either from their own efforts, or from other ways. They will treat you well. You might like it enough to send for your wife and son."

"No, I think it best if you go to the Mohawk." I gave him a hard stare and stomped off, knowing I had no control over my immediate future.

We walked for two more days, uphill and down, through forests of large trees and flat land that went for miles down long, wide valleys. We crossed many brooks and streams, which left our feet constantly wet. Large, painful blisters throbbed for hours after we stopped walking.

At mid-day on the second day, Philip sent a runner ahead with the message of his coming and the reason for his visit. A short time later, we came through large fields with corn stubble showing through the snow. The smell of wood smoke came to me, signaling that we were near the Mohawk village.

Half a dozen boys shooting with bows and arrows were the first to see us approach. They went running toward a large group of long houses a hundred yards away. Soon, a group of men gathered outside the houses and waited for us. Philip stopped when we were thirty feet away from them. Two men from the group came toward us. The first was about forty years old. He was a hard-looking man with a scraggly topknot that had several turkey feathers attached to it by a leather braid. The skin was tight to his face and he looked like he never smiled. The second man was younger, slender, and handsomer than the first. His forehead was painted red and his black hair was growing down over his left ear, with triangular pieces of blue shells hanging from his ears and tattoos covering his upper body.

“Shekon,” said the second man, which I came to learn was their greeting.

They looked us over for a couple of minutes before indicating that Philip and a few of his men should go to the central longhouse, always the largest building in an Indian village, the place where all important matters are discussed. We captives were herded off to an area at the edge of the village where the boys with the bows and arrows watched us. The other men with me didn't seem to care where we were. They acted as if life had no interest for them, which may very well have been the case.

Three women emerged from one of the wigwams and came to us. The oldest one went straight to the captive children, smiling at them. The children jerked back from her outstretched hand, not sure what to expect. The second went to the women and began talking to them in a soft, pleasant voice. The third and youngest came towards me. When she was a few feet away, her face lit up with a smile. I took a quick breath because she reminded me very much of Oota dabun. She had a special smile, too, that made you smile in return. She was very pretty with long black hair and perfect white teeth. Indians had much better teeth than any of us did. I hardly remember ever seeing an Indian woman with missing teeth. Most of our women, by the time they reached forty years old, had lost at least two or more teeth. Her name was Onatah, which, I later learned meant "of the earth."

When I asked if she spoke English, she replied she did, but not well. She spoke haltingly, trying to get each word right. Onatah and the other two women took us captives to one of the longhouses. Normally, several families live in a longhouse but there were only two in this one. We were given the first real, hot food we'd had in ten days, and told to sleep on the platforms around the edge of the house. The platforms were about three feet off the ground and covered with deer, bear, and wolf skins. We were all so tired that even a piece of soft ground would suffice, but this was almost as good as a real bed. To lie on skins six inches deep covered with warm, soft bearskin is wonderful. After the meal, we were all asleep within a few minutes.

The next day I had an opportunity to observe the Mohawk. Like the Wekapauge and Quaboag as well as other Nipmuck tribes, they treated the children well. The women worked hard while the men hunted or lounged about. In my time with them, I found them to be a good people, loving their families, protecting their children and giving them a good home filled with love and understanding. The one difference I noticed between the Mohawk and other Indians I knew was that anger seemed to smolder beneath the skin of the Mohawk men, taking only a small incident to make it burst forth.

Since the Mohawk were located to the east of the other Iroquois tribes, they were responsible for guarding the eastern part of the Iroquois territory. Years before the war, the Nipmuck, including the Quaboag and Wekapauge, attacked the Mohawk in a battle that lasted two days, but was a defeat for the Nipmuck. They were not well versed in warfare and easily beaten by the stronger, more numerous Mohawk.

While with the Mohawk, I learned that they called themselves the Kanienkehaka, which means "The People of the Flint." The village was located in a place called Kanatsiohareke, which means "The Place of The Clean Pot." It refers to a spot in a good-sized creek where the water carved perfectly round holes into the streambed. The Mohawk noticed that when the water ran downstream and into those holes, it swirled and churned around making it look like the water was scrubbing the inside of the potholes.

The Mohawk women treated us well, but several of their young men came around to sneer at us and taunt us with harsh words and threats. One of them took a strong disliking to me, though I could not figure out what I did to anger him.

The women and children captives were taken to another longhouse at the other side of the village, leaving me and the other two captive men alone. Unlike during our journey here, we were left free to wander about as we pleased but with the knowledge that there were many pairs of eyes watching us, making it clear we could not escape, and if we did, we wouldn't get very far.

I didn't see Philip for two days after we arrived because he was in council with the Mohawk sachem and other leaders, trying to convince them to join him in his war against the English. When I did see him on the third day, he looked troubled. He went to the far side of the village, climbed a small hill, and sat alone playing with his stone. He stayed there for a long time, looking up now and then. He was obviously considering what was best for his cause. Because I had nothing else to do, I sat on a rock outside the wigwam where we slept, enjoying the fair weather. The sky a was a beautiful pale blue with a light southwesterly breeze. The warmth of the day gave you the knowledge that spring was on its way, but the weather in this area could change in a moment, and I knew that there would be cold and snow again before the warm weather arrived. After a short while, I got up and went to Philip.

"Have they made a decision?" I asked.

He looked up, startled at the interruption. He turned away from me and tossed his stone in the air several times. "They will not join us. We are leaving tomorrow."

In one way, this was good news. Since the Mohawk would not join with Philip that meant the war would not be prolonged. In another way, it was worse because it meant I would have to stay with the Mohawk. I was not pleased with this.

"Take me with you. I want to go back," I said.

He shook his head. "No. You will stay here with the others."

"What will become of us? Will they make us slaves or sell us to some other tribe?" I asked, the anger in my voice growing. "Will they kill us when the food gets low?"

"While I can't answer for them, I know they will not harm any of you."

"Why don't you ransom us? I know Mr. Pynchon would pay for my release."

"Perhaps, but how much? And what of the others? Will anyone pay a ransom for them?" I looked down at my feet because I knew the others did not have much of anything and the reality was that even if they were offered ransom, no one they knew could pay it. I felt guilty knowing I could be freed, but not them.

"It is best if you stay here. I need to move to other places quickly and can't be taking care of a group of people that will get in the way."

I jumped up, angry. “You took us! Now you are leaving us because we’ll get in your way. What kind of plan was that?”

He didn’t say a word. He just looked at me with the steady gaze of a man who knows what he has done and that what he has started will not succeed.

“Now that the Mohawk will not join you, you will lose! You will lose soon and for what? All of this will be for nothing! There are already too many dead on both sides. What did this war change? What did it accomplish?”

He jumped up and faced me. His dark eyes flashed a burning anger. “Enough! What do you know? How can you possibly understand what our people have gone through? How dare you judge me and my people!”

I looked around and saw many of the Mohawk approaching as well as some of the captives.

“It is not for you to say what will be,” he continued. “Your predictions are wrong. We will win and drive you back to the sea. We will control our land again. We will not be subject to what the governor or anyone else says. It is not your right to tell us what we should do or the type of people we should be.” His chest was heaving and his jaw clenched. “You are just as ignorant as the rest, thinking you know what this is about but not having the slightest idea. You will stay here. You will not return to your home."

He flipped his hand backwards, dismissing me as if I was a servant. He walked away towards the Mohawk sachem as his final words rang in my ears. To me, it sounded like a death sentence.

That night there was a dance, although I didn't know what it was for. Perhaps the Mohawk, like other tribes I knew, needed to celebrate now and then. That night was such a time, with drums beginning just at sunset as the western sky turned pink under a band of dark, flat clouds. It began soft and slow, a single drummer beating out a simple rhythm as they gathered around a bonfire. Soon after, a second drummer joined the first followed by two more. Three of the men, dressed in skins and masks, held turtle shells full of stones or dried beans, shaking them in time to the drumming. As the music grew louder, the men began a dance, jumping around the fire, dipping their heads and swaying from one side to the other while shaking their rattles. Other men began dancing, with some women leaders joining in after a time. Soon the entire village was chanting as the drums beat a constant pulse. This went on for hours, and though I was tired, I sat watching, hypnotized by the flames licking into the air, feeling the beat of the drums in my body.

CHAPTER 7

When I awoke early the next morning, I learned that Philip and his men were gone. There was no hope for me now. I was trapped and could see no way out of the situation. The other captives and I knew we would find out about our future in the next day or two, so I went to find Onatah to see if she could give me a hint as to what was in store for us. I found her at the captive's longhouse, pounding corn into meal, preparing to make cakes on a flat stone next to the small fire.

I knelt down next to her. “Can you help me?”

“I don't know. What is it that you want?” She handed me a small piece of dried fish.

“I need to know what will happen to us now that Philip, I mean Metacomet, is gone. How will we be treated?”

She sat back, holding the long, round stone pestle in her hand and brushed the hair out of her eyes with the back of her hand. I swallowed the first bite waiting for her to answer.

“If you are all treated as others have been, you will not be harmed and will become part of our village.”

"Why have I not seen any other captives? What happened to them?"

She shook her head. "It's not my place to tell you these things. You must wait on the sachem to tell you."

"What is he like? Do you know him well?"

At this she laughed, catching me by surprise. I was wondering if I was going to die and she was laughing. "I don't see anything funny in my question," I snapped.

"I am not laughing at you. I know both sachems well because they are my father and mother," she said with a small smile. She went back to grinding her corn and I walked away, wandering around the village as I had since I got there, thinking of being home.

I came to learn that the Mohawk women or clan mothers were responsible for the farming, property, and family while the men were responsible for all hunting and military matters. The Mohawk were part of the Iroquois Confederacy. Only men could represent the Mohawk at the great tribal council but the women selected who the men would be. The women also selected the members of the tribal council that could be both men and women.

A constant, dull ache was in my heart. I couldn't stand being away from all I knew and loved, and not knowing if I would ever be there again. I thought about what my life would be like if I became a member of the tribe, realizing I would be given a woman and expected to raise a family, to help provide food, and work at whatever jobs were given to me. For all purposes, I would be a little better than a slave. My existence among the Indians would be a living death forever.

I sat in a solitary spot overlooking the river and wept for all I had lost. After a while, an anger rose up inside me and I didn't know which I was more angry with the situation or myself. No one could fix this except me. I vowed that I would see Becky and Sam again and do everything in my power to get back to them. From that moment on, I began plotting my escape.

Two days later, I received a shock when I saw the Narragansett Indian who killed the infant and taken my gun and powder from me walk into the village accompanied by three Mohawk men. They were talking and laughing, seemingly without a care in the world. His name, I learned later, was Matanaaga, which means "A man who fights." He turned my way and stopped, staring at me. He left his companions and hurried towards me with a fierce look in his eyes and his fists clenched. I stood ready, waiting for him to attack. When he was a few yards away, a short Mohawk with a large head stepped in his way, and put his right hand up, gesturing for him to stop. Matanaaga ignored him and started to go around him but stopped when the

Mohawk said something I did not understand. Matanaaga stopped, pointed at me, and said something in a loud voice. The Mohawk answered him and, putting a hand on Matanaaga's arm, turned him away from me and began walking toward the nearest longhouse. Matanaaga turned and glared at me, a look that told me he was not done with me.

It all came to a head a week later when Matanaaga came at me again, intending to beat me senseless. I was pounding corn and turned when I heard him yell. Everyone stopped what they were doing to watch. The Indians generally do not tolerate fighting in this fashion, unless it is for a something serious such as the murder of another Indian or a deep insult. Later I was told that they had never seen a fight between an Indian from another tribe and a white captive, so no one interfered. Matanaaga was lumbering at me, his head low, a tomahawk in his right hand that he whipped back and forth, cutting the air each time with a whistle. The only weapon I had was a ten-inch-long stone pestle. While it was heavy and could cause damage if you were hit with it, it was no match for a tomahawk. I crouched and waited for him, getting ready to defend myself as best I could. When he was almost upon me, he raised the tomahawk, ready to strike a killing blow. I ducked and smacked him in the stomach with the pestle, catching him by surprise. He grunted but did not stop.

Onatah was standing outside her longhouse watching the fight. She started to walk towards me but her father stopped her with a hand on her arm. Matanaaga came at me again, slashing the tomahawk from the side. I stepped out of the way and hit his hand with the pestle, causing his weapon to go backwards thirty feet. He started to go after it but stopped and came at me again. He hit me in the jaw, sending me sprawling, and I landed in a heap. When I looked up he was rushing toward me again.
Without thinking, I got up and lowered my neck and shoulders and charged into him, thumping into his stomach. I caught him just right because he came up off the ground a few inches, almost balancing on my right shoulder. I stood to push him off me but somehow flipped him up and over me. He crashed to the ground, landing on his back, and a let out a loud grunt. The Mohawk were amused at how I bested him and some were laughing. He struggled to his feet, wincing in pain, and looking for his tomahawk. I realized I still had the pestle in my hand and brought it down, aiming for his head. He raised his arm to block it so I hit him between the wrist and elbow. He dropped his arm as if it was broken and scrambled away from me. I watched him walk past the Mohawk men, shouting at them as he did.

Onatah was at my side in a minute to see if I was hurt, but I was fine considering I escaped being tomahawked to death.

Her father called to her and she left me, looking back once as she walked away.

The next day, I began looking for a chance to escape. One of the other male captives, John Stuart, ran from the village in the early morning, along the river, heading toward the woods. It was a stupid, clumsy attempt that resulted in him being caught and dragged back. He was beaten until blood flowed from every part of his body and left where he fell.

All of the Mohawk were now alert to the possibility of another escape attempt, keeping an even more watchful eye on us. I decided to bide my time until a good opportunity came about.

It didn't take long, for most of the Mohawk men went on a big hunt, so there were only a few boys and older men left in the village. I decided to slip away that night.

When everyone was asleep, I slowly made my way outside after taking the wolf skin I slept on and a leather bag full of meal from where it hung near the door. I looked around, letting my eyes get accustomed to the darkness. It was clear and cold with no moon. Much of the snow had melted over the last few days, leaving a good part of the ground bare and free of snow, so the traveling would be easier. Trying to escape in the snow was a foolish thing to attempt because it would be easy for anyone to track the footprints. I looked around once more and began walking away, all the while expecting to hear someone make a noise at my escape but it was quiet. I planned to go southeast, since Philip had brought us in a northwest direction. I did not know what I would do when I got to the big river but I knew I would figure something out.

I walked all night through forests and fields, making good time and putting some distance between the village and myself. With each step, I thought that it was possible I would get away. I stopped near dawn to rest and eat. I figured I had traveled at least twenty miles and, if I could do another thirty miles before sunset, I should be far enough away for the Mohawk not to come after me. Even if they did, I had what I thought was a good start on them. After a few minutes, I started on my way again, picking up the pace, and moving as fast as I could over unfamiliar territory. By late afternoon, I was sure I would be home soon. It all seemed so easy, just walking away. Within an hour, I found out that my situation was not as good as I thought it was.

I heard voices off to my left, coming from the other side of a small hill. I walked in the opposite direction, taking every care to make no noise. The voices were closer, so I looked behind me and fell, tripping over a small bush. I landed with a grunt and crashed into another bush. When I looked up, five Mohawk were standing over me. One, taller than the rest, motioned for me to get up. They took me back to where they were making a camp for the night and tied my legs so I couldn't try to escape. I gave them my bag of meal and lay down near the fire, exhausted from my effort, and slept.

We made it back to the village in two days, with the meat from five deer. I was given the happy chore of carrying as much of the meat as possible hanging from a stout pole on my shoulders. The bark bit into my shirt and rubbed the skin raw. There was no way I could shift the pole so that it did not cause me pain. By the time we got back, my shoulders were raw and bleeding, and the cold made it sting like fire. That was a minor issue compared to what came next.

The Mohawk and other war-like Indians have a punishment that, while very simple, is one of the worst you can endure. I was stripped naked before the entire village that formed two lines stretching from one end of the village to the other. Each man, woman, and child had a branch or reed in their hand, ready to hit me. I was told that I must go from one end to the other, through the gauntlet, to be beaten for my attempted escape. I saw the women and children jeering and taunting me, eager to whip me, with a fierce look in their eye. I do not know how it happened, but I stumbled and was pushed into the line. I ran as fast as I could, which was not very fast because of my weakened physical state from walking over two hundred miles in four days and the injuries from carrying the deer meat. The branches and reeds slashed across my neck, shoulders, back, and behind. The stinging pain rippled through my body. I tripped and fell, but that only caused them to increase the beating. I made it to the end, dropping to the ground, feeling the blood flowing from the hundreds of small slashes in my skin. After a few minutes, Onatah came and helped me up and, with another woman, brought me to a small wigwam. There they laid me down and washed me before slathering something that smelled bad enough to make me want to vomit but relieved the pain from my wounds.

Onatah stayed after the other woman left and sat down next to me with an angry scowl on her face.

"It was stupid of you to try to escape. My father and the other leaders decided you would be adopted into the tribe. You will be the son of a family that had one of its young men killed … you will take his place." She sat there, staring at me. "Do you realize how close you came to being tortured to death? You could be out there with all your fingers cut off, the children stabbing your feet with knives, everyone else waiting until the night to burn you until your skin falls off." She stormed out, leaving me to consider this sudden change in my fate.

Three days later, John Stuart tried to escape again. This time he made it a few miles before he was caught by some of the Mohawk men. He was brought back, his clothes were torn off, and he was tied to a post. The entire village was in an uproar, rushing towards the scene of the excitement. Two Mohawk came up to him and, after one put John's right hand against the post, the other cut it off with a long knife. He screamed an ungodly scream that only caused the tribe to yell even louder, demanding more. The fingers of his other hand were slit with the edge of a shell lengthwise before he was placed on a scaffold under which a fire was built. I couldn't watch anymore and turned away, trying to get away from the sound but I couldn't escape it. The torture continued for hours and the screams seemed like they would never stop. Finally, sometime during the late night, a loud yell went up from the tribe and I knew he was finally dead. Even after all these years, I can still hear the horrid sounds echoing in my ears, the incessant gabble and joyous shrieks of the women and children forever burned into my memory.

It was enough to make any man wonder if it could get any worse. What was to befall me was the last thing I would have expected.

I lay awake all night considering what to do. I didn't know if I should attempt another escape or be thankful I was not tortured. I could not get the thought of Becky and Sam out of my mind. It was difficult to contemplate that I might never see them again. I could not accept that.

All the next day, my mind gnawed at the problem while I worked at one menial job after another. As I looked around at the Indians, I saw them in a different way than I had two days before. They were unbelievably cruel and would relish the sight of me being tortured. I didn't sleep the next night either, thinking it over, weighing the possibility of seeing my wife and son again against the certainty of unspeakable torture if I was caught. I made my decision during the morning. I would escape and make sure I was not caught. I slept very well that night.

The following day, Matanaaga appeared beside me as I was pounding and scraping a deer hide, which was considered women's work, an act to humiliate me before the tribe. He said it would give him great pleasure to see me burned with fire sticks for hours before my skin was cut off. He told me I should run away, because if I did, he would catch me and bring me back so he could watch me die. He laughed when he walked away.

Three weeks went by, my life with the family that had lost a son being one unending torment day after day. I marked the days until my escape. I hid small amounts of corn meal in a leather pouch I was given. Much of the snow melted and the ground was dry and bare. That would allow me to make better distance with less chance of being tracked. When all was ready, I decided to go the next day.

When Indian tribes war on each other, they generally attack just before dawn as that is the time most people are still asleep and they have enough light to see to begin their attack. That is the time when I chose to leave, just before even a faint light began appearing on the horizon. I knew the area around the village well enough to be confident of not running into any hazards that would raise an alarm.

I stepped out of the longhouse, making no noise because I was wearing a pair of moccasins made for me by the mother of the family whose son I would replace. I took a small leather pouch of meal and a squirrel robe that hung from one shoulder and came down to the waist. It was warm while I was sleeping but not heavy enough to provide much protection from the cold. I slipped into the field next to the longhouse, staying near the edge, away from open areas where I might leave marks they could use to track me. I knew I had to move fast and leave as little sign of my passing as possible. I decided that I would do whatever was necessary to regain my freedom.

There are days when it is beautiful and cloudless with barely enough wind to stir a leaf. Many people marvel at such days, but those of us who are out in the weather daily know that these days are weather-breeders, forerunners of storms. It is difficult to distinguish between a fine day and a weather-breeder but I always explain that if it is too good a day, a bad storm will happen within the next two days. When the sun rose, I saw that the day would be perfect, a little too perfect. While a storm would slow me down, it would also help cover my trail, making it more difficult to find me, and let me get further away.

After a time, I was at least ten miles from the village, moving southeast and keeping a good, ground-eating pace. I learned the trick from Philip's warriors, how they moved at just such a pace as to travel long distances without stopping, able to cover fifty miles or more in a day. I estimated it was about two days' hard travel to get to the river. Once there, I had to find a canoe. From what I saw on the journey with Philip, Indians hid canoes all up and down the river to make crossing as easy as possible. I learned that when Indians want to get somewhere, they do not like to dawdle but get to their destination as soon as possible.

I stayed to the areas with rock and moss and walked down the ice cold water of the many streams I came upon, leaving as faint a trail as I possibly could. I blundered into a swamp and stumbled through it, water up to my waist, the intense cold slowing down my movements. My feet kept getting caught on the roots of long dead trees and I fell a couple of times, coming up coughing water, soaked from head to foot. I made it to a small island a hundred yards from the nearest solid ground and rested there for a short time, after which I walked back into the water, heading for a small field on the other side.

When I got to it, I took my clothes off. The cold air started to freeze the water on my body. As I shivered, I squeezed as much water from my sodden clothes as possible. My skin stung with the cold and putting the less wet clothes back on helped, but not much. I looked for a place to spend the night, some place that was out of the wind where I could build a lean-to of branches and pine boughs. My stomach rumbled as the hunger gnawed at me, making me shiver even more. The meal in my pouch had dissolved into mush but it was all the food I had, so I ate two handfuls and left the rest of it for morning. As I made my way toward a group of large rocks near the bottom of a small hill, I looked around, getting a feel for my location and the distance I had traveled. When I got to the rocks, I found the hill blocked the wind well and there was a large group of spruce trees at the edge of the woods, not more than fifty feet away, which was good because I did not think I had the strength to go any further than that. Another large rock, taller than me, was a few feet to the left of the other rocks. As I began to stagger behind it, with the cold freezing my ripped clothes, my heart stopped and fear washed over me when I saw the remains of a small fire behind it. I looked around in the fading light, trying to see if there was anyone near the area, someone who might have stayed there and, for some reason, might come back. The fire looked to have been out for a while so I felt the rocks around the pile of ashes. Since they were still warm, I knew that someone had left this area a couple of hours ago. I decided to build a small fire, stripping pieces of bark from a nearby birch tree and adding two pinecones, blowing gently on the few small coals hidden under the ash. The fire smoked for a moment but then began to burn. I was taking a terrible chance that someone would see the fire or smell the smoke, but I was too cold and afraid of dying in the night if I did not get warm.

There was no other shelter that I could see so I decided to spend the night. I hurried to the woods as best as I could, gathering an armload of spruce boughs for a bed and to put between the rocks and hillside to keep as much of the cold out, and as much of my body heat in, as possible. I dragged the three largest rocks to my miserable shelter and hugged them, trying to absorb any warmth that might still be in them. I covered myself with dead oak leaves and fell asleep a short time later, waking every little bit, the cold biting into me. The last time I woke up dawn was just beginning. The clothes on my back had frozen during the night, sticking to my skin in places, pulling at it every time I moved. I ate a handful of mush and set out for the river.

My pace was not as good as the day before, since the exertion and cold were taking their toll on my endurance. I used every advantage I could think of to stay out of the wind as much as possible. Around noon, I stopped and looked back, trying to judge the distance I'd made over the last few hours. There was a long narrow field with a stream running alongside. In my position, I could see three miles behind me. As I looked, I saw movement at the very far end of the field, moving in my direction. At first, I thought it was an animal, perhaps a moose or large deer, but as I watched, I realized it was a man, moving at a good pace. He walked at the edge of the field next to the stream, looked around every few minutes, and then resumed walking after scanning the ground. I lost my breath when I realized that it was an Indian after me. The Mohawk had probably sent a few of their men in different directions in hopes that one of them would pick up my trail. This had never occurred to me, and I cursed myself for it but realized I had no time to waste. I could think of only two courses of action: the first was to find a place where I could ambush my pursuer, and the second was to move as fast as I could, putting as much distance between us as possible. I decided against the first option because, in my weakened condition, I stood almost no chance in a hand-to-hand fight with a well-fed Indian. I turned and made my way into the woods, skirting the side of the hill, before moving to the southwest again. I made no effort to hide my trail, for this Indian, whoever he was, picked up the tracks I had made when I tried my best to conceal them. Now it was a matter of speed. If I could make it to the river ahead of him, it gave me a chance to get across and hide. I thought he might give up his pursuit if he saw I was across the river, though it was a slim possibility at best.

An hour later, I saw the river from the edge of a wooded hillside and knew it was only a couple of miles away. I kept a watchful eye and ear for my follower but nothing alerted me to any danger. I moved faster now, knowing I could be on the other side before nightfall. I was a mile from the river when, out of the corner of my right eye, I caught movement two hundred yards to my right. I crouched, watching for whatever I had seen. I waited a good amount of time and was just about to start when an Indian emerged from the woods across a small glade, no more than fifty yards away. I was shocked when I saw it was Matanaaga who was following me. I thought of his promise to bring me back to watch me die.

I could either attack him or race to the river. Like my consideration of the night before, I knew he could overpower me so I waited until he moved off to my left before I made my way down the hillside, staying behind rock and trees, showing as little of myself as I could. When I was down the hill, I made my way directly for the river. Only a short distance separated me from the water when I heard a noise behind me. I turned to see Matanaaga approaching, war club in his hand, flipping it back and forth, as he did with the tomahawk. I had nowhere to go, so I faced him, waiting for him to attack.

He stopped and laughed. "You thought you could escape but not from me," he said as he moved around to my right, trying to get between the river and me. "I told the Mohawk to not bother wasting their time chasing you, that I would find you and bring you back," he said with a hideous grin. "But we are not going back. I am going to enjoy watching you die." He began walking toward me, moving the club in a small circular motion, getting ready to strike. "I told you I hoped you would escape so I could find you and kill you, you miserable English, and now I will." He charged at me, the club raised above his head, his dark face contorted with hate, yelling as he came on. I ducked as he swung and having no weapon of my own, stuck my foot out and tripped him. It seems like a simple thing to do and it is, but he fell hard, the club slipping from his hand. I reached out and was able to grab it. He was on his feet in a second, coming at me like a demon from hell, ready to kill me with his bare hands. I yelled and swung with all my might, hitting him with a glancing blow to the right side of his head. He fell to his knees, grunting in surprise. As I began to pull the club up, he grabbed it, trying to wrest it from my hand. I fell on him and we rolled through the dry, cold, beaten grass to a small dirt area next to the water. He flipped me over onto my back and, just as he was about to jump on me, I rolled again away from him. The club thudded down into the ground next to my head. I grasped it, pulling him off balance, seeing him land on his side facing away from me. I jumped on him, the shaft of the club in my hands. When he rolled over, I leapt on him and shoved the handle of the club against his throat. To this day, I do not know where my strength came from, but I pushed it into his throat, trying with all my might to cut off his air and suffocate him. He was a big man and, with what I hoped was his last breath, threw me off and reached out for me. His hands closed around the front of my shirt, lifting me up before dropping me in the water. When he landed on me, I punched him in the throat and dug at his eyes with my fingers. I poked him in one eye and he fell off me. I threw my weight on him and we landed in the water a couple of feet from shore, struggling to pin each other. I found a small rock and hit him in the head with it. He yelled in pain and I turned him over so he was face down in the river. I sat on his back, pushing his head into the water. He lashed at me with his arms but I would not move. He tried heaving to his knees, but I kicked his legs with my heels and he dropped back into the water. I put both hands on the back of his head and pushed with all my remaining strength. I was straining so hard and weak from the cold and lack of food, that I started to lose my grip on him, and blackness began to descend on me. I felt faint and knew that if he got up, he would kill me in a minute. I shook my head, the blackness fading a bit, gave a wild yell, and pushed as hard as I could. His movements grew weaker until he kicked and squirmed few more times, and thrashed with his arms, then lay still. I leapt off him, waiting for him to resume the fight but he did not move. I fell into the water, staggering from the exertion, my mind blank. I kicked at him to turn him over. When I saw his face, I knew he was dead. I collapsed to the ground, exhausted. I stared at the dead body, watching the water lap onto the deerskin leggings and moosehide moccasins. I scrambled to the body and worked the leggings, shirt, moccasins, and blanket off of him, and took the small bag of meal hanging from a belt on his waist. The clothes I wore, except for the moccasins, were those I had on the day I was taken captive, and were ragged with large holes in the leggings and shirt. The moccasins I had were poorly made, partly because of the Mohawk mother's failing eyesight, and Matanaagas' while too large for me, fit fine if I wore them over my own. I put the shirt and leggings on and squeezed as much water as I could out of the blanket. I pushed his body into the water and watched it float downstream.

My search for a canoe took me upstream two miles. It was hidden in four feet of water, three rocks holding it down in an area just below the riverbank. I found a long branch and, by leaning over, hooked the broken end of the branch around the front of the canoe. Getting my arm wet to the shoulder, I was able to pull it up and dump the water out. I tossed the rocks into the river and found a paddle lashed to the gunwale with grapevine. Luck was with me, I thought. Dreams of getting home floated in my head.

Chunks of ice, some large and some small, floated in the river, which could easily rip a hole in the thin elm bark canoe. My strength was not enough to get me straight across, so I did as best I could, avoiding the ice, and floating downstream while I dug into the water, pushing hard to reach the other shore. The current was strong and swept me down river towards a large tree that had come down in a storm. The base of the trunk pointed at the eastern shore while the branches, half out of the water, reached far out into the water. I dug with the paddle to get far enough across to land against the trunk from where I could ease my way to shore. I wasn't able to and the canoe headed for the branches. I saw Matanaaga's body caught against the branches, bobbing up and down. I could do nothing to prevent the canoe from hitting the body. The canoe thudded into the body, somehow flipping it over so his face stared at the sky. I took the paddle and gave it a good shove but it made no difference. I made the shore a short while later, although it felt like a couple of hours. My arms throbbed and my shoulders ached but I was free from my captives.

Chapter 8

I knew that Springfield was three, maybe four days' travel to the east. I didn't think I would be able to travel very fast, but I vowed to myself that I would not stop until I reached it.

The next day started out fine with a clear blue sky and a southwest wind, but by late morning, gray streamers of clouds had moved in from the northeast. The wind picked up, shifted out of the north and the temperature dropped until, within a few minutes, it was cold enough to chill your hands and face. I rested for a bit, catching my breath and summoning the energy to go on. As soon as I started walking, the snow started, softly at first, a few flakes coming down but it stopped within an hour or so. Within a short time, it began to rain. The storm was doing its best to prevent me from getting home as fast as I wanted.

There are times when I wonder which type of weather is worst, whether it is the bone chilling bitter cold of winter with its wind-driven blizzards, or the insufferable heat and humidity of summer with its torrential earth shattering thunderstorms. After all my considerations, I have decided that it is a cold, dismal rain that will sink a person's feelings lower than any other type of weather. The ground turns to muck, causing your feet to sink into the ever-deepening mud, sloshing and sucking at you as you try to move along. Slogging along on such a day, you will see steam rising off your body as the rain runs into your clothing, wetting you to the skin.

It was a cold and mournful rain. Its cheerlessness was not relieved by the appearance of the brown and barren country. What was not brown was gray. Small trees were scattered about, looking as if they were starved.

Each minute of every hour that afternoon and night went by with agonizing slowness, a trickle of time that never seemed to move forward. The afternoon was filled with a sky of flat gray from which the cold rain fell and never seemed to stop. It was as if the day stopped, although I knew that could not be the case because at some point, after interminable minutes and hours, the dark of night would descend. The night seemed to move slower than the day. This is when it was the worst, for I could not travel and never seemed to be any closer to my home, my wife, and my son.

During the night, from want of food and exposure to the cold and rain, I became delusional, convinced the Mohawk were on my trail, getting closer with each hour. I knew that was a foolish thought, for Indians almost never travel at night because they feared Abamacho, the devil who would claim them if they are caught. Their fear was so great, it kept them in their wigwams. But, these were not ordinary times and the warriors' fears may be little compared to the humiliation they suffered because of my second escape. So strong was the feeling that, against all better judgment, I went back on my trail that night like a fool, moving slowly to not make any noise. Such was the strain on me that my thoughts were so muddled. After I had gone a mile or more in the pouring rain, and saw what I thought was a flicker of light dancing off the gray tree trunks. As I made my way around to the right and up a small slope, I saw it was nothing more than a large group of yellowed beech leaves on a branch twirling in the wind. The idea of a fire made me think of roasting meat and the memory of the smell of cooking meat came to me. My rumbling stomach reminding me of how hungry I was, since I had nothing to eat for two days. I made a shelter out of dead branches in an area behind a rock, out of the wind. As I lay there, my thoughts were of Becky, who I missed so much. We had been apart for months at a time before but the difference this time was that I did not know if I would live to see her again and she probably thought I was dead. My son Sam needed me even though he did not know it, and I needed him more than he would ever know.

"I am on my way home to you, Becky," I said aloud. "I am on my way home." Within a minute, I was asleep.

The next morning was colder, much colder, and in just a couple of hours the temperature dropped so quickly that I was forced to slow down. Hurrying in such weather with only soaking wet deerskin leggings, shirt, moccasins, and a small blanket wrapped about my shoulders was taking its toll on me. The wind shifted around to the northeast again, cutting through me like a knife. It began snowing around midmorning, a light, soft snow that I knew was the beginning of a strong storm. The wind picked up from a light breeze that swirled the snowflakes to a strong wind that blew them at an angle. The snow stung my eyes, so that I kept my head down, seeing only the base of trees to either side and the ground in front of me. The ground, wet from rain, turned to mud in places, which froze, making travel even more difficult.

I walked for as long as I could in the snow but had to stop after a while to find a place to spend the night. I found a good spot under two large pines trees that grew on the side of a hill. The pines needles on the ground made a soft bed and the hill blocked some of the wind. I gathered spruce boughs to make a lean-to and as many sticks and dry branches as I could. I found that Matanaaga had a flint and steel buried in the bottom of his meal bag, something he must have gotten in trade, so now I would be able to make a fire. My luck got better when, coming back with my fourth load of wood for the fire, I spotted a fat raccoon by a small brook. It didn't notice me so I grabbed a thick branch about four feet long and killed it with a few blows. When I got back to the lean-to, I made a small fire and skinned the raccoon with the flint. It was not the best knife but it worked well enough. Soon, I had pieces of meat cooking, the fat sizzling and dripping into the fire. The smell caused my stomach to rumble and gurgle as it never had before. I ate only a few small pieces because I didn't want to make myself sick by gorging since I had been without food for so long. I put a few medium sized branches on the fire and fell asleep exhausted.

When I woke it was still dark. The wind startled me, for it increased to such strength and power as I have never seen. I have been through storms that froze everything in its path, to thunderstorms that had lighting strikes so close that the hair on my arms and head stood on end, to terrific wind and rain in late summer that made you wonder if the world was about to end, but I never saw a storm of such power as that night alone in the woods.

My fire went out and there was no hope of having one, not in that gale, so I didn't even try to start one. I was hungry and ate some of the uncooked raccoon. The snow had continued to fall heavily overnight and in the morning light, I saw drifts of a couple feet all around me. The wind sculpted the snow into waves ranging from a foot high to over six feet. I sat shivering and watched the snow come down because there was nothing else I could do. When it finally stopped in the afternoon, the wind increased, toppling trees all around me. I lay down, curled into a ball, and hugged myself to keep warm as I felt the pine trees quiver, shaking the ground with their swaying. If one of them came down it would almost certainly kill me. I was still freezing, even though I had the Indian's wool blanket, or duffel as it was then called, to wrap myself in. If I could have had three more, it would have pleased me fine and I would have gladly taken them. The snow drifted around my lean-to. I shoveled it out with a piece of bark but, as it drifted up the back, it cut the wind so that I was able to start a small fire with large twigs. I kept it burning but just so, husbanding the wood I had left, but it went out after a short while. I was sure that I was going to die.

I sat thinking of Becky and Sam. The more I thought, the more my anger began to build. I questioned why I was in this situation, why me, until I realized that way of thinking did no good. I could not change my situation and my aim was to make it back to Springfield alive. I had been gone eight weeks, at least that is what I guessed, and swore to myself that I would somehow be home before another week was gone.

The wind stopped a few hours after dark and I itched to be on my way. A full moon rose, lighting the snow with such strong light it was almost daylight. I cooked what was left of the meat, put it in the pouch, and began walking. I could see well, marveling at the drifts. I walked all night, but my progress was slow, having to wade through the smaller drifts and around the larger ones. The wind had toppled many trees. Climbing over or going around them took even more time. The wet snow melted from my exertion and froze on my arms and legs. I made no more than three miles that night.

When the sun came up, I rested for a while, wishing I had some more of the cold raccoon meat before pressing on, but it had fallen out of the pouch one of the many times I tripped and fell. I walked through the heavy snow until my legs felt as if they would fall off although they were so cold I was sure I wouldn't feel it if they did. The moccasins were pulled off my feet by the snow every few minutes. Slogging through snow as heavy as that reminded me of walking through deep sand back in Ipswich. It was exhausting and slowed you to a crawl. I was still moving forward when darkness fell. I found some pine branches and tried to make snowshoes as I had seen some Indians do but it was a useless effort. It began to snow again but lasted only a couple of hours, amounting to no more than a few inches, which made no difference to me since I was already facing three feet of snow.

I walked all the next day, stopping now and then from exhaustion, not believing I would be able to continue but somehow I did. I came to a large stream that had ice on both banks. I went upstream to where there were large rocks across it. I had no choice so I waded into the stream, the cold water stinging my already numb feet and legs. It was so cold that it took my breath away, and, for a moment, made catching my breath difficult. The shock was as if a vise was clamped on my chest. There was crispness to the moss on the rocks showed it was needled with ice flakes. I slipped off the rocks twice landing in the water, taking skin off my right hand when I tried to catch myself. I had to stomp to break through the ice on the other side. When I got out and walked a dozen steps, I saw the blood in the snow. My feet were cut and bleeding and the moccasins were in tatters.

I became convinced that I would die in that cold and snow but the thought of seeing Becky again, of feeling her warm next to me, of smelling her special smell, of holding Sam in my arms, gave me the strength to go on. As I went on, I thought of the smell and taste of food, of the warmth from a big fire and the luxury of sleeping in my own bed, my arms wrapped around Becky, cuddling with her through the night.

I continued on, stumbling every ten or so steps, falling onto the snow, forcing myself to get up, to go on. All that day and all the next I went on, plodding with each step, one foot in front of the other, until I walked, or tried to, in a daze, my brain and body numb from cold and exhaustion. When I was sure I could go no further, I went to sit down but fell over. I lay with my face, now covered in a heavy beard, against the snow. At that moment, I almost gave up and let myself die, but something inside of me would not let go. Life clung to me and would not leave me.

I was confused. My mind was full of fog and sawdust and blank spots were in my memory as waves of exhaustion swept over me. In my mind were scenes from my childhood, seeing friends and places I had not seen for many years. I saw my mother, standing outside our home in Ipswich, calling to me, telling me to come home. The thought faded but came back clearer than any before. I saw her clearly, as if I was standing a few feet in front of her. She was wiping her hands on her apron, something she did many times a day, looking at me with an overpowering love and affection. She came to me and put her arms around me, slowly rocking from side to side telling me everything would be all right. I could feel her as I did when I was a little boy and she comforted me when I was sick or frightened. She stepped back from me, holding onto my shoulders, and looked at me, clear and knowing.

"You need to get home, Jack," she told me. "Becky and Sam are waiting for you. You have to go on."

I saw my father come to her side and smile at me. "Be strong, son," he said. "You must be stronger now more than you have ever been in your entire life. Your family needs you." He put his arm around her and pulled her close.

My mother smiled again. "Go home now," she said. "Go home to your wife and son."

I tried to answer them but couldn't. My head hurt and I could hear a buzzing in my ears as the sight of them faded. I heaved myself onto my back and opened my eyes, wondering whether it was a dream or if it was the first step of dying in the cold wasteland in which I found myself. I pushed myself up and staggered forward, lunging through every foot of snow in my way. I walked as if I was drunk, raising my knees high, not sure of where to put my feet. There were blank spots in my mind for long stretches and periods when I felt light and unreal so my feet seemed to skim to ground, and other times my feet felt huge and heavy, as if they were anvils. I wondered, not for the first time, whether I was fated to wander through the woods for the rest of my days.

In the late afternoon, I fell once more as I had a hundred times. When I looked up, I saw the carcass of a small deer fifty feet ahead of me. I scrabbled over the snow to it. I could tell that wolves killed it because the belly was torn out and the throat ripped open, two sure signs of a wolf kill.

Since those days, I have heard many people spout on about the nature of hunger, which I find interesting because most of these people have never known true hunger. Yet they go on, telling the world what hunger is. While I forgive them to a point but when they start holding themselves out as an expert, I must stop them for I have some knowledge of hunger and am able to recognize ignorance on the subject.

Hunger is deceptive for, unlike thirst that leaves agony in your throat and belly, it slowly robs you of strength, making you trip and fall. The weakness grows almost unnoticed until you realize your strength is almost gone and you do not have the power to endure much more cold or heat.

My hands were so cold, I had trouble pulling the flint out of the pouch. I could barely use my fingers. I hacked off a large piece of frozen meat and began ripping it with my teeth, swallowing almost without chewing. After the third bite, I heard an angry, low-pitched growl. I looked up to see a lone wolf, head down, beginning to circle me. I was eating its kill and it would stop me. I looked around for a stick or stone to use as a weapon but saw nothing. I spit the meat out and crouched low, ready to do something to defend myself, which I now find curious since I barely had the strength to stand. The wolf continued growling, its head dropping even lower, the fangs showing through the quivering lips. It stopped and raised its ears, turned to its left, listening at something that I could not hear. It moved back a few steps growling again. It was getting ready to strike, when a loud boom seemed to shatter the forest. The wolf yelped in pain and dropped on its side. I stayed there, my cold weary mind trying to make sense of what happened. Two men came walking towards me. They both had wool coats wrapped around them and both were wearing wools hats and carrying guns. They approached me slowly, looking at me and then at each other.

"Help me," I croaked. "Please." They rushed to my side and took me by the arms before everything went black.

When I awoke, I was laying on a straw-covered pallet near a warm fire. I saw a ceiling and heard voices coming towards me. I tried to sit up but a pain shot through my head and dropped me back to the mattress.

My head felt as if it would explode. My feet and hands throbbed, the pain coursing through me. A young woman came and knelt by my side, asking if I was hungry.

"Yes, I am … very hungry." My stomach felt hollow. When I raised my hand I saw how my skin was taut, the bones almost visible. The tips of my fingers were black as were my toes. She put warm rags around them trying to get them better. I could feel a slight tingling in my feet and hands that I took as a good sign. They had dressed me in old wool pants and a jerkin and gave me a worn pair of shoes. The woman came back with a small bowl filled with something that smelled wonderful.

"You can only have a few spoonfuls at a time now or you'll get sick," she said. I opened my mouth in response, like a baby bird. She fed me a light broth that tasted better than anything I had eaten in a long, long time. One of the men who found me knelt on my other side. He was tall with a dark, well-trimmed beard, and a friendly face.

"What's your name?" he asked.

"Jack Parker. I was taken by the Indians when part of a hunting party. We were in Springfield. Where am I now?"

"You're in Westfield. I am Sheldon Hubbard and this is my daughter Ellen. My brother and I found you two days ago about eight miles west of here. You have been sleeping since we got you here. I never thought something could look as bad as you and still be alive. What happened to you?" I took another spoon of soup before answering him.

"I escaped from the Indians and made my way back. I don't know how long it took me, maybe ten days or two weeks. I lost track of the days." He put his hand on my shoulder and smiled.

"You rest now and we'll talk later."

"I need to get word to my wife that I am alive. Mr. Pynchon, too."

"You'll see your wife soon enough, because once the ice is gone from the river, we'll get across. By that time, you will be well enough to go."

"How long will it be before the ice is gone?"

"Another three, maybe four weeks."

This news filled me with sadness because I was so close but still too far away to let even Becky know I was alive. I was determined not to wait for the ice to go out before I crossed that river.

CHAPTER 9

It was a glorious day when I left the Hubbard's house a week later on my final walk to Springfield. The sun was shining with not a cloud in the sky with a light southwesterly breeze and warmth that let me know spring was on its way.

I could not believe that I was on my way home. During the few days I had been with them, I slept most of the time and ate the rest so that I felt much better. I guess I did not look very good. One of the first things I was going to do when I got back was to shave the itchy, dirty beard off my face. I never liked facial hair and had no desire to grow any. Before I left, I asked Sheldon what day it was and when he told me it was Friday, I realized that I was going home two weeks to the day after I promised myself I would, four months after being captured. I was thrilled to be just a short time away from seeing Becky but wondered how she would respond to seeing me, if I looked half as bad as I felt and the Hubbard's said I looked.

When I got to the west side of the river, I could see the town on the other side. Smoke was curling from all the chimneys and people were moving about outside the palisade. Nothing was going to keep me from getting home. I walked across the ice, a foolhardy thing no doubt but I was not going to let three hundred yards of ice stop me, not after everything I had been through.

As I made my way onto the ice, it began to boom under me. For someone who has never been on an iced over lake or pond, the sounds it makes is frightening. As I stepped forward, I had to climb over chunks of ice that accumulated in spots, as if they were rocks sticking out of a flat field. I slipped on the way down the second massive chunk, a little more than 100 yards from the western shore, falling on my back before sliding down, feeling a sharp pain on the right side of my upper back. I picked myself up and began walking again only to feel the ice crack beneath my feet. As I watched, the ice off to my right toward the middle of the river split open a few inches wide with a noise so loud it reminded me of summer thunder. I stopped for a moment, catching my breath, determined not to turn back but concerned about what was ahead. I made my way, knowing that my weight was insignificant in relation to the massive ice covering the river, and that there was no way I was heavy enough to cause the ice to split. I continued on, at times struggling to keep my balance on the surface. I realized the warmth and sun were melting the ice, and that it opened enough in one spot to allow the water to seep up making it treacherous. I walked up the river, looking for a dry place to continue my trek but found it even worse, the water deep enough to cover my ankles. I went downstream a half mile before finding a section still covered in snow, but deep enough for me to walk through. I got fifty yards from shore when I felt the ice underneath me move, seeming to float. I realized that the piece I was on had separated from the other ice and was slowly drifting downstream. It was a large piece of ice, sixty feet across but was not large enough for me. My only hope was to wait until it banged into another solid section. I stood very still watching the shoreline slowly slide by. Luckily, I did not have to float for more than a few minutes before it ground to a halt, sliding over a solid sheet of ice. I made my way to the piece and got to shore, falling on my knees when I tried to climb the bank that was thirty feet high. I grabbed some branches of shrubs and pulled myself up, falling again as I reached the top. After catching my breath again, I turned and looked back at the frozen river, seeing my footprints. I started toward the town, now only a few minutes away.

I stopped halfway there, looking around, not quite believing that I was there and that I made it back alive. Several people whom I recognized but did not know watched me as I walked on, my ragged appearance catching their attention. When I got to the tavern, I opened the door and slipped inside. Jeremiah was the only person in the room, sweeping the floor and humming a hymn. He stopped sweeping, looked up for a second, and went back to sweeping. He moved the broom back and forth a couple times before he stopped and looked at me again.

"Jack? Is it you, Jack? Is it really you?" He rushed to me, putting his hand on my shoulder and guiding me to a chair near the fireplace. "Let me get you a mug, uh, no, I should tell Mary, um, oh, does Mr. Pynchon know," he said, not sure which of several things to do first. I watched him dither about like a flustered housewife.

"Where is Becky?" I asked.

He looked at me in surprise. "Of course, of course," he said. "She's in the back room with Samuel." I stood up, walked to the door of the room, and heard Becky talking softly. I opened the door and saw her in a chair, her left side towards me, feeding Sam. I stood there watching her, my wife, the woman I missed so much holding my son, our son. I stayed there for a few minutes, watching the dust motes in the sunlight coming through the window, falling softly on her. I opened the door all the way and stood there.

"Becky," I said in a low voice. She turned and looked at me. Her mouth opened wide in surprise.

"Jack! Oh, Jack!" she cried getting up from the chair and coming to me. "Oh, Jack, you're alive! You're alive. Thank you, God for hearing my prayers. You're alive!" She lifted Sam in her arms with tears streaming down her face. “Sam, your father is back, he came back to you.”

“I came back to both of you,” I said.

She put her arm around me, crying into my shoulder. I began to cry, too, as we held each other.

In the next couple of hours, everyone in Springfield heard of my return. It was a bit of a celebration, with people crowding into the tavern to welcome me back. After I saw everyone, I washed my entire body, something not done by most people. I saw the Wekapauge, Quaboag, and Mohawk do it and they were free from lice, something that could not be said of many people at that time. I shaved the matted, tangled beard from my face, and slept for several hours. When I woke, Becky was sitting in a chair next to the bed holding my hand and Sam was asleep in his cradle.

“I thought I would never see you again,” she said as she squeezed my hand three times, our little way of saying I love you. “I cried myself to sleep every night for the first two weeks, then I knew that somehow you would come back to me, to us,” she said, pointing at Sam. I pulled her onto the bed and held her for a long time, until we both fell asleep. Sam made sure we woke to take care of his needs.

When Sam was fed and changed, we sat and talked about what happened both to me and in Springfield while I was gone. Becky was as interested in my being with Philip as she was horrified at the torture of poor John Stuart.

"They wanted me to become a member of the tribe," I told her. "They wanted to replace a son who was killed a few weeks before I arrived." I looked at her as I had a thousand times and saw before me the woman I considered the most beautiful and most wonderful I could ever hope to know. I stopped listening as I concentrated on the golden dust of freckles across her nose, the green eyes that sparkled when she was playful, the line that appeared between her eyebrows when she got peeved, her soft lips. I took it all in.

She lightly slapped my arm. "Are you listening to me?"

"What? Yes, I was. No, no I was not." I laughed for the first time in a long time. "I was thinking how beautiful you are."

She smiled a warm, loving smile that filled my heart with happiness.

"I need to go see Mr. Pynchon before I do anything else."

I made my way slowly down the stairs for I was still feeling bruised and beaten. There was a group of people in the tavern room, more than I would expect at this time of the week. They began to crowd around me, asking questions, offering to buy me rum, congratulating me on my escape and return. I declined the rum, told them I would answer all their questions later, and thanked them for their good wishes as I made my way outside. On the short walk to Mr. Pynchon's house, I had several other people welcome me back. All in all, it made me feel wanted and needed, something I had not felt for a while.

Mr. Pynchon's wife greeted me at the door with a small hug, which caught me by surprise because such contact between men and women was far from normal, especially with someone like me who worked for her husband at times.

"Oh, Jack," she said, touching my arm. "You have no idea how worried we were about you. John didn't think you would survive, but I knew better," she said with a big smile. "He's in his room. He did not want to bother you until you felt better. He was planning to see you this afternoon." She led me down the hall to the closed door of his room. I could hear men talking and didn't want to interrupt them. She ignored my suggestion that I come back when he wasn't busy and opened the door wide.

"You have a special visitor," she said to her husband. "Jack has come to see you."

Mr. Pynchon rose from behind the large wooden table and came to me, hand outstretched, with a large smile on his face and a happy look in his eyes. He took my hand in both of his and stood looking at me for a moment.

"You have no idea how good it is to see you," he said. "We weren't sure we would ever see you again. I sat up nights worrying about you, trying to think of some way to get you back." He shook my hand again. "Sit down, sit down." He told his business associates he would meet them tomorrow to finish their discussion.

When they left, he looked at me for a long moment. "You have come to mean much to me. I hope you know that. Never did I think that the young man who brought me a letter one night, years ago, would be the man sitting in front of me now. You have been through a lot Jack, more in your years than people three times your age." He got up and stirred the fire, adding another log. "I have been very lucky that my father left me all his interests, though I worked hard to increase them. I do all that I can for the community, for the villages I created, and for the people who live in them. I feel powerless now because of this war. I cannot get the things we need to continue. People want to leave but they are afraid of having even less wherever they go. That, plus the danger of traveling … you never know where the savages are lurking, waiting for a chance to inflict harm." He wandered about the room, looking out the windows before turning back to me. "Of course, I don't have to tell you about that now do I?"

"I met Philip," I said. He leaned forward and turned his head to the side as if he misheard me.

"What did you say? You met Philip? How?"

"It was he and his warriors that captured me." I dropped my head, thinking of poor John Stuart. "It was horrible."

"Tell me all about it," he said.

In the course of an hour, I related everything that happened to me after I left on that hunting party. When I finished, he sat drumming his fingers on the table, deep in thought, looking around at his finely appointed room, before staring at the floor.

"You know I am not a man to give things away. I never thought it necessary and never will. Although at times, I make arrangements that are not always advantageous to me. I have a grant of land in Hatfield, over 100 acres, that borders the river. When you are ready, I will sell you some of it, perhaps 20 acres. We'll discuss the terms at a later time but I want you to know of my offer."

"Thank you, Sir. That is very generous of you." My smile turned to a frown at my next thought. "I worry for my family … for my wife and new son. Will this war ever stop?"

"Yes, it will stop, at some point, when I don't know, but it will stop. The Indians will not be able to continue this struggle for more than a few more months. Philip going to the Mohawk is proof of that. They cannot win without outside forces. We will survive, all of us, and when we do, your family and everyone else's will prosper. That I believe with my whole heart." He turned and looked out the window. "You know I am a man of deep conviction. This war is God's punishment on us. It is something we brought on ourselves. Is it horrible? Yes, it is, but it is also the judgment of the Supreme Lord on our failings."

I looked at him for a moment, seeing in him the man who provided me with opportunities I would not otherwise have had. He was a good man, a kind man, well-versed in all aspects of business and politics, a man who wanted nothing more than for his endeavors to succeed. I admired him more with each passing year. The strain of the years had taken but a small toll on him, except for a few wrinkles around his eyes and a few more pounds on his frame, but he was just as I remembered him the night we first met.

When Brookfield was attacked and the village destroyed, he was shocked. When Springfield, the town his father founded forty years before, was attacked and almost destroyed with only a few buildings remaining, he was heartbroken to see all that he worked so hard to achieve come crashing down in the space of a few hours. He cared deeply about all of the people who lived in the six towns he began and suffered through the catastrophes with them. Mr. Pynchon was a wealthy man, certainly focused on increasing his business interests while allowing the people in his towns to make a better life for themselves and their children. He was one of the wealthiest men in the Massachusetts Bay Colony, and possibly the other Colonies also, but to sit with him as I did then, you would not have known it. In many ways, he reminded me of a kindly uncle. I was grateful that on this and many other occasions, he took such a strong interest in me.

"You need to go before the selectmen and tell them what you've learned about Philip and anything you may have picked up while you were captured that could aid our defense. I will write Governor Leverett as well as Governor Winthrop in the Connecticut Colony. You are back, bruised but alive, for which we are all thankful to God."

That all sounded fine to me, but I had more immediate things on my mind. "So what do we do now?" I asked.

"Well, the Indians are still wandering up and down the Valley. There are reports of them near Deerfield again, Northfield, and Hatfield. Captain Morgan has the soldiers ready to fight on a moment's notice." He leaned forward, putting his hands on his knees. "Now what about you? What do you want to do?" I considered his question, although I asked myself that several times over the last two days.

"I want to spend some time with Becky and Sam but I am ready to fight if I'm needed."

"You are a good man, Jack, a good man. Hopefully, there will be no need for anyone to fight soon, although I doubt I am right about that."

I shook his hand and took my leave of him, walking around what was left of the fort, seeing the small efforts made while I was gone, most to shore up the limited remaining defenses. I wasn't sure, but I thought that if 400 or 500 Indians attacked us, we would not be able to stand the onslaught and the result would be the largest loss of life of the war. Anger rose up inside of me at the waste of human life and the unnecessary destruction of years of hard work by people who wanted to provide for themselves and their families the same as the Indians did. I made my way back to the tavern. My right hip, injured on the journey home, began to hurt so I knew it was going to rain.

I found out about all that happened while I was gone. In February, the Nipmucks attacked Lancaster and took a woman, Mary Rowlandson, and her three children, captive. At the end of the month, Philip and the Wampanoags attacked Northampton while the Nipmucks attacked Medfield. It got so bad that there was talk of building a wall around Boston to protect it from attack because Indians assaulted sites within ten miles. March was no better, with the Nipmucks attacking Groton and English soldiers near Sudbury. The Wampanoag attacked Rehoboth and destroyed Providence. Marlborough and Simsbury were attacked and the week before I returned, the Pocumtuck fought the Springfield soldiers in a battle in Longmeadow, six miles south of Springfield. The attacks continued, and from what I heard, the slaughter was increasing. Stories of brutality abounded, tales too horrible to believe.

It took me two weeks to recover fully from my ordeal. I tried to put it all behind me and get on with life. However, there are still times, although they are less frequent than before, when I can still see and hear John Stuart writhing and screaming under the Indian's torture. That scene haunts me still.

One night in bed, after Sam was put in his cradle, we lay there talking as husbands and wives do. I told Becky that, after everything I had been through, I could stand at the gates of hell and nothing would frighten me again.

"I thought you were dead," Becky said through soft tears. "I didn't think I'd ever see you again. When I saw you watching Sam and me, it was one of the most joyous moments of my life. I thought our dreams were gone and we would never know what it would be like to have our farm and family."

"The rest of our family," I corrected her, nodding to Sam, sound asleep in his cradle. She gave me a weak smile.

"Yes, the rest of our family … you're right." She moved closer to me and put her head on my shoulder and her arm across my waist. "I love you, Jack, more than you can ever know, more than I can ever tell you." We lay there quietly for a time before I leaned over and kissed her on the forehead.

There are times when I lie in bed, staring at the ceiling in the gray light of dawn and think of how much I missed my wife and son. A feeling of tremendous love and gratitude comes over me at those times. I watch Becky sleeping, the slow rise and fall of her breathing is hypnotic, and I hold her close against me, realizing all that she means to me. I would, at any time, give my life for her and my child. I turn and watch Sam in his cradle, fidgeting and squirming a bit, before making a face and rolling onto his side with a sigh and sleeping the sleep of babies. I am awake until long after the hour when good people should be asleep.

The love we feel for others sometime fills us to bursting. It is at those times that I give Becky a kiss on the neck and slowly slide out of bed so I do not wake her.

Before the first light of dawn reached the sky, I made my way down the stairs and out the door, stepping softly so as to not wake anyone. I made my way to the river's edge, a place that always soothes me even to this day. It was a cold morning. The stars were twinkling and the three-quarter moon was near the horizon in the western sky. I wrapped my arms around myself to help ward off the chill. The sunlight, coming up on the other side of the hill behind me, slowly spread across the land, lighting the hills and fields in the distance. I watched as the colors of the trees, the tall grass on the other side of the river, and the river itself, became visible. Though I could see smoke rising from the chimneys, there was no one about. I felt like I was the last man on earth, a feeling that I suffered through a short time before. I wandered back and forth, up and down the riverbank, listening to the water gurgle as it slid past, coming from somewhere far away, and making its way to the sea.

A great many things go through my mind at times like these, some of great importance and others of no consequence, just thoughts that need to be sorted through. After reflecting on my past, I began to think of the future. Mr. Pynchon's offer was something I knew I would accept, a big farm being part of our dream. My thoughts ran ahead a few years, seeing more children running through the field, Becky under an apple tree near the house on a fine summer day, the house and barn I built with my own hands, and the life we would have. The thought of it made me smile for there was a certainty about this part of my life, that I would somehow be able to accomplish all that I wanted to do, to achieve my dream. My reverie broke apart at the sound of a drum.

I turned and heard the warning drum, something done when an attack is imminent. I rushed back, looking for someone who could tell me what was happening. I came upon Captain Morgan yelling for men to assemble on the square in front of the tavern. When I caught up with him, he was giving orders to various sergeants and corporals.

"Captain, what is it?" I asked.

"A rider just came in … a group of Indians was spotted at Hatfield heading this way. Get with the other soldiers," he said before moving onto someone else. While I intended to help defend the fort, I first ran back to our room to wake Becky and tell her to get to Pynchon's house.

After a lot of rushing around and a few tense moments, it turned out to be a false alarm when another rider came in with news that Indians went east.

CHAPTER 10

As the spring season progressed, the snow melted and supplies came in from the east and the Connecticut Colony. We began farming again, although under guard, with at least a dozen armed militia protecting six or eight men planting crops. While the threat of attack lessened with decisive battles against the enemy becoming more frequent, it looked like the war would end soon, but not soon enough.

A soldier, Thomas Reede, captured in early April and lucky enough to escape unharmed a month later, made it to Hadley with news that Indians gathered at one of their favorite fishing areas at the great falls on the Peskeompskut river where it narrowed and the water plunged over a fifty-foot drop. He told us that they were catching and curing fish to fortify themselves for another campaign in the summer. Others would be planting in the abandoned fields in Deerfield with plans to harvest a crop in the late summer.

On Wednesday, May 13, two days after Reede made it back to Springfield, warriors raided three farms in Hatfield and stole seventy or eighty head of cattle, including eight prime oxen.

It was clear they would drive them to the campsite at the falls. The farmers were determined to recover their cattle.

Within two days, a plan was made for an attack against the Indian campsite. Mr. Pynchon, as the colonel of the First Hampshire Regiment and commander of all troops in the area, ordered Lieutenant Sam Holyoke to gather the men and plan the attack. Sam was young, only twenty-eight, but determined to succeed in all he did. Captain Turner, or Bill to everyone that knew him, longed to direct a battle and pleaded with Mr. Pynchon for the chance. Turner was ill, enfeebled by sickness for over a month, and was too weak to fight. Because of that, Mr. Pynchon declined his request, but Turner insisted on leading the troops. Mr. Pynchon gave in, and it was a decision he would come to regret. He allowed Turner to command half of the 160 men, half soldiers and half militia, who gathered for the fight.

We set out from Hatfield a couple of hours after sunset on a cool and damp May 18, a Monday that began with sunshine. We wanted to get within striking distance of the village by dawn. We were a mix of men, some who were experienced in battle like me, and others, some just boys, who had never fired a gun at another person. Unlike other expeditions where we had many guides and scouts, this time we had only two, Experience Hinsdell and Ben Wait, who knew the area better than anyone else did. We followed the Pocumtuck path, an ox-cart trail up to Deerfield, which was deserted for months after the last brutal attack. It was an odd feeling seeing the burned remains of the houses and barns that sagged from the weight of the winter snow. We sloshed across a small stream, the Weequioannuck, and continued through the woods to Bloody Brook, the site of the ambush and massacre of Captain Lathrop's men in September.

I rode beside Lt. Holyoke, talking about the war, and how it seemed it would never end. He asked about my time with the Mohawk. I told him some but did not want to re-live the scenes of torture that continued to haunt my dreams.

"Sam, this is an old Pocumtuck fishing village, right?"

"Yes, it is. Why are you asking?" I shifted in my saddle and ran a hand down Bubs' neck.

"I'm concerned it could be a trap or that there won't be any men there. You know that since the war started, the women and children do most of the fishing. I want to make sure our attack will be successful but only if it cuts their strength and ends the war quicker than it would if we didn't attack."

I hesitated for a bit, letting the thoughts roll around in my mind.

"What is it, Jack? There's something on your mind."

"Sam, I want to make sure we won't slaughter a village of women and children. That would be horrible to start with but it would also inflame Philip and the other sachems. Besides being completely wrong, it would work against us. I just want to make sure that's all."

Sam leaned back in his saddle and stretched his arms. "Reede is certain that it is a couple of large war parties. This is our chance to strike a blow, not wait for them to attack us. This could be a decisive battle, possibly *the* decisive battle, Jack. This could break them."

"I hope you're right, because I am sick and tired of fighting."

No one spoke as we moved forward, each deep in our own thoughts about how this was like so many other towns and villages in the colony. A shiver ran down my back as I rode through, with memories of the fires raging through our homes in Brookfield, the crackling sound of the flames, and watching all we worked for over those years disappear into the fires when Springfield burned that fateful night.

We rode on. The horses were even quiet as if they knew the importance of the silence, while the men whispered in low tones if they talked at all. The wind swished through the needles of gigantic pine trees as we closed in on the Indian village.

Crossing a brook at night in an area you are familiar with is perhaps an easy thing to do, but for most of us who never were in that area before, it was harrowing. None of us wanted to have our horse step into a hole or some other thing that would cause us to topple into the water. Captain Turner picked a place for us to dismount and assigned men to guard the horses.

We slowly made our way forward, making sure to step carefully on the damp ground. The good thing was that the ground was soft enough from the evening fog that we could move quietly through the edge of the woods. The bad thing was that the fog makes sounds carry further than they would if the air was dry, so any noise we made might alarm the Indians. Ben Wait came back to us, having been ahead scouting out the village.

"It's a few hundred yards ahead," he said. "All quiet, no scouts, no sentries, and no dogs either."

That told us that the Indians were suffering from hunger for dogs not only played with the children and guarded the camp, but were also food when there were lean times. The fact that there were no dogs meant they ate them.

"We should split up here," Ben said to Turner. "There are two trails leading right around the village."

Turner, who was leaning against a tree so he would not fall down, agreed with Ben's suggestion. It was clear his strength was almost gone from the ride and mile walk. He was far too sick to be with us and was more of a danger to us because he coughed every few minutes, a deep, hacking sound, and it was loud enough to give our position away. The last thing we needed was to be ambushed because one of our commanders was sick. Turner ordered everyone to move on, and for his men to take the left trail and Sam's men the right. Before we moved, we checked to make sure our powder wasn't dampened by the fog.

It took us only a short time to get to the village of a dozen wigwams and four longhouses. I figured about 150 Indians were there, and the quiet indicated they were asleep. It was still foggy and beginning to getting light. We crept closer and closer, all the while expecting a shot to ring out or an Indian scream to alert the others, but it was deathly quiet. We waited what seemed like a long time, although it probably wasn't more than a few minutes before we heard Captain Turner's signal, a loud whistle that pierced through the fog. We charged into the village and some of the soldiers began to yell but the mist and the lack of response from the wigwams and longhouses quieted them. For a moment, I thought the village was empty but soon heard shots coming from the far side. Three men emerged from the wigwam in front of me, guns in hand and ready to fight. I shot one who dropped to the ground with a thud. A second came at me, and, dodging his gun that he used like a club, I hit him in the side of the head with my gun barrel. I looked up and saw the third, his gun leveled at my chest with a hateful look in his eye. I started to bring my rifle up but it felt like it was forty pounds of lead. I was moving too slowly, my rifle seeming never to move, everything sluggish like I was under water. I was sure I was going to die from the Indian not twenty feet away. A shot blasted the air near my right ear, stunning me. The Indian sank to the ground, one hand on his stomach as blood seeped into his deerskin shirt. I turned to see Ben Wait reloading as he made his way to the next wigwam. Two children, a boy and girl no more than ten years old came out and were shot dead by soldiers to my left. I looked around and saw the same senseless slaughter in the other parts of the camp. Women and children were being killed, dragged from their wigwams before being shot or beaten to death. I ran to the next wigwam where I heard children screaming, looking for other soldiers. There was none. I pulled the three children out and huddled them around me. Their mother lay dead near the small fire. I heard a loud coughing and choking so I knew Captain Turner was near me.

"Kill them," he ordered. I saw half a dozen soldiers behind him. I looked at them and then down at the children in my arms.

"No," I said. "I will not slaughter children. They have done nothing to us. We are not at war with children. It's the men, the warriors we want. Put the children and women in one side of the camp. We can use prisoners to our advantage. We can bargain with Philip and the other sachems."

Turner gave me a cold, hard stare. "I said kill them."

When I didn't move, he raised his sword. "If you won't, then I will."

"Captain!" I yelled over the growing din of the attack, "I will not kill them and I will not let you or anyone else here do it either." As I said that, I heard a high-pitched scream, and turned to see a woman followed by a young girl and little boy running from three soldiers.

The soldier nearest the boy stuck his bayonet into the boy's back skewering him like a fish. The next soldier clubbed the girl until she did not move while the last soldier ran the woman down and shot her in the head.

I yelled to Captain Turner again to have him stop the slaughter of the women and children. He began coughing again before he could respond. As he opened his mouth, a bullet hit him on the outside of the left arm, high near the shoulder. He yelled and grabbed his arm. I hustled the children to a large group of rocks behind huge pine trees. I pushed them into a cleft in the biggest rock, almost a cave, and told them to be still and quiet. The heart wrenching look they gave me, their eyes full of sorrow and pain, would stay with me for the rest of my life.

I returned to the battle and ran towards the falls, where I saw another group of young girls. As I got near, two of them jumped into the river to escape and were swept over the falls to an almost certain death. Two warriors went bolting by me, intent on reaching the canoes along the bank. One of them slowed and shot at one of the youngest soldiers, missing him by a few inches. I brought my gun up and fired, hitting the Indian in the back. I reloaded as I moved closer to the remaining group of children but was hit by a glancing blow to the head. I fell, dropping my gun, and rolled over to see a large Indian raise his war club high over his head, preparing to bring it down on me. I rolled to the right and grabbed my gun by the barrel and, jumping up, my head swimming with pain, swung it as hard as I could and caught the Indian on the left temple, caving his skull in.

As I went on, I told all the soldiers that Turner ordered us not to kill the women or children. Some stopped what they were doing and looked at me.

"Bring the women and children to that side," I yelled, pointing to an area away from where I hid the children. Some men began to herd the Indians where I directed while others stood looking wild-eyed, caught in the heat of their first battle, unsure of what to do.

I looked around and saw the slaughter continuing. I found two children and three women and brought them to the large rock.

"Stay here!" I hollered. "I'll get you to safety." I left them and ran back to the village just as a large group of warriors appeared from the woods nearby and began to shoot at us. With ball and arrows landing all around us, a group of soldiers split off from the main body and headed towards the planting fields in which beans, squash, and corn were just beginning to grow while others began burning the longhouses, which contained whatever food they had been able to gather. I, and a few others, ripped down the smoking racks they used for fish.

We came upon two forges set up to repair guns and make ammunition. We destroyed them and threw two large blocks of lead, each weighing close to forty pounds, into the river.

The shooting went on for several more minutes before it was clear most of the Indians were dead. The campsite was totally destroyed and the smoke from the burning frames of wigwams drifted across the area. It became quiet as we all realized there was no one left to shoot at. I looked towards the rocks several times to reassure myself that the women and children I hid were not hurt, but I didn't see them. I grew anxious and started to move towards them when shots rang out, whistling through the air above us and slicing small pine branches that drifted down to land around us.

There was a commotion at the other end of the village. I couldn't see what was going on. Men started yelling and firing their guns while moving backward towards me.

"Get ready!" Ben Wait yelled as he moved past me. "There's more coming!"

"What's going on?" I asked.

"Must have been another group up the river that heard the shots. They came out of nowhere. Where is Turner?"

"I don't know. I haven't seen him."

"Stupid man will get us all killed," he muttered before gathering the others to retreat.

A shot slammed into the bark of a pine tree a foot from my face. I ran towards the rock to tell the women and children to stay where they were and that they would be safe but they began to move toward me just as the shots came on faster. At that moment, Captain Turner ordered a retreat as more warriors came upon us, bent on revenge for the destruction we caused.

As we began the retreat, I saw Ahanu, in a small group of Indians ahead and to my right. Although I knew it might draw fire, I decided to send the children and women to him if I could get his attention.

"Ahanu! Ahanu!" I yelled, hoping he would hear me over the noise of men yelling and shooting, but he didn't. When I yelled again, he looked up and but didn't see me. He was about to shoot when he recognized me. A hard look was on his face, not surprised that we would meet in a fight. He lowered his gun and slipped behind an oak tree.

"Take the children! Take them!" I yelled, pointing to the women and children. I turned to them and grabbed the oldest boy by the arm. "Go to him. Take the others and run to him!"

They stood looking at me, fear and confusion on their faces. "Go! Run!" With a quick glance back at me, they ran around to the right, skirting behind several large trees towards Ahanu. They made it to him unhurt. Our eyes met and Ahanu nodded, a look of appreciation and respect on his face.

The sound of a shot whistling by my head brought my attention back to the battle. I scrambled to check that my gun was loaded while feeling, rather than seeing, the mass of men behind me yelling, fumbling backwards in retreat, firing haphazardly, and hitting nothing. They were just wasting powder and ball and making noise as the number of Indian attackers grew. The retreat grew into a race for my life as the Indians pressed the attack upon us. Several men dropped around me, and I expected to be shot too but through some miracle, I was not. The Indians were getting closer, so I began to run, gripping my gun tight.

When I got to the other side of the campsite, soldiers were going in three different directions, all trying to get back to the horses by the shortest route possible. I knew which way we had come, so I told the others to follow me.

"It's this way!" I yelled, waving my arm in the direction of the horses. Some followed me but many others did not. I found Ben Wait a short distance ahead.

"You're one of the few who knows what he's doing," he said to me.

"Yeah, well, right now I would rather be anyplace else but here. Those men are going to be cut down if they don't come this way."

He put his hand on my arm. "Nothing we can do about it. Let's go." There were about two dozen of us now all heading in the same direction. I thought we were safe but that idea changed when I heard a shot and felt a hot sting in my left arm. Having been shot once before, I knew what it was without having to look. A ball skimmed my arm, from wrist to elbow, ripping my jerkin, taking skin off an inch wide. While it was not bleeding badly, it hurt badly. We got behind a large gnarled oak tree that, from the look of it, toppled over a couple of years before. About 100 feet away was a large rock, almost as big as a house, behind which were a group of Indians who knew how to shoot well for they kept us behind the tree for several minutes as the balls slapped into the bark, sending slivers and chips flying into our hair and eyes.

When they stopped firing to reload, we jumped up and let off a few shots, killing two of them and wounding two more. The shooting did not resume after a short time, so we looked around the edge of the tree trunk and saw that they were gone. We picked up our guns and took off running toward the horses. We heard shots coming from where the horses were and our fear increased that they would be gone, scattered by the Indians by the time we got there. The horses were in a bowl shaped field that was near the edge of the woods. To get to it, we came down a small hill, leaped over the edge of the field, slid to the bottom, and found our horses. Bubs was agitated, prancing back and forth, his eyes wide, wanting to go. I jumped on him in a single bound and, looking around to see if the other men made it, headed Bubs towards Hatfield. We hadn't gone more than a few hundred yards when we heard screams coming from 100 feet on our right on the other side of a brook surrounded by pine trees. Four of our men were running along the brook, all without their guns, followed by half a dozen warriors swinging war clubs and tomahawks. Jacob Brown was tackled by a small Indian who looked no more than fourteen years old. The boy brought his club down on Jacob's head three times. We heard a thud with each blow and knew he was dead. I brought my gun around, took quick aim, and shot the Indian. Young or not, he killed one of our men and was the enemy. We cut our horses in behind the three men and charged toward the Indians who fled. The three men found their horses and took off at a gallop for Hatfield.

We weren't sure whether to head for Hatfield or ride back toward where we last saw the other men, so we milled about for a minute, looking around in all directions, making sure we were not in danger. There was no sound of yelling or screaming. There were no men in sight, neither the enemy's nor ours. Suddenly, we heard a series of whoops and saw the rest of the horses, fifty or more, take off down the field followed by a group of Indians excited at their success. Without waiting, we all rode toward them, barreling down on them, the anger growing inside me. It was a burning desire to kill each of them to avenge what they had done for months, killing innocent people all over the colony. My anger dropped as suddenly as it rose at the memory of what we did to them just a short time before. I slowed Bubs when the Indians took off heading for the woods. It was so quiet, it was difficult to believe the area had been full of men just a short time ago. We turned toward Hatfield and rode on.

CHAPTER 11

We were one of the first groups back to Hatfield. Others came back in small groups, dribbling in a few at a time or walking in alone. By dusk, there were sixty-eight of us. Sam Holyoke was one of the last men into the town. We gathered at a few different houses just outside the palisade. I was at Sam Belding's with about two dozen others, some in the house, some in the barn, and some of us outside. The rest were at Sam Kellogg's, Obadiah Dickinson's and John Allis's. Some talked about what they had seen and done, getting over their first time in battle, while those of us who had seen more bloodshed than we ever wanted to, sat wondering about those that didn't come back. We spoke about going to look for them in the morning but the way they were running, they could have been anywhere by then. The good thing was that there were not enough Indians to track down all our men. Forty–five men were missing, almost one third of those that set out. Among them were nineteen year old Josiah Leonard, fifty-one year old Joseph Kellogg who had twenty children and ran the ferry between Hadley and Northampton, and twenty-four year old Tom Miller. Tom was the son of Tom Miller, the Springfield constable who was attacked and killed with Tom Cooper. Captain Turner was killed but his body was not found until a month later, when a large scouting party went out to find those who were not accounted for. He was buried where they found him.

We learned later that we killed Sancumachu, the Pocumtuck sachem, one of those who led the successful attacks on Northfield and Deerfield early in the war.

I sat brooding with my back against the barn, away from the others, listening to snatches of conversation around me. I was tired of the killing and I could not get the thoughts of what I had seen some of these men do only hours before to young children and elderly women. I was revolted by their actions and by mine. When I first went to Quaboag a few years before and there were discussions during militia training about what to do in case of an attack, I never thought I would ever kill a man and here I was, having brought death to so many. Granted, some deserved it for they were evil and would have killed innocent people, and others would gladly have taken my life if I had not taken theirs. Yes, it was a war and I was lucky to be alive, especially after all I had been through. As I sat there, my bandaged arm in my lap, I realized I missed Becky and Sam so much it hurt. I wanted to be with them in peace and build our farm, see my family grow and prosper, and not have to worry about more attacks. I was weary of the fighting and longed for an end to the conflict. I had been involved in this war for almost a year and I was sick and tired of it.

As I sat there, the rich smell of the land drifted by me, as the soft south wind touched my face. I looked into the sky and saw stars stretching from horizon to horizon. I could hear the water in the river gurgling and chuckling along, the same river I crossed less than two months ago when it was covered in ice. It was hard to believe it was the same river. Hatfield was a pretty place right beside the river so I knew it would have good soil. Once the war was over, it might be a good place to have our farm. With that thought in my head, I took my gun and made my way to where Bubs was tied under a tree. Knowing I was not going anywhere, I rubbed him with my hands like my father taught me. I took his head and buried it in my shoulder as my father had done with him so many times when Bubs was a little more than a yearling.

"Oh, we've been through a lot, haven't we, boy?" I asked him. "More than I ever thought we would. We'll get back to Springfield in the next day or two, and then you will able to rest." I put my blanket on the ground next to him and, after reloading my gun out of habit, fell asleep in seconds.

Several of us, including Lt. Holyoke, made it back to Springfield the next day, leaving Hatfield as the sun crested the horizon. As we made our way to the tavern, people gathered around us asking questions, chattering at us like squirrels, wanting to know if what they heard was true. I ignored them and went to find my wife and son.

Becky was in the back room and came out when she heard me calling for her. There have been times when she looked beautiful to me, although she would tell you she certainly didn't feel that way, but this was one of those times she looked the most beautiful. I took her in my arms, forgetting that I was injured.

"Oh Jack, never leave me again. Please don't ever go away again," she said, her forehead pressed against mine. "I am so afraid you'll go and never come back, that someone will bring me word that you were killed and then our son would not have a father. I can't bear the thought of that happening." She sniffled and wiped here eyes.

I kissed her on the nose. "I am tired of all of this fighting. I have no plans on going to fight again. I am done with it."

People came into the room, crowding around us, waiting for us to tell about the battle. Holyoke began telling them all about it, not leaving anything out. I know he, like all of us, was tired but there was a sorrow in his voice that I will never forget.

He stared at the floor, his mug of rum untouched, relating how well the surprise attack went. The room went quiet as he began to talk about the killing of the women and children. The images flitted through my mind, one horrid scene after another, bringing me back to a place I did not want to go.

"There is one man among us who was not afraid to fight and killed several of the enemy, but refused to harm the women or children." He nodded towards me. "Jack put himself in constant danger to save some of the women and children." He looked at me for a moment before continuing. "I wish I was as strong as you." His face was overcast with thought and introspection. A murmur of derision went round the room.

"What are you talking about Sam?" asked John Farnsworth, who came up from the Hartford area just after I got home from my escape. "He let them get away?" He rounded on me with an angry look in his eyes. "You didn't kill some of the Indians? What kind of a man are you? They are all evil devils and every one of them needs to be destroyed, men, women, and children. It is a sin against God to let any of the enemy live. What kind of man would do that?"

I saw some of the people, those I recognized but didn't really know, nodding in agreement with his view. "He's probably afraid of Indians, doesn't like to see blood spilled," he said to the man next to him with a chuckle.

"I am not afraid of any man, Indian or English," I said, a slow anger beginning to grow.

"Then why did you let them go? Tell me that if you are not afraid of them."

"There were three women and five young children. I was not going to murder them when they did nothing against us. I put bullets into the heads and bodies of the enemy without blinking. I killed several, knowing I was doing right, and not sinning against God."

"Who cares if they were women and children? They were Indians and should have been killed. If you are really on our side you wouldn't have helped them." I stood up scraping the chair legs against the floor. Becky stood up and put her hand on my chest to stop me from going to him.

"You have no idea what you are talking about," she said to him. "As a matter of fact, the more I hear you talk, the more I think you're an idiot." Her words hung in the air. Many women were not outspoken and did not offer their opinions outside the home. Becky never had been that way and did not hesitate to speak her mind, something that was not always taken well by those on the receiving end of her sharp words.

"What did you say?" Farnsworth asked.

"I said that I think you are an idiot. And just so you know, Mr. Farnsworth," she said contemptuously, "my husband and I were two of the ninety-nine people trapped in the tavern at Brookfield while 400 Indians tried to kill us for three days last August. Jack protected us, along with the others, and had no problem killing any of the enemy. Also, for your information, he was captured by King Philip in January and held captive by the Mohawk for two months before he escaped and made his way back here. So don't you dare question my husband's actions."

Farnsworth dismissed her comments with a wave of his hand. "I listen to no woman, especially about anything to do with this war." People shifted on their feet and fidgeted in their chairs uncomfortable with where this was heading.

"And just where were you when all this was happening?" a voice boomed from inside the door. When I looked up, I saw a huge beast of a man, towering above everyone else. His shoulders were as wide as two men's put together. He had a burly round face with a big, bushy beard and arms like young tree trunks He was dressed in rough clothing with a rope tied around his waist to keep his breeches up. He rubbed his face with one of his huge hands while he waited for an answer.

"Well, were you with him?" he asked, pointing at me while continued to stare at Farnsworth.

"Uh, no, I, uh, wasn't with him," Farnsworth replied. "I don't see what interest it is of yours anyway, whoever you are."

"I am Ezekiel Huff."

Everyone just stood there looking at him for a moment until Becky broke the silence.

"Thank you, Mr. Huff for standing up for my husband."

"I don't know your husband from Adam, but I didn't like the way this was going. I learned that those who complain about someone not doing something have less courage than those who do it. And it takes courage to fight man to man. So, little man, why weren't you at the battle? Where were you?"

"I was here."

"Of course you were. Get out of my sight, you loud-mouthed coward." He waved a meaty arm toward the door to show Farnsworth the way out. As people began to leave, he came over to Becky and me and sat down, the bench almost breaking under his weight.

"I'll have rum!" he called to Jeremiah. "And not a small one, either. Make it three times the amount of a normal mug. I'm thirsty." He turned to us. "And who are you?"

"I'm Jack Parker and this is my wife Becky. You didn't have to get in the middle of that, you know. I could have handled it fine on my own."

"I don't doubt that you could and I didn't mean to interfere, but I didn't like the look of that fellow. Looks like a pissant."

Just then, Sam started crying from the back room. "And that," Becky said as she stood, "is our son Sam."

As time went on, Ezekiel and I became good friends. Of his background, not much was known. He told people he was born on a ship that his father captained but could not give them the name of the ship or his father. He said he came from Connecticut but I also heard him tell a group of men lounging at the tavern that he was from the Indian country in New York.

Drinking was a favorite pastime of his and together we spent a few long nights at the tavern. Ezekiel could drink more than any other man I have ever known and he ate like an ox. He could eat a whole deer haunch without a problem.

For all of his rough manners, he was gentle and affectionate with most women and all children except those that annoyed him, which happened with some regularity. He doted on Becky and Sam.

Ezekiel got angry easily. The surest sign was when he started rubbing his face with both hands. When that happened, he was ready to let someone have it. He could lift a full size man off his feet with one hand. When he spoke, he bellowed and his whisper was the same volume as a normal person's voice. In some ways, he was like a big child always looking for fun wherever he could find it. In other ways, he was the meanest, most violent man I had ever met, especially when upset by something he viewed as an injustice. Threats of having a finger cut off or having his nose slit as a punishment for his thievery did not faze him. "Let 'em try it," was his standard response for he knew no man or group of men could contain him long enough to give him punishment. He disliked authority, though he was humbled when Mr. Pynchon, whom he viewed with a sense of awe, addressed him in public. Over our years as friends, more than once in our adventures, he saved my life and I saved his.

"So how were you captured by the Mohawk?" he asked, taking a big slurp of rum from his mug. He studied me closely as I related the experience to him, leaning forward to rest his elbows on the table as I described my escape and subsequent ordeal.

"Huh," he said when I finished. "Sounds like you know your way around the Indians."

"Where are you from, Ezekiel?"

He gave me a sharp look, his eyes narrowing before he rubbed his face with one meaty paw. "Oh, here and there. A little bit of everywhere."

"Where were you born and raised?"

"I don't know. I spent my first couple of years with an old woman who took me in when my parents abandoned me. She got sick and I was passed from family to family, some related to me, some not, until I was twelve or thereabouts when I took off on my own."

"How old are you now?"

"Don't rightly know. No one knew what day or year I was born. It doesn't matter anyway … at least not to me." He emptied his mug in one swig and motioned for Jeremiah to bring us two more. He cocked his head to one side while giving me a quizzical look.

"You wouldn't be interested in going to Hatfield with me in a couple of days would you?" he asked.

"Well, I don't know. I've had my share of Hatfield for the time being although it is a beautiful place, lots of nice land along the river. Why are you going to Hatfield?"

"I need to see someone," was all he said. He went and came back in a day and I never learned why he went.

Twelve days later, we learned of another horrible attack against Hatfield when 700 Indians descended on the town. Everyone got into the stockade, not daring to attack such a large enemy force. The savages were free to burn the houses and barns outside the stockade and collect whatever plunder they could find. Twenty-five men from Hadley attempted to assist their neighbors but were attacked by 150 Indians that were not taking part in the burning. When the Hadley men got near the gate, the Hatfield men rushed out to their aid. The Indians fought desperately, our men killing twenty-five of them. Most of the cattle were killed and all the sheep ran off. The fires consumed twelve houses and barns. Five men were killed and four others wounded.

Two weeks later, 250 of the enemy attacked Hadley. Major John Talcott of Connecticut and 250 troopers from towns on Long island, along with 200 friendly Pequot, Mohegan, and Niantic Indians, arrived on June 8. They rushed to Hadley and easily defeated the attack. It turned out to be the last battle of the war in Hampshire County, something for which we are all eternally grateful.

CHAPTER 12

It was late June when Mr. Pynchon asked that I ride to Boston with information on the state of affairs for the governor. I left early in the morning and would be away for the night. I didn't want to leave Becky and Sam alone for more than that. I kissed them good-bye and set off. I found myself anxious the closer I got to Brookfield. For some reason, whether a bout of melancholy or just curiosity, I wanted to see Brookfield again. In some ways, I wanted to see what it was like and in other ways I really did not.

It was a fine day, warm but not too warm, a light breeze from the west, a few white, puffy clouds here and there. The color of the sky was a blue that you only get in New England at that time of year. Bubs was in fine form, though older like all of us, he was ready to run that day. He acted as if he was only a few years old.. He could not wait to be off.

When I got a few miles from the village, I slowed Bubs to a walk. I came up the road, now more a path with weeds growing along the edges spreading into the road, to the Wekapauge village. There was nothing left. The place was desolate, with the crooked frames of three wigwams standing. I thought about my times there and how happy they were. My memories took hold of me and I could see in my mind's eye the children playing as the women worked in the garden. I smelled the roasting meat and saw Oota coming out of her wigwam, giving me her beautiful smile. I could also see Kanti waving at me as I rode by, and a memory of William standing, watching me approach. I shook myself out of my reverie and looked at the unhappy sight before me, a scar on the earth. I was sad for what was and would never be again. I gave Bubs a nudge in the flanks. As we went on, I leaned over and patted his neck. He had been through all of this with me too, had seen it all, and suffered as we did though in different ways.

After a few minutes of contemplation, I turned and rode towards the village. I realized that I might not come this way again for quite a while so I decided to make a full tour. I headed to the millpond, curious if anything was left of it. I know Mr. Pynchon would be interested in the state of things. I rode by the deserted fields and saw weeds growing where good strong crops grew less than a year before. A few corn plants, sown from the seed of last year's abandoned crop, grew in small patches amongst the weeds that were slowly but surely taking over the land.

There was hardly a sign that another person was ever here.

I turned Bubs down the millpond path and was there in a few minutes. The millstones lay on top of each other supporting the blackened timbers, all that was left of the gristmill. The water had overflowed the dam at some point, washing away the dirt below it. Just like at the planting field, weeds grew along the cart path. Shaking my head, I turned and headed toward the village.

I went up the hill slowly, taking it all in. When I got to the top, I saw the burned out remains of each family's house and barn, just a pile of burned rubble in the middle with four corner frame posts three feet high, burned at the top and pointing to the sky like fingers, the cellar holes gaped at me like an open mouth. I walked to where our house stood and, looking down, saw something glinting in the sunlight. I let go of the reins and hopped into the cellar. Digging through the rubble, I found my mother's pewter spoon. It was my most prized possession. I thought I had lost it during the siege and spent hours looking for it but finally gave up the hope that I would ever see it again. I turned it over in my hand, thinking about my childhood and the times with my mother and father. I clenched it tight for a minute then put it in my bag.

I heard a screech and when I looked up, there was a big hawk floating on the wind, just like on the day we first came to the village. I wondered if it was the same bird, looking down on me again. I watched him circle higher and higher until he was only a speck in the sky. I realized that I had not heard any sound other than the hawk, except for the light, lazy wind. It was completely quiet and still, the silence seeming to extend to the horizon and beyond.

I watched as a chickadee flew from the edge of the woods to the wild grapevine growing over the charred remains of the tavern wall and trailing off into the cellar hole. The bird picked at the bugs on the vine and, at the push of a strong breeze, took off for the small tree by the road. A movement caught my eye and I saw a wolf trot over a pile of stones and into the edge of the field moving slowly and eyeing all that was ahead. Insects chirped, flew, and hopped to the small plants growing out of the stone wall edging the road. The tall grass in the fields bent and swayed as the breeze blew showing the path of the wind. Nature had reclaimed what was hers.

I picked up the reins and led Bubs down the road.

The tavern was completely gone, having burned to the ground. There were a few small piles of broken boards and a pile of charcoal, but that was all. I walked around it, remembering the Indians shooting at us from behind the big rock and Ayres barn. I looked up and saw where the Indians, led by Matchithew, caught Sam Prichard and beheaded him, and where his head had been stuck on a pole. I turned around and looked toward the corner where Sarah Coy had given birth to twin boys that we heard only lived a month. I could hear Becky asking me in a whisper, holding my arms tight, if we would live through this and hearing the fear in her voice. I could not believe that ninety-nine of us stayed in that four-room building for three harrowing days, men getting shot, babies being born, fires being put out every few hours, and almost no sleep or food. A strong sadness washed over me. I stood there wondering how in God's name we survived that horrendous time.

Realizing it was time I left this place, I got on Bubs and rode up and down the road twice, looking things over, shaking my head all the while at the destruction and waste that lay all around me.

I wondered how long the land would sleep under the beautiful blue skies of summer and the raging snowstorms of winter before it was scratched by plow or trod by humans or animals again. Little did I know that I would be a part of it.

Chapter 13

I made it to Boston by late afternoon. I delivered the letters to the governor at his home, and, as I came down the steps, I saw a man coming towards me who I recognized as my old friend Ephraim Curtis. He was not looking in my direction so I stepped directly in front of where he would walk.

He stepped back in surprise when he saw me. "Jack! What are you doing here?" he asked, a big smile appearing on his face.

I shook his hand. "I delivered letters to the governor for Mr. Pynchon."

We made our way down the street to a tavern.

"We all wondered what happened to you," I said. "I heard you made it to Marlborough safely."

"It was a difficult day. I ran most of the way. When I got there I found that someone already got word of the attack."

I was amazed. "You ran twenty-six miles?"

"Most of it," he said with humility.

"How did you get away?"

"I tried to sneak away but almost had to come back twice. The second time I was within 100 yards of the tavern for over an hour. I finally made it to Hovey's place and thought I was clear of the Indians and on my way when I heard voices, I crawled over a large rock and there were seven of them sitting around a small fire not fifteen feet away. I didn't dare move because if I did they would have heard me and I would not be sitting here talking to you." He finished his mug and signaled to the tavern keeper for another for each of us.

I thought of my own recent adventure. "How did you finally get by them?"

"I lay there, waiting for them to go to sleep or move off. Finally, the fire died down and they were quiet. I moved back a few feet and very slowly moved around to one side. I never walked more softly or quietly in my life. When I got fifty yards away from them, I started moving faster. They heard me and came running. I jumped into the stream and went under. I never held my breath for so long. I didn't have a chance to do anything before I slid into the water. It was dark and the water was muddy – I couldn't see a thing. I made my way toward the bank where there were a few overhanging bushes. I came up for air right underneath them. I heard something move right next to me. I looked up and saw and Indian standing there, not two feet from my head. If he looked down, he probably would have seen me."

I gave an account of our lives since we last saw him, relating our going to Springfield, the birth of Sam, the attacks, and my capture and escape. He was very interested in my talks with Philip. He hadn't gone back to Quinsigamond since his house was burned the past year.

One of the tragedies of the war was the number of unfortunates on both sides who were hurt by the fighting. It was common for a hundred Indians to be rounded up and brought to the prisons in Boston where they were left to die with no food or clothing. Almost 400 were put on Deer Island in November 1675, given no shelter, food, or clothing so they could die a slow and horrible death. It was approved of by most people, but I saw it for the cruelty it was. I kept my mouth shut to avoid the same fate as the Quakers, whose opinion was similar to my own, and were exiled from the Bay Colony almost immediately after their religious beliefs were known. Stating my opinion to anyone but Becky would get me nothing but trouble. Many other Indians were sold into slavery for the West Indies, which, while a horrible fate, may have been better than watching your family slowly starve in the brutally cold winter.

I went to the jail on Prison Lane, not more than a mile from Gurdon Goodfield's place. He was the greedy and brutal merchant of whom I apprenticed for two long, seemingly unending years. The prison was menacing, with outer walls of stone at least three feet thick, its unglazed windows barred with iron, and the doors covered with iron spikes.

The guards would not let me see William at first but relented when I argued with them.

"Mr. John Pynchon, magistrate of Springfield, directed me to see William of Wekapauge," I lied, knowing it was the only way I would get to see him.

"Show us the paper," a short, ugly guard grunted. I doubted that he could read so even if I had any piece of paper, he wouldn't have known what it was. Since I did not have anything like that, I decided to bluff.

"I don't have it. I lost it on my way here," I told him.

He sneered at me, showing the stubs of blackened teeth. "You don't get to see anyone unless you got a piece of paper."

I pulled myself to my full height and stared down at the squat, smelly man. "I will go to the governor," I threatened, "who is a good friend of Mr. Pynchon's and get his approval to see the prisoner." I tried not to wince at having to call my friend by such a term.

He stood there, scratching his behind first, then his neck, wondering if I meant what I said.

"Let me in now," I directed him, "or the governor will be informed of your stupidity and you will be out of a job."

He grunted again and let me pass, following me through the dark, dank, smelly passage.

The guard stopped and pointed at a room, the door closed tight with a small, narrow opening at the top. He opened the door with a large key from around his neck. The stench was overpowering. He stuck his head inside and looked around as I wondered how he could see anything with so little light.

"You," he said, moving into the room filled with Indian men, women, and children of all ages. They were in rags and near starvation, some barely able to move, many sitting on the floor staring at me. A man slowly stood and made his way from the other side of the room towards me. "Out," the guard spat at him, taking him by the emaciated arm, and roughly pulling him into the passageway before slamming the door shut. It took me a moment until I realized that the man standing before me was William from the Wekapauge village, son of Kanti and cousin of Oota-dabun. His eyes, normally bright and inquisitive, were sunken into his head, his arms covered in sores and his skin was tight against his bones.

"William?" I asked. "Is that you?"

He stood looking at me as if trying to place me. He wavered reaching for the wall to steady himself.

"William, it's Jack." His dull eyes were on me but there was no spark of recognition in them. I took him by the arm and led him toward the entrance, hoping more light would allow him to see me better.

"Here now," the guard protested, "What do you think you are doing?"

I ignored him, taking William by the hand, leading him along. As we got to the light, he looked at me with the utmost sorrow I have ever seen.

"Jack," he whispered, dropping his head.

"William," I said, "you will not stay here, not if I can do anything about it."

The guard chucked his thumb at me, turning to another guard that walked in. "This one thinks he can just come in and take any prisoner he wants."

I stared the filthy little man down. I turned back to William.

"My mother?" he asked.

"I was captured by Philip but escaped. Ahanu was with him. He told me that Kanti and Oota are safe in the north."

I looked him up and down, my nose crinkling at the powerful smell coming from him. I thought of all those imprisoned with him and understood that I could do nothing for them. But I might be able to do something about William. "I will try to get you out of here."

He just stood there, staring blankly at me. It was difficult for me to believe this was the same man who was my friend less than two years ago. If I didn't do something, I knew he would be dead within two months, if he lasted that long. I didn't know what I could do. I had no money to buy him food. The best I could do was get back to Springfield to plead with Mr. Pynchon to help get him released.

I made it back to Springfield by noon the next day and went to see Mr. Pynchon right away. I had to wait to see him and I spent the time pacing back and forth, my impatience getting the better of me. All the way back, all I could think of how beaten and starved William looked. I shuddered every time I thought of it. At last I got to see Mr. Pynchon. I explained the situation as best I could, but when I asked for his help, he shook his head.

"Jack, why do you ask me to interfere in something that is not my business or yours either. If these savages were captured, then it is God's will that it be so."

I stood there watching him, my arms crossed over my chest, my mouth drawn tight, angry as I had ever been.

"You see," he said in a tone as if he were teaching an unruly child, "these savages must be dealt with, and if that is what the authorities decided, then it is best."

I shook my head and dropped my arms.

"No, it isn't best," I said, causing him to look sharply at me. "It is not best," I repeated. "He's done nothing wrong and ended up in the English prison. You are one of the authorities Mr. Pynchon. Is this what you want? Is this what you think is best for every Indian regardless of his alliance before and during the war?" I moved to the other side of the room. "Mr. Pynchon, Sir, in all the time we've known each other I've only asked a couple of things of you but I ask now that you use your power and influence to save the life of one of my good friends who did not fight against us. He endured outrage and suffering from his own people only to be captured by us. If there is only one thing I could ask of you for the rest of my life it would be this."

He studied me for a few moments, looking hard at me with a mixture of anger and doubt passing over his face.

"Let me think about this, Jack. Come see me in two days and I will give you my answer." I was discouraged to say the least. My hopes of a speedy return to rescue William were dashed.

He didn't give me an answer in two days. It took me almost a week to convince him to write the letter.

"I will write a letter to the governor," he finally agreed, "asking that he consider releasing him, but that is all I will do. Do you understand? I have my position to consider you know."

"I do understand, Sir and can ask no more of you. May I wait for the letter?"

"Why do you want to do that? I will have it ready later today."

"I am going back to Boston, as soon as possible," I told him. He stared at me for a moment before taking his quill, dipped in into the inkwell, and scribbled a few lines on a small piece of paper before handing it to me.

"Thank you so much, Mr. Pynchon. This means a great deal to me."

"Jack," he said as I was on my way out the door, "You need to know that my letter may make no impression on the governor and your friend will stay in jail for the rest of his life, however long that might be."

I just nodded and left.

I was on my way well before daylight, hoping to get to Boston by early afternoon. It was a cloudy, gray day and the weather matched my mood for I couldn't help but think of what would happen to William if I could not get him released.

I arrived in Boston ten days from when I last saw William. I got to the governor's house at mid-afternoon. He wasn't home so I had the choice of either waiting for him or going to the prison to see if I could convince the jail keeper to let me see William again to tell him what I hoped was good news. I chose to go to the prison.

The same guard was there as before. When I approached him, he held up his hand.

"You need to see Mr. Buttrick if you want to see your Indian again," he said. Mr. Buttrick was the jail keeper, a heavyset man with a stupid expression on his face, who barely listened to my request before replying.

"You can't see him."

"Why not?" I asked.

"He's not here."

"Where is he?"

"Gone. They all went on the ship this morning."

"What ship?"

"The one to the islands. Where else would they send slaves?" he asked with a laugh, shaking his head as if not believing my stupidity.

"Do you know the name of the ship?"

"It is the Destiny, I think," he replied.

I ran to the docks that were only a short distance from the prison. I looked around at the several ships tied up at the wharf, trying to see if any of them were the Destiny. There were men going back and forth on a few, either taking things from the ship or bringing supplies to it. A man was at the end of the dock, watching a ship that was just making its way into the harbor. I ran to him.

"Is the Destiny here?" I asked. He looked me up and down.

"It's right there," he said pointing at the ship under sail. "It left a short while ago, on its way to the plantations in Barbados."

The breath went out of me at the realization that I was too late to help William. I was powerless to do anything as he sailed away to a certain death. I took Mr. Pynchon's letter and threw it in the water.

CHAPTER 14

The war changed Mr. Pynchon in ways it did not change others. It had a very strong affect on everyone throughout New England and most of all for those of us in the Bay Colony. He went from a strong, vibrant man to a seemingly beaten one. The gleam gone from his eye. In all the time I knew him, he was, for the most part, a serious-minded man as good merchants generally are. This made him believe he was the cause of the Indian uprising, lamenting that if he were a better man, God would not have let the war happen. He told me each time I saw him that the war was God's punishment on us. He became more serious. He didn't smile or joke anymore and sometimes acted cold-hearted to those he helped before the war. It was difficult to watch him and see the anguish and doubt consume him. He even became short with me, which was something I never expected. It happened in October 1676 following the end of the war.

One morning I saw Mr. Pynchon coming out of his house. I walked toward him intending to say hello. He stopped me before I could get a word out.

"What is it?" he snapped. I was taken aback at his abrupt tone.

"I just wanted to say hello to you and Mrs. Pynchon. Maybe spend a few minutes visiting with you, Sir."

He shot me a sideways glance as he walked past. "I'm a busy man and don't have time for idle chatter."

I stood there, rooted to the spot and stunned at his manner. Never before had he treated me this way. He just walked away. I was flabbergasted, unable to understand the cause of him acting this way. I wasn't sure whether to run to catch up with him or let him be. I decided that it was best to try to visit with him another time. I watched him continue speaking to people was he went by, some stopping what they were doing to watch him, a puzzled look on their faces. I saw two or three men shake their head before going back to whatever they were doing.

I went to visit Jeremiah and Mary at the tavern to see if they could explain the odd treatment I received. The room was empty when I came in with only Mary at the fireplace, stirring something in a large kettle that smelled good. She turned to me, setting a large spoon down next to the side of the fireplace.

"Jack, how are you??" she asked.

"I am fine," I said a smile on my face. "And how is my favorite tavernkeeper's wife?"

She laughed as she fixed her cap, her mass of gray hair starting to spill out one side. I leaned against one of the tables and was about to ask her if she noticed a change in Mr. Pynchon when Jeremiah came in.

"I just saw Mr. Pynchon," I told them. "He was very abrupt. He asked me what I wanted, not even calling me by my name. He's never done that in all the years he and I have known each other."

They looked at each other before shifting their glances toward the floor. Jeremiah pulled out a bench and sat down rubbing his hands in circles around the tabletop. "He's changed," he said, looking at his hand moving over the table. "He is more direct and aggressive to almost everyone, so it's not just you."

Mary shifted from one foot to the other still trying to keep her hair under her cap. "He ignored me the other day when I said hello to him … walked right by me. He was never like this before."

I sat down across from Jeremiah. "You mean before the war, don't you?"

"Yes, that's what I mean." He sat forward, putting his elbows on the table, leaning toward me. "He's gotten stern, even speaking to his wife in a harsh tone when they were out." He shook his head. "God save him from further strife."

"He's a different man," Mary added. "He thinks the war is his own fault. He has also said that if we were better people, worked harder, and all went to Sabbath meeting every week, the war would not have happened. He believes it is God's punishment against us and that the Indians were acting out His will."

Jeremiah stood up, pushing the bench back under the table. "You can't argue with a man who thinks that way, not that I would ever argue or even discuss it with him. That is not my place by any means."

Mary flashed me a smile, showing the four remaining teeth she had. "Will you stay for a bit and have a bite to eat?" She waved the linen cloth she had in her hand at her husband. "Jeremiah, get him something to drink," she directed.

I stood up, concerned that Mr. Pynchon was causing himself unnecessary upset with his beliefs.

"No, that's all right," I said. I began walking toward the door, lost in thought. I turned toward them after opening the door. "Maybe he is right. Maybe that is why the war happened … but I don't think so. No matter what we did, no matter how hard we worked, no matter if every person in the Bay went to Sabbath every time, I think the Indians would have attacked."

They both took a few quick steps towards me, Mary slinging the cloth over her shoulder. "Don't be saying that out there," Mary warned, pointing out the door. "There are many people who think the same as Mr. Pynchon. You say those things and you will cause trouble for yourself."

Jeremiah nodded in agreement. "If you know what is good for you and your family, you'll keep your thoughts to yourself and your tongue in your head."

"I understand," I said before closing the door behind me. I was troubled by what I learned about the man I thought I knew so well, the man who married Becky and me, and helped me in many ways over the last nine years.

CHAPTER 15

With the war over, the people of Hatfield began to rebuild their lives. I bought twenty acres of land bordering the river from Mr. Pynchon. It was the best land I had ever seen, fertile and rich with a deep smell that made you know anything would grow well. I had ten fathoms of wampum that I used for supplies.

It was July 27, 1676 when I began to build the house. It took four weeks with the help of several of the other men in town, giving me their time as they could. After our house was finished, I spent the next four months helping several other men build their houses and barns. We spent a great deal of time building barns, houses, and fences. At times, it seemed as if there would be no end to it.

The barns took longer, but when the frames of the first three were up, we had a celebration, as was the custom. All the townspeople brought food, and the those of us who did the building supplied the rum and cider. It was a fine afternoon … until the storm hit.

After everyone left, I looked to the sky and saw big, rolling black clouds coming in from the west, cutting out all the light. A moment later, everything went quiet. The birds stopped singing and the crickets stopped chirping. What little wind there was became still, and the backs of the leaves, silver against the green, started swirling under a fresh breeze while the clouds got darker. The wind began to howl and lightning stabbed from the clouds, flashing against the sky, followed by thunder that boomed so loud the ground shook, like a giant trying to crash through the gates of Hell. White streamers came out of black clouds twirling towards the ground. The rain began pouring down as if the heavens opened and every drop of water in the sky fell on us, coming down so hard you couldn't see across the yard and couldn't see the barn from the house. The storm lasted a good part of the night, the wind bringing down branches and leaves. The next morning was bright and clear, everything washed clean by the wind and rain. It made me feel like it was a new beginning.

We farmed together and saw a good harvest. The wheat and corn was better than any of us remembered. I cared for three milk cows, two oxen and four sheep that belonged to Mr. Pynchon, with the agreement that we each get half of new animals and the animals be returned to Mr. Pynchon at the end of two years.

It was in mid-August when we heard of King Philip's death. He and his remaining warriors retreated to a fortified village in Rhode Island. Benjamin Church, a great military leader, along with over a hundred soldiers and Indian allies found the village and killed Philip in addition to many other Indians. Philip was beheaded and his body drawn and quartered. His head was put on a pole and displayed in Plymouth for many years. Soldiers took his fingers as trophies of war. There was great rejoicing when we learned of his death. Although he was responsible for my being left with the Mohawk, I was not as cheerful as the rest, thinking of my time with him and knowing that he did not look to lead a war but understood it had to be fought.

The next year was peaceful and it went by quickly. Even if it was not as good as I remember, it seemed very good compared to everything we had been through. The peace after the war was like a sunny, warm spring and summer after a long, cold, brutal winter. What is ordinary was good, because through the war everything was so out of the ordinary.

We faced many tough times rebuilding what was lost and we all helped each other as we could. Hatfield suffered a greater burden than any other town in the colony, except for the abandoned towns of Deerfield and Northfield. Twenty-seven people were killed, over a third of the houses burned, and most of the cows, swine, sheep and horses were killed or taken by the enemy. With so many soldiers quartered in the town during the war, many of the people were almost destitute as a result of having to feed and board those men and their horses. A petition was sent to the general court asking for relief from the tax rates and thankfully, it was granted. It was a difficult time for all.

One morning in May, I noticed that Becky was starting to look different. I couldn't figure out what it was, so I watched her for a day or two and the look remained, a happy, radiant look that everything was well. When I asked her why she was so happy, she wouldn't tell me, and when I became frustrated, she only laughed. The next morning after breakfast, she told me she was pregnant. It was a wonderful day for us. We looked forward to another child. Sam was growing fast. He was starting to run, bumping off the table and chairs several times a day. He had little accidents like when he fell and caught his chin on the bench. He got a cut that bled for a while but he cried for what seemed like hours. He was talking, mixing real words with a stream of gibberish. His first word was "me" that he said early one morning. He latched onto it and repeated it a hundred times that day and the next. That changed into "carry me," which he said as he raised his arms up for you to hold him, something I could never refuse.

Becky began teaching him to read, or so she said even though I thought it was too early for it, by having him sit on her lap as she read the Bible aloud. There were times when he would sit and listen, watching her and looking at the book, and other times when he would squirm and want to get down to see something that attracted his attention and then, at other times, he would fall asleep in her arms, his head lolling back onto her shoulder.

As for me, I was working from early morning until night every day, getting my fingers dirty with the soil, smelling the fresh earth as it was plowed, feeling the sun on my shoulders and watching the nourishing rains fall on the crops.

Peace and prosperity were very welcome. All in all, it was a good time.

CHAPTER 16

It was a glorious fall morning. The sky was a pale shade of blue and the bright sunshine carried with it a soft breeze. It was a special morning because Becky and I woke up before Sam and made love, which was all the more special because she was now four months along. I watched her begin her day and saw the quiet beauty in her face. I never tired of looking at this wonderful woman who was my wife, making me realize how blessed I was to have someone like her. I couldn't pull my gaze from her as she built up the fire and began making breakfast. She caught me looking at her.

She gave me a sly smile. "What are you looking at?"

"Just the woman I love, that's all." I went up behind her and wrapped my arms around her, pulling her to me. I kissed her neck and felt her belly, letting my hands wander.

"Don't you start again," she said with a laugh. "I have things to do."

"Fine. Let your work come before me, your adoring husband." I kissed her once more on the neck and tickled her before letting her go.

"Stop that!" she laughed. "What am I going to do with you, Jack Parker?"

"Oh, I don't know … love me forever?"

She put her hand on my arm and kissed me.

After we finished breakfast, Sam came into the room rubbing the sleep from his eyes. I picked him up and swung him around and gave him a big hug and a kiss. "How's my boy this morning?" I asked as I put him down.

He started to walk away but stopped, turned and put out his arms for me to hold him again. After I lifted him up with my right arm, he put his head on my shoulders and gave me a hug. Becky looked at me, shrugging her shoulders as I pointed to Sam with my left hand, wondering where this came from. After a minute, he got down and started playing with one of the toys I made him, a carved wooden horse that was a bad likeness of Bubs.

"I have to go," I told Becky, taking the pot from her and placing it on the table. I hugged her again and told her I loved her.

"I love you too," she said, giving me a quick kiss. I turned before walking out the door and looked at them, Becky getting ready to make bread and Sam playing with his toy horse. I smiled, happier than I had been in a long time. I grabbed my corn knife from the barn and headed to the South Meadow.

Stephen Jennings, Sam Belden, and John Coleman met me as I started down the lane toward the Meadow. We talked as we went about the wonderful crop and good weather. Our conversation turned to the six Mohawks who had spent the night outside the palisade.

"One of those Mohawks had a scalp hanging from his belt," Sam said, "and he was proud of it."

"I saw that too but they were heading back to New York. The women were not Mohawks but Naticks," I said. "Not sure how they got mixed up with the Mohawks."

Sam shook his head. "They all looked like they were hiding something, like they shared a secret. Something about them bothers me but I can't put my finger on it." He swung his scythe onto his shoulder and looked at me. "You have more experience with the Mohawk than most of us. What do you think they're up to?"

"I don't know," I answered. "They looked like they wanted to be on their way home." I pondered my experience with the Mohawk and shuddered slightly. "The Mohawk are the most brutal of all the Indians I've known. They would spend three days slowly torturing you and enjoy every minute of it."

"Well, I am glad we sent a rider to Worshipful John," John chimed in, referring to Mr. Pynchon. "You never know what might happen. It's best to keep him informed, just in case. Better to be prepared than not."

We all nodded in agreement.

John kicked a stone as we walked. "I would be happy if I never saw another Indian again."

We began cutting the corn as a few other men joined us, working in silence for the most part, except when we took a short break.

It was near noon when Sam, working three rows to my left, dropped his scythe. I looked up at the sound of it hitting the ground and saw smoke rising from one of the houses. It took just a moment for us to realize the village was being attacked. Two shots, followed by a third, rippled through the quiet. We took off at a run. None of us had our guns with us since we didn't see the need to carry them while we were working in the meadows now that the war was over. I first thought that maybe it was just one house that caught fire as that sometimes happens. A spark from the fireplace lands on something and a fire starts spreading to the whole house in a few moments. I knew I was wrong as I saw a second house, Sam Belden's, begin to burn. As we got closer, we could hear the yelling and whooping of Indians as well as the screams of our families. I tripped and fell face first into the corn stubble but pulled myself up and ran as fast as I could.

My thoughts were of Becky and Sam, a fear washing over me at the idea they might be killed or captured. I pushed myself hard and ran faster, getting to the village ahead of the others.

Ben Wait ran by me. “It’s the Mohawk, I’ll bet!” he yelled as he ran to his house. Four buildings were burning now, and the sound of shots at the end of the North Meadow made the hair on my neck stand up.

As I got to our house, I saw the door open and Sam’s toy horse in the dirt near the barn. I rushed into the house. The fire was still burning in the fireplace with a pot of bubbling stew hanging over it and slices of pumpkin were on the table, which Becky would use for a pie. One of our knives, smeared with blood, lay on the floor. I ran through the rest of the house, calling for her and Sam. They were gone.

My heart came to a sudden stop at the thought of never seeing them alive again. I pushed the thought away as I heard yelling outside. I ran out the door to find Sam Kellogg, Obadiah Dickinson, John Coleman, and Ben Wait’s houses burning, the flames engulfing each building as the smoke poured into the blue sky. John Alliss’s barn fell onto one side, the fire weakening the beams and roof. Some of the dead lay near their homes, others in the lane. I came upon Hannah Coleman and her infant daughter lying side by side in the lane, their skulls bashed in. Four men, including brothers John and Isaac Graves, John Atchisson, and John Cooper, who were building a house for John Graves and his soon-to-be-wife, were shot as they worked and lay where they fell. Elizabeth Russell and her three-year-old son Stephen were clubbed to death, their faces mangled by the spikes from a war club. Sam Belden's wife died when their house burned. A little two-year-old blond-haired girl, Elizabeth Wells, was shot in the throat with an arrow. Several people were wounded, some seriously, some not.

I stood there dumbfounded, looking at the death and destruction, taking it all in. After fourteen months of peace, the war came back like a bad dream that would not leave me. I realized I had Sam's toy horse in my hand and clutched it tighter.

"I will come and get you," I promised them, "I will bring you home." A flame of anger and hatred ran through me as I cursed the savages that caused the ruin of the village.

We got to work, tending to the wounded and began burying the dead. We did things without much talk, each of us going through the motions in a daze. Coffins were built by several men while others went to the burial ground to dig the graves. By the time the coffins were finished, the graves were ready. The dead were cleaned and wrapped in shrouds, by whom I cannot remember, it just seemed that the dead were not wrapped one minute and the next they were, before being placed into a coffin. I got Bubs and the cart and began, with Ben's help, loading the coffins into it. The cart took six at a time, stacked two high. Stephen Jennings, Ben, John Coleman, Philip Russell, Sam Foote, John Wells, Will Bartholomew, and I headed to the burial ground. I led Bubs while the others walked along, shovels and picks over their shoulders. It was a horrid sight, the coffins containing the bodies of those we knew bouncing along. Elizabeth Wells' coffin began to slide off the cart when I went over a bump but her father gently caught it, holding it in his arms for a moment before placing it back into the wagon. One of us got into each grave and took the coffin, lowering it to the bottom of the grave. By the time the horrible job was done, twilight was coming on. We got back to what was left of the village, numb from the shock of what happened.

I went into the house expecting Becky to be there as she had been a thousand times before. The realization that they were taken captive hit me as I sat at the table. Ben knocked on the open door and came in.

"They took seventeen captive," he said. "They took my whole family … and yours too."

I sat there, nodding at what he said, but I was barely listening.

"John Alliss is on his way to tell Worshipful John about the attack and to get help just in case they come back, although why they would, I don't know."

"Stay here tonight, Ben. Everyone can if they want."

He looked at me before hanging his head and shaking it from side to side. "Thank you, Jack. I'll tell the others."

As he got up to go, Stephen Jennings came in, gun in hand.

"I'm not going anywhere without it," he said as he and Ben sat down. I poured them some rum from the small bottle I kept. After we drank in silence for a minute, we all looked at each other at the same time.

"I'm going after them tomorrow," I said.

"I'm going too," Stephen said. "We'll get thirty or forty soldiers to help us."

"It's not that easy," Ben told us. "We don't know which Indians attacked. My guess is that it was the Mohawk but I'm not sure."

"What difference does it make?" Stephen asked. "We send out three scouting parties to find where they went and then go get them."

"I agree," I said. "And we shouldn't wait. They either went north or east toward Wachusett. They won't be able to move fast with that many captives, especially since ten of them are young children."

"You're assuming they kept all of them alive," Ben said.

The thought that Sam could be laying somewhere dead, killed because he annoyed one of the savages, shot through my mind.

"What do you suggest?"

"First, we need to figure out which tribe took them. Then we need to get money for a ransom. Then go get them." Stephen shifted in his chair and finished his rum in one swallow. "We don't want to wait until they are too far way. The more time we give them, the more difficult it will be to get them back."

His words would prove prophetic.

"All right, I can ride to see Mr. Pynchon tomorrow about the ransom," I told them. "He may be able to give us what we need, although I am not sure. Much of what he owned was destroyed last year. If he can't, he'll help us get it, I know that."

"I'm going to Albany," Ben told us. "I want to know if it was the Mohawk. They have been friendly for too long to do something like this. But, if it was them, then maybe we can begin negotiating a ransom. I am leaving at first light so let Worshipful John know when you see him."

There was nothing else to say. Sam Foote joined us since his house was also burned.

While I should have slept from exhaustion, I tossed and turned all night until an hour or so before dawn, when I gave up on sleep altogether. Ben was up, getting ready to leave.

"I should be back in a week," he said. "See what you and Stephen can do about a ransom." We watched him ride off.

I was saddling Bubs when a shadow fell on me. I turned to see Ezekiel, his big form blocking out the sunlight behind me.

"I came as soon as I heard," he said. "When are we going after the bastards?"

I told him about Ben going to Albany and my going to see Mr. Pynchon about a ransom.

"For the sake of Almighty God, we can't wait forever … they'll get away! We find them savages, kill them, and bring everyone home. The hell with a ransom, if all of us go, we can overtake them and get your people back," he bellowed.

"It's not that simple. As much as it frustrates me to do nothing, we need authority from the governor before we just take off after them. Soldiers should be here today, probably under Captain Watts. If they get here soon, you and the others can go with them. We need to get ransom money. It makes no sense to find them and not be able to bring them back because we don't have a ransom. I have to go."

Several others gathered around us, probably attracted by the noise he was making.

"It is going to take time, Ezekiel. Now, I know you're not a patient man but we have to do this right."

He turned and glared at the others. "Do all of you think the same thing?" When they murmured their agreement, he began to thunder.

"What is wrong with you men? Don't you want your families back? Are they not worth doing everything you can to get them back? Why in God's good name would you wait until someone tells you that you can do something?" He scratched his head with one big hand before rubbing it over his face. "I don't understand it," he mumbled as he walked toward my house.

"Stay here," I told him. "I should be back later this afternoon." I rode off, leaving him there, standing next to my empty house.

I arrived at Mr. Pynchon's house three hours later and went right in after tying the reins to a post. Mr. Pynchon was coming down the stairs just as I entered the door.

"Jack, what happened?" The concern in his voice was unmistakable.

"Indians attacked while most of us men were working in the south meadow. They killed twelve and took seventeen others captive, including Becky and Sam."

"Gracious God, spare us any more trouble. I sent to Connecticut last night for help. I received a message a little while ago that forty soldiers will be here by noon. I will send them on to Hatfield right away. I also dispatched a messenger to the governor letting him know of the attack."

"I'll wait for the soldiers. They can ride back with me."

There were dark circles under his eyes and he looked like he had not slept well in a long time. There were more lines and wrinkles on his face than I remembered.

"Will this ever end, Jack?"

"It has to, Sir. Ben left for Albany this morning. He wants to make sure it was not the Mohawk. He doesn't think it was them, but I am not so sure."

"It doesn't surprise me that he's gone."

"Ben, Stephen Jennings, and I are going after them. We will get our families back. We need to be able to offer a ransom. That's what I came to talk to you about."

"Come in and sit down." He motioned me into his business room. He slumped into a chair behind a big table and shook his head.

"How much do you think we would need to offer?" I asked.

"I don't know. It depends on what the savages want … sometimes it is not just money, you know."

"I am aware of that. Can you give us the money we need?"

"Jack, I lost most everything when the town was destroyed. Some of it is rebuilt but I have little funds to give you. I wish the circumstances were different, but I do not have anything to offer as a ransom."

"So what do we do? Where can we get it?"

"Well, the very first thing you need to do is get authority from Governor Leverett to go after them. I doubt he will authorize a group of soldiers to keep after them; the cost would be too great. If they are on their way to Canada, perhaps he can give you a letter of credit to use with the authorities there. I know the colony has almost no funds available either. The cost of the war depleted everything."

"Can you write a letter to the governor explaining what I need?"

"Of course." He stared at the floor, deep in thought for a moment. "This bothers me more than anything else over the last two years. They are innocent of everything. The women and children in Hatfield never did anything against the Indians. It makes my blood boil." His shoulders slumped and he put his hand to his face. "I am sorry I can't help you more, Jack. I feel like I am of no use to you, or anyone else, when you need it most."

"No sir, you needn't feel that way. You've done a great deal for us. Why you married us right in that room," I said, pointing in the direction of large room across the hall.

He gave a weak smile. "Yes, I know. It was a howling snowstorm and we went to the tavern afterwards. Tom Cooper, your friend and mine, God rest his soul, was there, too." He sprung out of the chair. "But, these memories do us no good now. Give me a few minutes to write the letter."

I went outside and looked around at the town. All signs of the destruction Mr. Pynchon spoke of were gone and some of the buildings had been rebuilt.

As I saw the various buildings and remembered the times when Becky and I were here. My thoughts turned to her and Sam.

"Dear God in Heaven, please protect them," I prayed aloud. "Let me find them safe and unharmed. I ask this of you." I went to Bubs and rubbed his neck up and down. He lifted his head and gave me a knowing look. While I know some people would think I imagine it, there are times when I think Bubs talks to me with his eyes. The look he gave me told me that he would bring me wherever I needed to help find them. It was as if he was telling me that Becky and Sam are his family too. My thoughts were interrupted by Mr. Pynchon.

"Here is the letter. I explained the situation to him and asked that he give you, Ben, and Stephen, and anyone else who joins you, whatever assistance he can."

"Thank you, Sir. Your support means a great deal to me. I honestly don't know what my life would have been like if I had never met you." I shook his hand and thanked him again before going to the tavern to wait for the soldiers.

I waited less than an hour before they arrived. Captain Watts reported to Mr. Pynchon, who, until recently, was the ranking military officer in the western part of the colony. There were twenty-two soldiers accompanying the captain. He was experienced in Indian warfare, having fought in several battles. Another eight men from Springfield volunteered to go with us.

We were on our way within a short time of their arrival. I gave Captain Watts the details of the raid before we set out for Hatfield.

"Where do you think they went? Which Indians were they?"

"I think they went north or toward Wachusett, but I'm not sure. Ben Wait left for Albany this morning to see if it was the Mohawk. I think it might have been them but he doesn't. It might be a mixed group … Nipmuck, Mohawk, maybe Narragansett, too, but we don't know. There was nothing I saw or anything they left that would let me say it was this tribe or that."

"Let's get there and see what we can find," he said mounting his horse.

We were halfway there when a rider came galloping toward us, in a big hurry to get somewhere. He pulled up aside of us, looking like he had ridden a distance, covered with dust. His horse was panting, looking strained.

"They attacked Deerfield last night," he told us. "They killed John Root and took Benoni Stebbins, Quintin Stockwell, and Sam Russell, Phil Russell's boy. He is only eight or nine. I'm on my way to tell Mr. Pynchon."

Captain Watts looked over at me.

"I think you are right. They are headed north to Canada. They may not stop until they get there since there are no other places to attack."

My heart sunk with the possibility that Becky and Sam could end up in Canada. That would make getting them back even more difficult assuming they survived the ordeal.

"Go tell Mr. Pynchon," Captain Watts told the rider. "Let him know I will return when I have news." The rider nodded and kicked his horse in the flanks and tore off towards Springfield.

Arriving a couple hours later, we found the ruins of the burnt houses and barns. It being too late in the day to start our search, we talked for hours about why the Indians raided us and Deerfield, the horror of the killings of our neighbors and friends, the worries about our families, and what we can do to get them back.

Ezekiel was unusually quiet. He was not joining in the conversation except to add a minor comment here or there. When the soldiers sitting at our table began getting ready to sleep on the floor, I leaned over to find out what was wrong.

"Why are you so quiet?"

He turned to face me and laid his meaty arms on the table.

"Because we are not moving fast enough to catch them. By the time the good Captain gets going tomorrow, those rotten Indians could be halfway to Canada. Don't you want your wife and son back as quick as possible?"

"Of course I do. What kind of question is that? We'll know more when Ben gets back in a few days."

"A few days! This could go on for weeks before anyone starts doing anything. The longer we wait the less likely it is you will ever see Becky and Sam again. You do know that don't you?"

I didn't answer him but sat brooding over the delay that I knew would take even longer than it had already. I did not expect that it would take as long as it did though.

We sat there, taking turns at the fire, melting lead and pouring it into moulds, making balls for we wanted to have as many as we could carry.

Just after dawn the next morning, several men came in from Hadley and Northampton, so with the soldiers, men from Springfield, and those of us from Hatfield, thirty-five of us set out to see if we could find where the Indians and our families went. We were all well armed, most having a large powder horn full and a leather bag packed with shot. I carried my short sword on my right side and, on my left side, a war club I took off the first Indian I ever killed at the ambush in Brookfield. The club was about 30 inches long and heavy, made from the root of an oak tree, the roots sharpened into lethal prongs. It whispered "death" to me the first time I saw it, as it sliced the air an inch from my face, and I hoped it would do more to the savage that took my wife and son.

We rode to the north most of the morning, past Deerfield and the old Pocumtuck Indian village, on toward the abandoned Indian village of Squakeag without finding any sign. Two Indian scouts were with us, although how good they were I didn't know, never having seen or heard of them before. Captain Watts didn't trust them or any other Indians, and only took them because the Connecticut governor insisted they were loyal to us and that they go along. From what I saw, they did not seem to be trying too hard to find anything. They told us twice they knew the Indians were in the area but gave no proof of it. Most of us believed it was a tactic to allow the captors more time to get further away.

The only thing our efforts were giving us was an increasing amount of frustration. When we stopped for a rest, I pulled Ezekiel, Stephen Jennings, John Coleman, Philip Russell, Sam Foote, John Wells, and Will Bartholomew off to the side.

"This is useless," I told them. "Going along like this is not going to get us anywhere."

"That's right, it won't," Ezekiel chimed in. I shot him a look that told him to hold his comments until I was done.

"If we go off on our own, just the eight of us, we can cover more ground faster than these others who don't have nearly as much interest at finding our families than we do. What do you think? Do you agree?"

They all nodded.

"I think it is a good idea, Jack," Stephen said.

"Me too," Phil added.

The others murmured their agreement.

I turned toward Ezekiel. "What about you?" I asked.

"After all I told you last night, you think you have to ask me what I want to do?" he bellowed. "Good God, Jack, either you had too much to drink or you just weren't listening to me."

"Hard to believe you couldn't hear him," Will said with a smirk.

"I'm already angered up little man," Ezekiel said to Will who was at least a foot shorter than him, "so don't push me any farther or you'll end up in that tree." He pointed to a large oak tree to our right and Will walked back to his horse.

"That was a smart thing to do, little man," Ezekiel hollered at him.

Captain Watts strode over at the sudden noise. "What's going on here?"

"We want to go out on our own, Captain. We can cover more ground faster and we know the area better than anyone you have with you."

"Well, I don't know. I want us to stay together in case of trouble. You men don't want to be ambushed do you? What if you run into the savages and they attack? What will you do?"

"We'll fight them," I said, "or anything else we need to do to get our families back."

"No, I want you to stay with us."

"Captain, these are our wives and children," Stephen said. "We want them back soon and we will do whatever it takes to get them back to Hatfield."

Captain Watts did not appear moved by our argument.

"No, you will ride with us."

For all of his clumsy, sometime brutish ways, Ezekiel can have moments of inspiration. Seeing nothing else was working, he moved his bulk next to the captain, and stood looking down on him. Ezekiel weighed at least 100 pounds or more than the captain, was twice as broad, and towered over him by a good foot. His hands were the size of the captain's head. "Captain, with all due respect, I think you need to reconsider your decision. We are not looking to cause any trouble. We want to find our people soon and not follow behind those scouts, who don't seem to know what they are doing." He moved another couple of inches closer to the captain until they were almost touching. Looking down on him once more, Ezekiel said only one more thing.

"I think you need to let us go," he said in a low, somewhat threatening tone.

The captain looked up at him for a full minute. "All right, go. You'll have a few more hours to ride before dark. We'll head northwest. There's a stream on the far side of a big meadow ten miles or so in that direction isn't there?"

"Yes, sir," Stephen answered. "It's on the other side of a big hill after you cross a rocky stream with large, moss covered rocks around it."

"Fine. Meet us there before sunset."

We went back to our horses and took off at a gallop.

Within the first five miles, we began to pick up little signs. Something shiny caught Will's eye that turned out to be a button. A little further along, Sam Foote found a small area where the ground had been turned up as if there was a scuffle. A half a mile from there, we found a handprint in blood on the smooth bark of a young beech tree. The last thing we found was Becky's white cap. I sat on the ground holding it, turning it around in my hands, looking at it, smelling it, and thinking of her and the wonderful morning we had before I went to the meadow on the day of the attack. I held it tight in my hand all the way to our meeting place with Captain Watts and his men.

They were waiting for us, sitting around two small fires in a flat area in the middle of the meadow. We told them of our discovery and that we knew they were headed northwest. Pleased with our success and glad that he decided to let us go out on our own, he agreed to allow us to lead the search the next day. Ezekiel, never one for holding back, congratulated him.

"Best decision you ever made, Captain," he said with a grin. "Glad you talked us into it." The rest of us chuckled a bit but our mood turned somber as we remembered the reason for our search.

The captain's men had food for only two days, so they would leave for Springfield the next afternoon. We decided that the eight of us would press on until we either found them or lost the trail for good. I was optimistic that we would get closer to the captors the next morning. I was anxious to get going and didn't sleep much. When I lay down, I clutched Becky's cap in my hand and fell asleep smelling her special smell.

We were on the move before dawn, picking our way through the forest, looking for the trail they made. After three hours, one of the captain's men found a small piece of leather with beadwork on it. It looked like it had been there for at least two weeks, maybe longer. I took it from the man and examined it closely.

"It's Pocumtuck, a part of the covering of a quiver," I told them. "But it may not be from the ones who attacked us. One of the tribe could have had it drop off when he was out hunting." Stephen looked at me with a jaundiced eye.

"None of the Indians around here have been doing much hunting. This came from one of the enemy that took our families. I have no doubt about it."

The rest of the day we found nothing, no trace of anyone passing through, and no more signs of our families. It was as if they disappeared, as if the woods and field swallowed them up.

When it came time for the captain and his men to head back, we were tired and discouraged, and wondered aloud whether we should go on or return to Hatfield. In our search, we covered well over fifty miles and were getting far from home without enough supplies to go on much further. If we were attacked, the eight of us would not be able to defend ourselves well. The further from home we got, the greater became the chances of something bad happening. We would be of no use to anyone if we were killed, so we decided to return.

The mood in Hatfield was one of dejection and hopelessness. No one had any ideas as to what else we could do. It was three days since the attack and there had been no message or ransom demand from the captors. Things continued like this, with us going back to the field and meadows to finish the harvest. We went on, working listlessly, our hearts and minds not in it, doing it only because it needed to be done. Every time I walked into our house, everything there reminded me of Becky and Sam. I sat by the fire each night, feeling hollow, as if someone ripped the biggest part of my life out of me, casting me away to live the remainder of my days alone. One night, I cried as I lay in bed, the fear of never seeing them again came over me and wouldn't leave. I was hollow-eyed when I got up the next morning from lack of sleep and constant worry.

Ezekiel stayed with me but didn't intrude on my sadness. At night, he went up to the loft and slept on an old corn husk and straw mattress. In the morning, he got the fire going and cooked us breakfast, asking what else he could do to help.

James McDevitt from Hadley came in the mid-afternoon the next day to tell us that five Indians surrendered to the few soldiers at the mill garrison and that they confessed to being part of the group that attacked Hatfield. They said they tried to burn the mill but failed and that struck us as odd because it had been clear, dry weather and, had they done it as they did to so many other buildings, the mill should have easily gone up in flames. Within minutes, the eight of us were riding to Hadley.

It was less than ten miles and took only fifteen minutes to get to the ferry at the river. It could take only two of us over at a time, and in another hour we were all across and at the mill.

The five Indians were all young men, no older than in their early twenties, with a haughty air about them. They told us that they were part of the group that attacked and were sorry for taking part in it. They said they were duped into it by a group of Nipmucks and would not have done it on their own. I did not care for their reasons but thought several times about taking them out and shooting each one for what they did. Stephen and Will felt the same way with Ezekiel and Sam Foote calling for calm, asking that we learn as much as we could before doing anything. It was good that my emotions did not rule the day for the Indians told us they could help get our families released.

"Where are they?" I demanded. One of them, tall and long-faced, was the leader.

"Four days north. I will help with getting your families ransomed. I do not know what the Nipmucks will demand to let them go. We can take a message to them."

We discussed this for a few moments before deciding that it was the best chance we had so far, and to let them go only if they promised to meet again in a week in Hadley to which they agreed. Ezekiel was suspicious of the whole situation.

"They wanted to be captured," he said. "They just walked to the mill and didn't get it to burn, and then didn't put up a fight? They are up to something no good. I can feel it in my bones."

"What are we supposed to do?" Stephen asked. "Keep them here? For what? We know more than we did two hours ago."

"Why would they want to get captured?" Sam asked.

"To set us up. To trick us." Ezekiel answered.

"But to what purpose? What would it accomplish?"

"Sam's right," I added. "They could have just as well sent one of them with the same message."

Stephen shook his head. "No, they were looking the mill over, checking out the defenses. They will be back to burn it. That's what they were really doing."

His words rang true. Three weeks later, a dozen Indians attacked early one morning and burned the mill to the ground.

October 4th was a cloudless, cool day with hard blue skies filled with bright sunshine. Around mid-morning, Ben rode into the village looking tired and bedraggled.

"It wasn't the Mohawk," he told us. "I met with Captain Sylvester, commander at Albany, and he sent out a messenger to the Mohawk. Three days later, two of them came to him and told us that they were not responsible for the attack. I asked if they knew who was. They said it was probably the Nipmuck or Pocumtuck under Ashpelon." He drained a mug of cider and wiped his mouth with the back of his hand. "I talked to Mr. Pynchon on my way here. Captain Sylvester wrote him a letter about it not being the Mohawk." He paused for a moment, looking around at us. "I want you to give me authority to go the governor and ask for permission for us to go after them, and for the colony to pay a ransom."

"When will you leave?" I asked. "Tomorrow?"

Ben shook his head. "Today, as soon as possible. If I ride hard I could be there late tonight."

"I will write up the request," I told everyone. I ran back to my house for the one piece of paper I had left. Ten minutes later, Ben had the document telling the governor we wanted to rescue our families and pleaded with him for the colony to provide a ransom sufficient to guarantee their release. I also gave him Mr. Pynchon's letter.

Ben went to his house, changed his clothes, grabbed some food, and was on his way to Boston, all within an hour of arriving from Albany.

No more than two hours later, Benoni Stebbins came running into the village, his dirty, ragged clothes flapping about him. He was one of the four men captured on the raid at Deerfield. He escaped two days ago from a group of Nipmuck near Wachusett. The Nipmuck left Canada with the attackers, a group of twenty-six Pocumtuck, eighteen men, five women, two young boys, and one Narragansett, but split off several days north of Hatfield and went off to Wachusett. The leader of the attackers, Ashpelon, sent two messengers and Benoni, to get the Nipmuck to return to the camp four days north. Benoni escaped and ran most of the way the last day and a half, a total of fifty miles. After Benoni ate some food and had a couple of mugs of cider while telling us of his adventure, we began asking him many questions.

"Is everyone still alive?" I asked.

"Yes, they are. No one has been hurt … yet."

"What do you mean?"

"The day before I left with the messengers, the warriors were all in a rage and threatened to burn three women and two men. Ashpelon talked them out of it, telling all of us to be quiet and not get them angry because, if we did, he would not be able to control them."

"Where are they going?" Will asked.

"Canada."

"Sweet mother," Ezekiel said, "I knew we should have stayed after the bastards. I say we go after them now. You can take us," he said, pointing at Benoni.

"They would kill every one of them before we got a chance to attack."

"We need to let Mr. Pynchon know," I said.

Stephen Jennings agreed to ride to Mr. Pynchon to give him the news and seek his advice. I thought of offering to go but decided I wanted to talk to Benoni some more. Stephen was gone in a few minutes, promising to be back after sunset.

"Benoni, tell me, how were Becky and Sam?" I was afraid of his answer.

"They were as good as they could be but so was everyone else. The Indians staked us down every night, tying our hands and feet with vines. They didn't have much food to share but gave us enough … we ate a little something every day."

Memories of my time with King Philip and the Mohawk flashed through my mind, the first time in well over a year. The thought of my wife and young son going through all that made me sick to my stomach. Then a red-hot anger sprouted inside of me and I wanted to go get the bastards then and there. I realized Benoni was right and there was no way we could rescue our families without most of them being killed. I could only hope that Ben would have luck with the governor approving our request, as it seemed like the only option remaining. I knew from what Benoni told us that the Indians would not come to Hadley as they promised and that there would be no way to ransom unless we went to Canada and brought them back.

Stephen was back shortly after sunset with news that Mr. Pynchon sent to Connecticut for assistance requesting a troop of men. He also was sending a messenger the next day to Captain Sylvester to ask that the Mohawks be incited to fight against the Pocumtuck and assist in getting the captives back.

CHAPTER 17

Captain Treat and forty men rode into Hatfield the following cold and windy afternoon. After we told him what happened, they rode off toward Deerfield. There was not much they could do except patrol through the area to protect us in some small way. They were back before sunset, not having seen a trace of other Indians. None of us in the village thought they would. They stayed the night, bedding down in the houses as best they could, and rode out again in the early morning. They stayed in Hadley for three nights before returning to Hatfield.

We spent several long days waiting for the Indians to return. They were supposed to come back on Sunday, the 14th but they didn't. This caused us great concern because when they did not do something they promised, it meant that they were planning to do something against you. The only question was what it would be. At that moment, I knew we had no choice but to go to Canada to get them and bring them home. Captain Treat and his men stayed for two more days and returned to Connecticut.

Things dragged on while we waited for Ben to return from Boston with word from the governor. We worked getting the harvest in, which helped not only to prepare for winter, but also to take our minds off our troubles, even if only for a short time.

It rained hard for the next three days straight. The river climbed up its' banks by three feet. There was no danger of flooding like there was in the spring because the season had been on the dry side. Ezekiel and I sat in my house with the door open watching the rain come down. I sat by the hearth and kept the small fire burning under a pot of stew while he brooded and grumbled about the lack of action.

"Jack, this is driving me to all frustration. I have to do something. I cannot sit here waiting and waiting day after day. We have to do something."

"I know," I replied "but what?"

He shrugged his shoulders and slumped back onto the bench.

"Only thing we can do is get ready. Ben has to be back in a couple of days at the latest."

He took a deep breath, filling his giant lungs with air. "Well we can't wait much longer because winter is coming on and I don't like the idea of traveling to Canada in the winter. Now in the summer it might be a lark, a good long walk, a good stretch of the legs. What can be taking him so long? He's been gone almost two weeks!"

I couldn't help but agree with him. The waiting was wearing on me, too.

On the third rainy day, I decided that we needed to be ready to go when Ben arrived so Ezekiel, Stephen, and I began getting our things ready. I cleaned my gun twice, once because it needed it, the other from sheer boredom. I filled my pack with the warmest clothes I had, put all the parched cornmeal into a pouch made from a woodchuck bladder so it would stay dry even if it fell into water. I filled my powder horn and spent two hours making balls, having over fifty, all that the shot pouch could hold. I sharpened my knife and short sword, put bear fat on my knee-high moccasins to waterproof them and gathered other odds and ends I thought I might need. All the while, I could not get my mind off Becky and Sam. I worried about them constantly, and got angrier and angrier at what happened and how helpless I felt. I ached to be off after them.

Between the three of us, we packed bags of cornmeal, dried sliced apples and pumpkin, dried peas, smoked venison pounded into thin strips, small dried biscuits, a favorite of Ezekiel's, and beans.

On the morning of the 22nd, I was in the barn feeding Bubs when I heard Ezekiel yelling. I rushed out, expecting the worst, but was relieved when I saw Ben ride into the village. Everyone came from their houses or barns out and gathered around him. He wasn't even off his horse before we began asking questions.

"It's been a long ride and I am tired … and thirsty," he said, squaring his shoulders. "I left Boston well before sunrise and pushed this poor beast all the way." He put his hand on the horse's neck as it stood there panting and blowing, little flecks of foam at the edges of its mouth.

We waited to hear what he had to say after a good long drink of cider. After he slaked his thirst, he began. "It took me a week to see the governor. I spent more time with assistants and clerks than I ever wanted to and none of them could help me. They kept explaining that the governor was the man to make the decision. When I finally got to see him, I asked him right out to make me the agent to get them released. He agreed and guaranteed to provide whatever amount is needed for a ransom. He also gave me letters for Captain Sylvester in Albany and the authorities in Canada. He told me the colony did not have any money, that it went to pay for the war." Several men grumbled at this for our county rate taxes had gone up four times in the last year to help pay for the cost of the war. He did give me a letter of credit to use in Canada and said the governor up there should help me. I'm off early tomorrow morning."

"You're not going alone," I told him. "Stephen, Ezekiel, and I are going too. We are all ready to go, and were just waiting for you."

"We almost left yesterday," Ezekiel grumbled, "since we were tired of waiting for you."

"We know where they are," Stephen added. "Benoni Stebbins escaped two weeks ago and made it back here the day you left. He said they were about sixty miles north of here, heading northwest. It was all Pocumtucks except for one Narragansett who attacked, only eighteen warriors. The rest were women and children."

"Where is he, now?" Ben asked. "What did he say about all of them?"

"He's in Hadley now." I related what Benoni said about our families and Ben accepted this as good news.

Most everyone drifted away after hearing Ben's report. It was just Ben, Stephen, Ezekiel and myself left in the room.

"We head to Albany first?" I asked.

"Albany? Why do we need to go to Albany?" Ezekiel bellowed. "That will take even more time, time that we don't have!"

Stephen made figures with his toe on the wood floor. He cocked an eye at Ezekiel. "You ever been north the way the Indians went?"

Ezekiel shook his head. "No, I haven't."

"Well, as far as I know, none of us have. We don't know the territory and it would be too risky. It makes more sense to go to Albany, get a guide or two, and push on from there."

"Besides," Ben added, "once you get five days north of here, you are in a place none of us have ever been. It would be too easy to get lost and then how would you feel, having to find our way back here, and then start out for Albany. We could lose two weeks."

Ezekiel sat on a bench against the wall and nodded. "Makes sense."

"Of course it does," Ben replied. "I need to deliver this letter to Captain Salisbury anyway so we have to go by way of Albany."

We looked at one another, acknowledging what we were about to do. We intended to travel for more than a month through forests unknown to any man we knew or ever heard of, with just a guide or two, to find our families and get them back.

"We can meet at my house first thing tomorrow," I told them.

The sun was just cracking the horizon when we set out, the cold promising a hard frost that night, and the air filled with the sweet scent of dying leaves. After talking the first couple of hours about nothing in particular, we fell into a comfortable silence broken when one of us had something he considered important to the group. We arrived in Albany on the 30th and it was then that our troubles began.

Captain Sylvester liked to show his importance as the top military authority for a hundred miles in any direction in the Albany area, mostly by making people wait. That is what he did for us, his aide turning us away after informing the captain of the purpose of our visit. We were told to come back in three days. Ben's visit with him a few weeks before did not go well either.

"He's a little weasel," Ben told us.

"I'll break him in half if he makes us wait anymore," Ezekiel blustered.

"You'll do no such thing," I said. "We need him."

"He didn't even want to talk to us," he replied.

"There's nothing we can do but wait," Stephen said. "Let's go to the tavern."

We walked to the place Ben directed us, De Hems Tavern. It was near the waterfront, a large place with a huge sign of a windmill hanging over the door. It was bright inside, the walls painted with whitewash and yellow paint around the windows and doors, and it was very clean. The floors were swept twice a day and the trenchers and mugs were washed and wiped clean. We got four pallets in a large sleeping room that had 10 pallets lined up along the walls. After getting settled, we went down to the big room and sat by the fire, drinking a mug of rum, which warmed us inside and out and smoked four of the clay pipes lined up on the end of the bar before ordering dinner. It was at that meal that I saw a fork for the first time.

That night I lay there, listening to all the others in the room snoring and mumbling as they slept, and thought of Becky. I was lonelier than I could ever imagine I would be. It was six weeks since they were taken and the hole in my heart was growing larger every day I was apart from them. I hungered for Becky's touch and longed to hold her close, to feel her body pressed against mine, to run my hands through her hair and listen to her sigh with pleasure. I wanted to pick my son up and lift him above me, see him smile and giggle, spin him around, then pull him to me and hold him, his little head against my shoulder, as I looked at Becky, with the love radiating from her. I thought of these things far into the night and finally fell asleep sometime before dawn.

On the third day, we went back to see Salisbury and were put off again. We were told that the captain was busy and would not be available for another three days. We felt time slipping away and decided to secure a guide before attempting to meet with Salisbury again. We made our way to Schenectady at the suggestion of the tavern keeper, where, according to him, there were four men, each of whom was an excellent guide and anyone of them would serve us well. We hired Christian Boeker, a man about my age who lived in the woods north of Albany his whole life. He assured us he had been north past two great lakes several times and could guide us to wherever we needed to go. Satisfied with him, we went back to the tavern. Within an hour of our arrival there, we were summoned to see Captain Salisbury.

He was a haunted little man with a pale face, fine white hair, and long bony fingers. He looked as unmilitary as any man could. He also was upset with us, although we couldn't figure out what we had done to cause him such upset.

"What do you think you are doing?" he asked us without any introduction.

"I have a letter for you from the governor of the Bay Colony," Ben replied, taking the letter out of his pouch.

"Keep your letter," Salisbury said, dismissing it with a wave of his hand. "You are under arrest."

We were stunned by his pronouncement.

"Arrest? What do you mean we're under arrest?" Ezekiel asked. "What did we do?" Salisbury stared at him until Ezekiel looked away.

"You did not meet with me before going out and seeking a guide. Now the talk is all about of this adventure you are about to start on. It will cause me trouble."

I was furious. "How will it cause you trouble? We are trying to save our families' lives."

He ignored me.

"I am the agent for the Massachusetts Bay Colony in the matter of ransoming the recent captives from Hatfield," Ben told him, his voice hard and determined. "I will not allow you to arrest us and further delay our efforts."

"It doesn't matter to me who you are an agent for or what matter you are engaged in. You did not request or receive my permission to proceed."

"Your permission?" Ben asked. "Why do we need your permission?"

"Because I am the military commander and any matters pertaining to military operations require my approval."

"Military operation?" Ezekiel asked, scratching his head and moving closer to Salisbury. "This isn't a military operation.

We are just trying to get our families and neighbors back from the Indians who took them. We are not asking for any of your soldiers to help us. All we want is a guide to get us north."

Salisbury pursed his lips and lifted up on his toes several times, before sitting at his desk.

I looked at the others and saw that they were getting as mad as I was. Here was this little man meddling in our affairs and frustrating us at every turn all because he needed to feel superior.

"Captain," I said, "my wife and two-year-old son were taken and I will get them back if I have to travel to Canada alone. Neither you nor anything you throw in my way will stop me. Do you understand me?"

"You should hold your tongue since it is obvious you don't know who you are dealing with."

"Yeah, well you don't know who you are dealing with, either," Ezekiel growled.

"You will go to New York to plead before Governor Brockholds to see if he will help you, which I doubt."

"Now wait," Ezekiel said loudly, "why do we have to see the governor? If he tells us we can get a guide and move ahead, we've wasted more time that we don't have. We need to get to Canada and soon. There were people taken captive by Pocumtucks and they are in Canada."

"I am not interested," Salisbury replied. "You will begin for New York tomorrow morning under a guard." With that, he dismissed us and left the room. Four guards came into the room, accompanied us back to the tavern, and kept us under guard until the morning.

It was mid-morning Tuesday, December 6, when we began our journey to New York. It took us two days by boat. We were admitted to see Governor Brockholds the morning after we arrived.

The governor was a good man, pleasant to look at with a broad smile on his round face. He understood the urgency of our effort and offered to help in any way he could.

"Salisbury is a difficult man," he said in a thick Dutch accent. "His dignity is ruffled at the slightest hint of what he considers trouble. I will make sure you get back to Albany as soon as you can." He was as good as his word, giving us a letter for Salisbury commanding him to provide any and all assistance to us, and arranging for a boat to take us back up the river.

CHAPTER 18

We got back to Albany on December 10. Salisbury was less than pleased with the support the governor gave us and read the letter quickly before tossing is aside.

"Now," Ben said, "I am the agent for the Massachusetts Bay Colony and we have the permission and support of Governor Brockholds. We will be leaving with our guide the day after tomorrow. We do not need to provide you with any other information or seek your approval for any of this. You will not interfere with us again. Is that understood?" Ben reached over, took the letter off the desk and we left the room.

Boeker, our guide, was ready before dawn on the 11th. The cold wind was coming at us from the north, swirling the dead leaves on the ground as we set out. We went through open fields and sparse forests. It felt good to be finally on our way. During the next three days, we skirted small lakes and swamps, went through spruce forest, and climbed a lot of hills. On the fourth day, we made our way down a long sloping hill until we came to a beautiful lake. The water was so clear, I could see the bottom. The wind chopped the surface into little waves. The bright blue sky reflected in the water made it look even bluer than it really was.

Boeker announced that night that he would be leaving us to go back to Albany but he secured the services of a Mohawk guide who would take us on from the lake. This Mohawk appeared from behind a small rise as if waiting for Boeker to mention him. The Indian bedded down on the other side of the fire from us. At first light, Boeker took his leave of us. The Indian began walking north along the lakeshore, and stopped after an hour.

He peeled a large piece of bark off a birch tree and, with a piece of charcoal, drew a map of what looked like two lakes. Since he didn't speak any English, he used what sign he could to make us understand that the two lakes were connected and each very long.

He then took us further up the shore where there were two canoes, both good size with two paddles in each one. Pointing up the lake, he gestured toward the canoe, making paddling motions. We examined each and put our things in them since his intent was that we travel by water. After a couple of attempts, we came to understand that it would take three days to paddle each lake. I questioned him on why there were only four paddles since he was guiding us to Canada. He shrugged but pointed to a large piece of ash wood that was being shaped into a paddle. We assumed he would finish that quickly and we would be off.

After a few minutes discussion among the four of us, we turned to ask a question and found he was gone. We were alone in a wilderness, a poor bark map as our only direction to Canada. Not having any choice, we got into the canoes and began paddling.

The wind picked up out of the northeast and the white caps grew larger. We stuck to shore and once we got into a rhythm, began making some speed. For half the day, we stroked the paddles, slicing the turbulent water. When mid-afternoon came, things changed. The wind began to howl and blew us against the shore. It became harder and harder to keep the canoes pointing straight ahead. After making little headway, we decided to camp for the night. Our lean-to, four large moose hides stitched together with deerskin laces, went up quickly and Ezekiel had a fire burning in no time. We ate sitting under the lean-to, the canoes overturned in front of us to block as much of the wind as possible. By the time the fire began to burn down, we were ready to sleep. Wrapping ourselves in our oversized double heavy woolen blankets sewn into a moose hide, we passed a fitful night, the sound of the wind keeping us from sleeping well.

The next day wasn't any better. The wind continued and a light rain began to fall within a few miles of us starting out. The rain grew heavy and within a short time, we were all wet to the skin and cold, getting colder by the minute. Since we were making little headway, we pulled in to shore and found a large stand of pine trees, their thick sweeping branches almost touching the ground. We sat in front of a fire, drying ourselves as best we could. When the rain and wind let up, we pushed on, stroking hard and fast, striving to make up for lost time. Our efforts were rewarded by reaching a large flat point of land sticking out into the lake. Hemlocks stood at the back of the point, giving us another dry area to set up for the night.

At the end of the fourth day it seemed like we were no closer to Canada then we were when we started out.

"I don't think this lake will ever end," Ezekiel commented as we were eating.

"Of course it ends," Ben replied, "it's just a big lake that's all."

"I hope it's not much bigger because my arms are starting to ache."

"All of us feel the same," I said, rubbing my left shoulder to reduce some of the ache.

"I wonder how big the next lake is," Stephen said. "It could be longer than this one." He shifted so he was closer to the fire as the cold was setting in good. It had gotten much colder in the last hour or two and would get even colder as the night went on. "Well, we'll see tomorrow."

We grunted in agreement and Ezekiel built up the fire before we lay down to sleep. The warmth, what little there was, came into the lean-to to keep us from shivering too badly.

That was the night the dreams began. They were always the same three dreams and left me with a feeling of dread. Becky and Sam were in two of the dreams but I could only see them in one. I knew they were in the second dream but were off to the side somewhere, out of sight, yet I could feel their presence.

I was a young boy eating dinner with my parents after fishing that day with my father. It was a happy moment from my childhood. Mr. Pynchon came into the house and announced that Becky was no longer there, that she left. All of this left me confused for I knew I was dreaming and it made no sense. I didn't meet Mr. Pynchon until after my parents died and Becky didn't become my wife for more than 10 years after that.

The next dream fluttered out of the first, slowly, like watching a butterfly. Becky and Sam were waiting for me up a dirt path. They both smiled and waved, glad to see me. I smiled, happy at being with them again. I kept walking but never seemed to get any closer to them. They didn't move, but I was still the same distance away. I began to run, slowly at first, then faster and faster but couldn't get close to them. They faded into the background as a beast roared to life from the woods on the left side of the road, a loud beast that got closer to me. I could feel it near me, the stench of death, and a deep, wet, throaty rumble when it breathed.

Next thing I knew, Ezekiel was shaking me. "Jack! Jack! Wake up! You were dreaming."

I sat up and looked around in the darkness. All three of them were watching me.

"Sorry," I said, "just a bad dream."

Stephen and Ben lay down again but Ezekiel sat watching me. "You all right?" he asked.

"Yes, I'm all right. Becky and Sam were in danger and I couldn't get to them, couldn't help them."

"Don't worry," he said, "we'll find them. Now get some sleep and if you're going to dream, do it quietly. If I don't sleep well, I get in a bad mood." With that, he lay down with a thump and was snoring within a minute.

I sat there with my blankets wrapped around me, thinking about the dreams but was too tired to give it much thought, so I slept until first light.

The snow began soon after we left camp and came down faster as the day wore on. We couldn't see far and paddled right next to the shore. Late in the afternoon, as the snow began falling heavily and the wind starting to blow hard from the northeast, we came to where the lake narrowed into a stream and after paddling for a few more miles, a large falls. As we got out of the canoes, Ezekiel was about to put the sack containing most of our food on the shore when he fell into the water and the sack tumbled over the falls. He scrambled to get it and when he came out of the stream, he and the sack were soaking wet. It was turning into a blizzard and we needed to find a place to stop, so we carried the canoes up a hill to a stand of pine trees. We put up the lean-to facing away from the wind, cut dozens of pine boughs to cover the lean-to, gathered as much firewood as we could, and got a big fire going to warm Ezekiel and dry his clothes. We were all hungry before we landed and now that our food was gone, we were starved.

"I'm going to look for something," I told them, picking up my gun. I reloaded it to make sure the powder was dry. "There has to be an animal bedded down here somewhere. Wouldn't a nice piece of deer meat taste good?" I asked.

Ezekiel looked up at me, his face full of sorrow. "I can't believe I ruined our food. I'm sorry and as soon as I dry out, I'll go find some animals out there. There has to be something we can eat out here."

"Why don't you try to catch some fish? There's two dozen feet of fine braided leather in my pack," I told him.

Ben and Stephen nodded at the idea.

"I have a few pins you can bend and use as hooks," Stephen offered.

Ben was mad at Ezekiel for being careless and offered no comment. He sat there scowling, throwing an angry look Ezekiel's way. I could tell that if he started to say something he would yell and it would only cause hurt feelings with Ezekiel.

"I'll be back," I said as I headed into the blinding snowstorm. I hadn't gone more than a hundred yards when a small deer popped out from under a hemlock tree and stood there. I brought my gun up and shot but missed. I watched the deer run into the woods. As I looked where it went, I saw a shape on the other side of the stand of hemlocks. Leaving the deer, I went over and found a deserted wigwam, dry and tight with a small ring of stones for a fire. Sleeping platforms were against the frame all the way around and three leather bags hung from the one of the poles used as part of the frame. I opened them and found two dozen hard biscuits, a full bottle of what smelled like brandy, and a couple pounds of Indian meal. When I got back to the lean-to, Ezekiel had five nice fat fish flopping on the ground as I approached.

"I found a wigwam!"

Ben could barely hear me over the wind. "What?" he yelled.

"I found an abandoned wigwam. Come on! It's dry and tight. Take down the lean-to. Bring the wood."

In a few minutes, we had everything packed up and were on the way to the wigwam.

"Jack," Ezekiel said, a smile breaking out on his face, "you're a savior."

"I don't know about that but let's get set up in here."

We made three trips to get all the wood, Ben got a nice fire going, Stephen got our blankets on the sleeping platforms, and Ezekiel made a few more trips to get wood. Soon we were warm and dry. We had a nice feast of fish and biscuits.

"Good thing you found this," Ben said, "or we would have frozen tonight." He lifted the piece of bark that served as a door and looked out. “This is turning into a real blizzard. We could be here a few days.”

“Another delay,” Stephen said. “What’s next? At this rate, it will be April before we see our families again.”

None of us said anything but sat staring into the fire watching the flames dance over the pieces of wood.

A different dream came to me that night. I was in a place I knew, although I could not identify it but it felt familiar. I tried to get somewhere but I couldn’t because something was always got in the way. I started out and then had to bring in hay. I would start out again and find myself mending a fence or working in the barn or something that kept me from where I had to be. This continued until I became fearful that I would never get to wherever it was I had to be. I woke up, even though it was cold in the wigwam, the fire having died down, drenched in sweat. I realized that these dreams were about my trying to get Becky and Sam back. I fell back and spent most of the night staring at the roof of the wigwam.

The next morning there was almost two feet of snow on the ground. The blizzard raged on, the snow coming down sideways, the wind howling against the wigwam. We kept our fire small so we did not use too much wood, not knowing how long we would be there. We spent the time sleeping, talking, cleaning our equipment, and staring at the roof. By the afternoon, we were bored. From the look of it, we were going to be there for another day, possibly more. Ezekiel took some of the meal, mixed it with snow in a small, dirty little pot he found under a pile of leaves in the corner, and made a tasteless but warm mush. The cornmeal was almost gone by the end of the third day. We cut back to one meal a day but with the four of us, it did not take long to eat the remaining biscuits.

At the end of the day, the wind died down but the snow kept on, drifting down softly. The snow was three feet deep and getting deeper, now up a third of the side of the wigwam. Lucky for us it was a soft, fluffy snow, so the weight was not great. That night the wind picked up again after the snow stopped. The wind blew the snow into drifts as tall as a man is in some places while in others the ground was swept bare. The sky cleared overnight, the temperature dropping to a bitter cold, so cold we could feel it slipping into the wigwam through little gaps in the bark. The next morning was filled with sunshine and blue sky. The light was so brilliant reflecting off the snow that it blinded me. Looking around, we saw that the canoes were completely covered, as was most everything. Ice formed on the lake and we knew that taking a bark canoe through ice that could slash the side like a knife was a fool's way to travel.

As we gathered outside, glad to be out of the confines of the wigwam, we considered our situation.

"Going by canoe isn't possible, " Ben said shaking his head. "Fastest way to travel too."

"Maybe we should stay here another couple of days to see if the ice melts a bit," Ezekiel suggested. "Walking through this," he said filling his big hands full of snow, "is going to be difficult. Might seem easy because it doesn't weigh much but you go through this for ten miles and you'll know it."

"We don't have many choices," I reminded them. "Either take the canoes or walk. Since the lake is ice, we walk."

"Nothing else we can do," Stephen said.

"Let's try walking on the lake. It's flat and may be easier than plodding through this snow."

"We have to find something to eat," Ezekiel said. "I'm starving."

Ben cocked an eye at him. "We had food but it all got wet when you dumped it in the stream, remember?"

Ezekiel scowled but did not reply, just swept the snow with his foot.

"We've had enough delays. Let's get our stuff and get going," I said, feeling like one more obstacle had been placed in our path. At times, it felt as if we would never reach Canada, as if the world was conspiring against us.

"We need to make snow rackets like the Indians use," Ben said.

"That could take another day or more," Stephen pointed out. "Besides we don't have any leather for the webbing."

At this point, another day won't make any difference," I said. "Besides, it would be much easier traveling with them than without them." We spent the next day fashioning snow rackets of spruce and hickory. They were clumsy lopsided things but prevented us from sinking through the snow.

We made poor time no matter how we traveled. Going was slow because wading through the drifts was like walking in sand, lifting your legs high, pushing through the drifts with your body. The glare off the snow became a problem as our eyes hurt and we were each having trouble seeing. By dusk, we traveled only a few miles. We were tired, cold, and hungry. Without a word, Ezekiel set off to find something to eat. A short while later, we heard a gunshot and when he made it back, there were three fat raccoons in his massive hand.

"Found them in a stump. Never knew what hit them," he said, rubbing his hands together in both happiness at having something to eat and to keep them warm.

Soon after clearing an area for the lean-to, we had a small fire going, ate one of the raccoons, and saved the other two. The frigid cold bit into us that night, so cold we couldn't sleep. A while after dark, we heard wolves howling as they moved through the area behind us, up a long hill. We reloaded our guns to make sure the powder was dry and kept them by our sides.

I knew Ezekiel dozed during the night because I heard him snoring. When he got up, there were icicles hanging from his beard. I started to laugh, a slightly deranged sound, jagged on the nerves until I felt them on my face too.

We cooked both raccoons and ate one for breakfast, keeping the other for the night's meal. We trudged on that day through the wind that sliced into you and the cold that froze you to your core. I started to lose the feeling in my fingers around mid-day. Ben was having the same problem. For an hour, we rested, made a large fire, and warmed ourselves as best we could.

Ezekiel sat thoughtful, staring into the flames.

"You men are lucky," he said.

We all looked up in surprise.

"How are we lucky?" Ben asked. "Wrestling with Satan as we are is lucky?"

"No. Because you have families, and had mothers and fathers and sisters and brothers."

Ben tilted his head to one side and gave me a questioning look. They did not know Ezekiel's story.

Ezekiel didn't look up from the flames. "I never had a mother."

"Everyone has a mother," Ben said.

"Yeah, but I never knew mine. She abandoned me after my father left … just disappeared one day. I barely remember her. I was ordered by the magistrates to live with another family, but I only stayed with them a few months when they realized the five pounds a year they were getting for me wouldn't cover how much food I ate. Not only was the food they were getting for me not contributing to their own sustenance, but I was eating some of their food. I went from home to home, never staying in one place very long. When I was taken in by the old woman, she treated me indifferently, never giving much compassion. It was a place to eat and sleep. I went to school for a bit. I enjoyed that, learning to read and write, being with other children, though I was larger than two of them put together." He wrapped his blanket around himself tightly and stared into the flames. "You're lucky, that's all."

Even though the lake was flat, breaking through snowdrifts as high as your waist takes a lot of work and makes you sweat, another problem we had. It was worse in the afternoon because we were dead tired and sweaty. The moisture dried quickly in the dry air but some of it froze onto our skin before it did, leaving small frozen patches that we rubbed so the skin would warm.

We found the ice buried under the snow had melted so our steps were falling into ice water. After a few hours, our heavy moccasins, and feet, were soaked through. We decided that we would get off the lake and travel over land.

We ran out of food the next day. There were no signs of any animals, not even a bird flew overhead. It was utterly quiet; the only sound was the wind moving through the pines trees. We went on all day, stopping twice to rest. We were hungry, but knew we would get something to eat at some point. We didn't know when, but we had hope. It was more important to us to continue moving north, toward our families.

Ben attributed our starvation as God's judgment against us.

"Why would God be against us? Are we not going on a mission to save our families and neighbors from the heathens? Why would he be against us?" Stephen asked.

Ezekiel gave a loud sigh. "To what else would you ascribe our troubles if not to God's judgment? How about plain bad luck?"

Ben didn't respond. He just kept walking ahead.

At the end of the second day without food, we were near exhaustion. Our clothes were becoming ragged, our hair and beards were tangled messes, there were dark hollows under our eyes, and our features were gaunt. All each of us could think of was food. We talked about food, the best things we ever ate, and our favorite foods.

"One of my favorites is raisin pie. Another is fish chowder or maybe fish balls cooked in fat," I told them, my mouth watering.

"A good piece of venison roasted over a small fire," Stephen said, a far off look in his eyes.

"My mother's corn and pumpkin bread," Ben said with a sigh. "She was one of the best cooks I knew."

"What about bread?" Ezekiel asked. "I love any type of bread, though my favorite is apple nut bread. The old woman who raised me made it. She didn't treat me well, but she did make good bread."

"How long were you with her?" Stephen asked, struggling through a mound of snow.

"Four years."

Water was the one thing we had plenty of whether from the snow or the frozen lake. We ate snow at first until we realized how cold it made us feel. After that, we began melting it over a small fire, filling our little cooking pot to the brim. Doing this twice a day helped us feel full even if we were not.

We were lucky that Ezekiel was strong enough and big enough to carry much of our load. He put the lean-to and the cast iron cooking pot on top of his blankets. Ben, Stephen, and I carried only our blankets, guns, powder, and ball. Ezekiel never complained about hefting the load all day long, not giving it up even when we told him we wanted to take some of it. He would not hear of it.

The weather turned warmer, causing the snow to begin melting, and that made traveling even more difficult. We knew that going over the lake would be even worse than it was before. Slogging through heavy, wet snow was more exhausting than making our way through the dry powder. Our pace slowed considerably to the point where we were making only a few miles a day. Food was still scarce. Ben shot a crow and an owl the day before. We made a weak soup out of the tiny bit of meat and bones. It didn't give us much nourishment since birds bones are hollow and contain no marrow. We needed meat with fat in it but it didn't look like we would get any soon.

I knew we were in trouble when Stephen collapsed late in the afternoon. He was last in line and talking to Ezekiel when he went quiet. We thought he just finished speaking until Ben looked around and saw Stephen lying face down in the snow. We rushed back to him, pulling him up and sitting him against a tree. The most difficult part was that we had no food to give him.

"I'll be all right," he said weakly, "just a little tired, that's all."

"You're not tired," Ezekiel bellowed, "You need something to eat. If I hadn't lost the food bag we'd be fine."

"No, we wouldn't," Ben cut in. "There wasn't much left anyway and it wouldn't have lasted more than a few days. We'd be in the same spot we are now."

Ezekiel looked out at the frozen lake. "Well, I don't know about that," he said, kicking snow with his foot.

"Well I do," Ben shot back. "I know that we would be in the same situation even if you had kept all the food. It was a bad idea for us to put it all together. We should have split it up."

"But we didn't and there is nothing we can do about it now," I said. "We need to find something to eat."

"You think I don't know that?" Ben said sharply.

Tempers were beginning to fray. The hardship was taking its toll on all of us. I was surprised it hadn't happened before then. Of the four of us, Ben was the best woodsman and scout. It was a natural ability he had, something he was born with. For him to be discouraged was a deep concern to me.

"Tomorrow Ben and I will go out hunting," I said. "Ezekiel, you will stay with Stephen."

"But, I should be the one to –"

"No," I said. "You are not the one to make up for losing the food. It doesn't help with you worrying over it like a dog does a bone. Ben is right. We'll get something tomorrow … maybe a couple of rabbits. Now, let's get settled for the night."

There was a large stand of white pine trees a couple hundred yards behind us. The ground there was covered with pine needles. I floundered back, pulled handfuls of needles off the branches, and put them in my pack. I never tried it, but I remembered my uncle Josiah talking about pine needle tea. I figured we had nothing left to lose. When I was about halfway back, it occurred to me in my muddled state that we should have camped under the pine trees since it was mostly dry and the ground was soft. I was going to tell the others about it but by the time I got to the where we camped, it was out of my mind completely. I couldn't even remember what I just did for a few minutes until I looked in my pack and saw the needles. I threw them into the melting water.

"What did you do?" Ezekiel asked in a tired voice.

"Pine needle tea," was all I could say.

Stephen and Ben just grunted.

When the water turned brown, I scooped as many needles out as I could with my hand. We took our leather cups and drank some. It had a pleasant taste that made us feel better. Ben and I went back to get more needles.

"How long do you think we can go on like this?" he asked.

"I don't know … maybe another few days. I'm worried about Stephen. He is failing fast."

"If we get any food, we should give him more than we take, he needs it more than we do."

When we had full packs, we headed back. Stephen was asleep next to the fire while Ezekiel sat with his back to a tree on the side of the lean-to. Even putting up the lean-to every afternoon was a struggle.

That night and every night after, we prayed to God to help us. Ben suggested it, saying that he was thinking of it a good part of the day. Surprisingly, Ezekiel agreed to the idea.

"I've never been a praying man or much of a religious one, but we need more help than we got and it's right that we ask for God's help."

We sat by the fire, heads bowed, as Ben began the prayer.

"Almighty God, King of all kings, and Governor of all things, Whose power no creature is able to resist, save and deliver us, we humbly beseech Thee, from the hands of our enemies; abate their pride, allay their malice, and confound their devices; that we, being armed with Thy defense, may be preserved evermore from all perils, to glorify Thee, Who art the only Giver of all victory. Ours is a just and righteous cause, to right a wrong done to us by a godless people who kill and destroy. Grant us Your help, see us through these hardships that are in our way, give us strength to carry on and bring us safely to our families and friends. We ask this through the merits of Thy Son, Jesus Christ our Lord. Amen."

It was just after sunrise that Ben and I headed out to hunt. We went up a hill to a flat area overlooking the lake. We walked for an hour without seeing so much as an animal track. There was nothing.

"I've never seen anything like this before," Ben said. "Where did all the animals go? I mean, they have to eat, too. I don't understand."

"Neither do I. I'm ready to eat one of the leather bags."

"It may come to that," he said with a rueful smile.

"Let's hope not."

We headed back after a while with nothing to show for our efforts.

"There is nothing around here," Ben said. "We'll move on tomorrow and hope we find something."

"There are no berries, no roots to eat, no animals, nothing," Ezekiel said with a look of worry crossing his face.

"This is what the Indians called the starving time," I said, instantly regretting it.

The three of them looked at me.

"We can't have that much further to go," I said, trying to recover from my blunder.

After going a couple of miles the next morning, we came to a great mass of grapevine that still had handfuls of dried, frozen grapes. We each got a handful. They were cold and but we didn't care.

I remembered my Indian friend William's mother Kanti talking about using the inner bark of trees like slippery elm to make coarse flour. It sounded like something we should try but we were so lethargic, we never did. The Indians also tapped the maple and sweet birch trees but not until the end of February or early March. I decided to try it and at the next maple tree we came to, I slashed the bark and saw a little sap flow out, but not enough to fill even a thimble. It was too cold for it to run.

The weather warmed to the point where I took off my coat and stuffed it into my pack. The others did the same. The problem we faced the next day was that overnight it got very cold and froze the melting snow to ice. Walking through it was like walking through glass, the little sharp edges of ice cutting into our heavy moose hide moccasins, the fur on the inside and the skin side out. They were tough but no match for the constant slashing of hardened ice. Slowly, they began to deteriorate. Our feet were constantly cold and each night, when we were done walking for the day, were numb. It was not a good sign and we all knew it.

After we decided on a spot to stop for the night, I spotted two squirrels in an oak tree. I motioned to Ben who shot one while I shot the other one.

Ezekiel and Stephen were glad to see the squirrels I held high as we made camp. Within a few minutes, Stephen had the animals gutted and cleaned while Ezekiel built up the fire. We roasted them and made a weak soup with the bones. While it was not much, it was the best thing we tasted in what seemed like a long time. Two squirrels are barely enough for a good meal for one man let alone four hungry men. It satisfied us but only for a few hours. I found that after a couple of days without food, I stopped feeling hungry.

It was early afternoon the next day when I smelled smoke.

"Do you smell that?" I asked

"Smell what?" Ben said.

"Smoke. It's coming from that direction," I said, pointing to the northeast.

The four of us stood there sniffing away, ready to drop from lack of food and exhaustion, but smiling because we knew that where there was fire, there was food.

"Let's go!" Ezekiel hollered, floundering ahead of the rest of us.

What we found was the small hamlet of Chamble, a poor village of ten smelly huts and ragged but happy people. Their houses were small with steep roofs.

The French inhabitants were very pleasant and helpful, feeding us what they could which was not much but better than anything we had eaten in more than two weeks, although it felt like a year. The most wonderful smell came from the houses, one that seemed to hang over the hamlet. It was a strong smell of onions boiling. I wasn't far wrong because they made a thick stew of potatoes, onions, garlic, herbs, and salmon. Though the villagers didn't have much for themselves, they shared with us what they did and were happy to do so.

We stayed four days, regaining our strength before pushing on to find our families. The villagers told us the Indians and captives came through over a month ago and were now at Sorel, a five-day walk.

Ezekiel was rude and uncouth and seldom a symbol of the polite side of society. I was a bit uneasy about him as he talked much of the way about how he doubted he would like the French because of his belief in their dirty, smelly ways. Whatever he was, he was my friend.

My concern grew when, on our third day in the village, we couldn't find him. Since there were so few houses, unless he wandered off, he had to be in one of them. A few minutes after I began to search, I heard him bellowing a song from the last house on the path north. As I got closer, I heard other voices singing.

I opened the door and made my way into a small hallway and then a warm, candlelit kitchen. Four people were sitting on the floor; Ezekiel, one of the villagers, a man of about forty years of age with a brown and wrinkled face and a long queue down his back. Across from him was his wife, a small woman, her hair wrapped around the top of her head with a long, colored cloth to hold it in place. A young boy of seven or eight was seated on Ezekiel's lap. The three French were all smoking short clay pipes, the smoke filling the air.

Ezekiel took a swig out of a bottle before he saw me. “Jack! Come join us … it’s a wonderful brandy. He says he made it himself.” He nodded at the man across from him.

“Where have you been?” I asked.

“Where have I been? Why, I’ve been right here visiting with my new friends,” he said, waving his arms and spilling some of the brandy on his shirt. “They’re good people once you get over the way their food smells. Horrible stuff, full of bitter roots and garlic.”

“You didn’t think it was horrible last night when you ate three bowls of it,” I said.

“I was hungry and there was nothing else to eat. What did you expect me to do? I didn’t want to appear ungrateful.”

He put his hand on the Frenchman’s head and used it to push himself up. He raised the bottle in salute to his new friends, took a big swig, and followed me into the cold.

Ezekiel said goodbye by hollering at them, believing that the louder he talked the easier it would be for someone who spoke a different language to understand him.

We started out on Tuesday, January 8, a cloudy, cold day with scattered snow showers. Luckily for us, it wasn’t windy so we made good time. A local man, Armand Pechin, acted as our guide. He was a short, stocky man with a pipe clenched in his mouth all the time except when he slept. He chatted in his language during our push to Sorel, calling it a "periple" which meant a voyage as best as we could understand. We trudged through the snow on the snowshoes the villagers gave us, it being only a few inches in one spot to a drift of three or four feet in another. Pechin grinned through it all, never slowing his pace, encouraging us to keep up with him.

We made our way along a wide river with tumbling rapids, the water boiling over rocks as big as a house. In other sections it was frozen solid and was tempting to walk on to make better time, to get to our families faster, but Pechin warned us against it. He threw a rock onto a large section where the ice looked thick. The rock hit with a smash, making a hole two feet wide and dropped into the river, water quickly bubbling up from the hole. It was clear that the unseen rapids would not support our weight for even a minute and would lead to disaster, so we kept on the snow-covered path.

CHAPTER 19

We went on to Sorel. Soon after we arrived, one of the inhabitants said there were captives and went to get them. After a few minutes of waiting, we heard a woman's voice, one that was familiar. Stephen stopped talking and listened at the sound. He rushed out of the hut followed by the three of us. As we came around the corner of the hut, his wife Hannah came down the path, and without saying a word, rushed to him. He hugged her and kissed her, she cried and he was smiling.

As I watched them, I heard a voice, almost a whisper. "Jack … Jack, oh Jack." I could not believe my eyes when I saw Becky come out of the hut at the far end of the path, walking slowly toward me as if in a dream. She had lost weight and looked haggard and gaunt. She wore the same dress she had on the day she was captured and it was now torn and ragged, but she was never more beautiful to me. I ran and caught her in my arms. We almost fell down, both of us weak, but were held upright by a thickset woman villager who flashed a toothless smile. I held Becky for what seemed like only a minute but was probably much longer.

"Sam?" I asked a great fear shooting through me at the thought something could have happened to my little boy.

"He's asleep, on the floor of that hut," she said pointing to the one she came from.

"The baby?" I asked, putting my hand on her belly.

"Kicked a lot this morning," she said, beginning to cry. I felt like crying too but the tears would not come. I just stood there holding my wife, cradling her in my arms.

There are times in your life when your heart aches from both joy and sadness. Mine ached that afternoon when I went into the hut where my son was sleeping, curled up on a bearskin with a rough wool blanket over him. He looked smaller than I remembered, and needed more food than he got. As he lay there, his hand curled up under his chin, I saw the soft rise and fall of his breathing. The world ceased to exist for me at that moment. He was so peaceful. I found myself fighting back tears. As I watched, his eyes opened slowly and he looked at me. He stood and put his arms out for me to pick him up. I knelt and picked him up into my arms, and pulled him close to me, Becky's hand on my shoulder. I held him, never wanting to let him go. I pulled Becky to me and slid my arm around her waist. Having my wife and son in my arms made the entire ordeal worthwhile. The hunger and pain, the waiting and haunted dreams all faded to insignificance.

"Where is everyone else?" I asked. "Was it the Nipmuck or Pocumtuck?"

"Both," she said. "I recognized two of them from Brookfield. They were with the ones that tried to burn down the tavern. They were two of the three that were with Matchitehew and his brother.

"They took everyone else to another village a few miles from here."

"Why are you and the others here?"

"They traded us for two kegs of liquor. We work for these people doing simple chores. I think they took pity on us. They treat us well enough but…" She began to cry. I gave Sam another hug and put him back on the bearskin.

"Oh, it was horrible," she said. "They fed us a little bit once a day and expected us to keep up with their pace. They killed Samuel Russell and Mary Foote because they got sick. They were only little children. They killed them and dumped them over a cliff." She began to sob at the thought of such cruelty. After a minute, she sniffled and wiped her nose with her sleeve. "That was only part of it," she continued after taking a deep breath. "They burned Sergeant Plympton at the stake. They made Obadiah Dickinson tie him to the stake and set him on fire." A shudder went through her entire body and she pressed close to me, shaking at the memory. "It was the most horrible thing I ever saw. I can't stop thinking about it. They made everyone watch, including the children." I held her in my arms for what seemed like hours. "He screamed for a long time and they laughed and cheered."

I thought of John Stuart at the Mohawk until Sam began pulling on my breeches. "I want to go home," he said, staring up at me.

I knelt on the floor next to him and let out a loud laugh, the first I had in months. "I know you do, we all do, but it will take some time. Some of us have to go meet with the Indians to see how to get you home. Don't you worry," I said kissing him on the forehead. "I'll get you home soon. I promise. I need to find Stephen, Ben, and Ezekiel. We need to find the Indians and tell them about the ransom."

"Ransom?" Becky asked. "They demanded a ransom?"

"No, they didn't. Ben met with Governor Leverett and got a letter to the French governor promising to pay 200 pounds for your release. We have to go to Quebec to meet with him after we talk to the Indians. You stay here. It's the safest place for you."

"I want to go with you."

"No, it will be too difficult. Stay here where you and Sam are safe."

Ben, Stephen, Ezekiel, and I started out the next morning. The villagers told us that the Indian village was two days north toward the great river. We did not know what river they were talking about, but we headed north and about twenty-five miles further on, we found the rest of the captives.

They were in the same condition as Becky, Sam and the Jennings family, ragged, gaunt, and underfed. The Indians were surprised when we walked into their village. When our neighbors saw us, they yelled in joy and came running to us.

A dozen of the Indian men rushed toward us, war clubs out, ready to pounce. Ezekiel was seething mad, ready to take on all twelve of them.

"Come on you heathen bastards," he growled. He stood to his full height, spread his arms and yelled, "Any one of you who attacks us will get his head crushed by me, between my hands!"

The fact that he was almost a foot taller than any one of them caused them to stop their advance.

"You cowardly abukcheech," he said, using their term for mice. The only thing that is a worse insult to an Indian man is to call him a woman. They began advancing despite his threat. A man I took to be a sachem emerged from one of the wigwams, telling his men not to fight as he came toward us.

"I am Ashpelon," he said, his English as good or better than many of the people back in the Bay Colony. It is interesting how quickly and well they learned our language.

"I am Ben Wait. This is Stephen Jennings, Jack Parker, and Ezekiel Huff. We come from Hatfield to ransom those you captured."

Ashpelon stood looking at us for a moment before he responded.

"What if we do not want to ransom them? What then?"

"We'll take them back with us!" Ezekiel yelled.

"Shut up!" I told him. "Stay out of this. Let Ben do the talking."

Ben shot a hard look at Ezekiel.

"I am the agent of the governor of the Massachusetts Bay Colony and come with a letter authorizing a 200 pound ransom.

We will go to Quebec to meet with the governor. He will pay you."

Ashpelon considered this for a moment then pointed toward a longhouse. "We should talk."

As we began walking towards the longhouse, Ben grabbed Ezekiel by the arm.

"You stay out here and keep your mouth closed. Don't fight with any of them either. Understand me?"

Ezekiel said nothing.

After getting settled, Ashpelon began to tell what happened.

"I was not in favor of attacking your village but I could not stop my men. They were determined to attack. I did not want to come here but knew that I must or they would harm your families."

"So you went along so they wouldn't harm them?" I asked.

"Yes."

"But that is not what happened to Mary Foote, Sam Russell, or Plympton. You killed two children and you burned Plympton at the stake."

Ben and Stephen bristled at the mention of this atrocity. Ben sat clenching his hands into fists, his anger growing.

"I tried to stop it but could not. There are certain of my men that are strong-minded and will not listen to reason, no matter how strong the argument. They persuaded several of the others to go along. It became a heated argument amongst us but there was no chance of changing their mind."

We weren't sure he was telling the truth, although I couldn't figure out what he would gain by lying to us.

"While it was an incident that should have been prevented, I was able to save the rest of your families and neighbors from any further harm. Torturing that one man seemed to satisfy their need for vengeance."

We didn't know what to say. In my mind's eye, I could see Plympton working the fields and raising a mug of rum with the rest of us.

"You must keep your people and our families and friends here while we go meet with the governor," Ben said.

Ashpelon did not respond for a while. He sat looking at the dirt floor. "I cannot make a promise for the others. I will try. Let me bring one of them in so you may speak with him." He went out and called to someone. By the time he sat down again, another Indian entered. He was tall and lean with an inscrutable face.

"This is Nootau," Ashpelon said.

Nootau stood looking down at us, glancing from one of us to the other.

"These men are here to ransom the captives," Ashpelon told him. "They will meet with the French governor soon. They ask that we keep the captives here until they return."

Nootau considered this for a moment. "We will, if there is enough food for us. We cannot provide for them unless we provide for ourselves first." He turned and left.

"If there isn't enough food, what will he do, let the captives starve? Go to Quebec?" Ben asked.

"They will not starve," Ashpelon assured us.

I felt anything but assured.

"How far is Quebec?" Stephen asked.

"If you go now while there is so much snow, it will be at least seven days travel. If you wait until much of the snow is gone, it will be an easy, three-day trip by canoe."

"We can't wait that long," I said. "We want to get home as soon as we can."

"We need a guide," Ben said. "Who here can take us?"

"One of my men or one of the villagers," Ashpelon replied.

"I wouldn't trust any one of your men as far as I could throw them," Ben declared. Ashpelon nodded in understanding.

“Let us see our people,” I said.

Ashpelon rose and escorted us to a large longhouse. As we entered, we saw it was crammed with over fifty people. Ours were at one end, crowded together, dirty, smelly, underfed, and ragged, and two Indian families were at the other end, clean, well-fed, and comfortable. Some sat huddled together in the corners while several stood staring at us, not recognizing us because of our slovenly appearance. Little Abigail Bartholomew, who was only eight years old, came slowly towards us, giving us a wondering look. Most of the others watched her, staring back and forth between her and us. When she was a few feet away, I saw the recognition spark in her eyes.

“Mr. Jennings! Mr. Wait! Mr. Parker! Ezekiel!” she cried. “It is you? It is really you?” She ran to us and threw her arms around Stephen, burying her head in his stomach. “You came for us!” she said in a joyful voice.

The others began moving toward us, Obadiah Dickinson in the lead.

“How did you get here? How did you find us?” he asked, reaching out to touch me as if to make sure we were real. They gathered quietly in a semi-circle in front of us, not sure of what to say. There were dark hollows under everyone’s eyes, their cheekbones prominent on their faces for lack of food. There was even a weakness even in the way they stood.

I looked at them in wonder, amazed that anyone as poorly clothed and fed as they were could make it so far and still be alive. I know how I felt, and I came prepared for a trek, but these people had no idea how far they would be going that beautiful September morning they were captured, a day that seemed so long ago. My heart hurt looking at them.

"It's a long story," Ben said, seeing his pregnant wife Martha for the first time. He walked through the group and swept his wife into his arms. She cried at the sight of him.

"Oh Ben, how I've missed you."

"I missed you too," he replied, touching her face with his fingers as he gazed lovingly at her dirt-streaked face. He caught himself, since he was not given to expressing his feelings in public. His three daughters rushed up to him and grabbed him around his legs.

After we all sat down around the small fire, we told them everything about our journey to find them. Once we finished our tale, they became more animated, asking of home and if any other attacks took place. We then said a prayer of thanksgiving, a prayer to God for seeing us through our difficulties and to our families.

The entire time we were talking with our people all of the Indians at the other end of the longhouse sat silently watching us with no emotion showing on their faces.

Everyone was hungry, so I began asking about food.

"They feed us when they want, which isn't often," Abigail Allis said. "And when they do, it's not much."

"That's right," Obadiah said, "but it is God's will that we suffer."

"Believe what you want, but I doubt it is God's will," Abigail said. "They are a bunch of thieving heathens," she spat, staring at the Indians at the other end of the longhouse. They stared back expressionless. One Indian woman, wearing a full-length deerskin dress and a headband of bright beadwork against her black hair, came down to our end. She stood for a moment looking at us.

"You are hungry?" she asked in broken English.

"Yes, we are," I said.

"I cannot give you much but will get what I can."

She came back a little while later with a medium sized clay pot full of a steaming gruel of Indian meal, bear fat and dried berries. There wasn't enough for all of us to have more than a mouthful, but it was enough. We took sticks and let the children and pregnant women eat first. Ezekiel did not take anything at all and later explained to me that he couldn't eat while everyone else was hungry and that he had enough meat on him to last a while.

We rested for four days, eating what little there was. Ben killed a small bear on the second day, not more than 100 pounds or so, but it was some of the best meat I tasted in a long time. We dried some of it over a small fire to mix with the fat and dried berries. We shared some of it, though not much, with the Indian families in the long house. Three of the men agreed to act as guides to Quebec.

Before we left Sorel, the four of us cleaned up as best we could. One of the villagers lent us a razor, a bit rusted and not the sharpest I ever used but it worked well enough. The Indians are a clean people and never have lice or other bugs on them or in their wigwams. They allowed all of the captives to clean themselves and to stay clean. The clothes they wore were ragged but it was all they had. We promised to see what we could get in Quebec.

Seven days after we left the village, we made it to Quebec. We came out to a great frozen river, wider than any I've ever seen, wider than the Connecticut and Muhhekunnetuk, the Great Mohegan as the Iroquois called it, that flowed by Albany. Ice floes were jammed up everywhere, sticking into the sky like huge frozen fingers pointing towards the heavens.

"There's no other way to get across?" Ezekiel asked.

One of our guides shook his head. He was the only one of the three who understood our language. Like many other Indians, he spoke very well. He told us he could also speak and write French.

"That's what I want to do," Ezekiel said, "I want to learn how to speak French," although he pronounced it Fronsh for some reason no one will ever know. It was just Ezekiel's way.

"Don't start learning until we're across," Ben said while giving Ezekiel an annoyed look. Ben never seemed to accept Ezekiel and his odd ways. Ben was a man not given to sudden outbursts of any type so Ezekiel's bursting forth with any idea or whim that struck him grated on Ben's nerves.

We could hear the constant booming and cracking of the ice. It sounded like large peals of thunder, never stopping, sometimes louder and sometimes softer, but always there. As we stood and looked at it, several large floes toward the middle were moving downstream at a good rate.

"We could get swept down the river," Stephen said. "Not a good way to do things. Is there a better place up or down river?" he asked our guides.

"Up the river," the English speaking guide said as he pointed to the northwest. "Might be better but we won't know until we get there. The problem here is that the river we came up flows into the fleuve Saint-Laurent and pushes the ice downstream."

"How far upstream might we have to go?" I asked.

"It could be a day, maybe two."

At this we all looked at each other. I, for one, had no intention of traveling another day or two to get across then have to travel back that distance before heading off to Quebec.

"I say we cross here," I said. Ben and Stephen eyed the river ice, considering the two options. Ben turned his face toward Stephen and nodded. Stephen considered for another minute then agreed it was best to try to cross from where we were.

"Good, we'll cross here," I told the guide.

"Don't I get a chance to tell you what I think?" Ezekiel boomed, indignant at not being consulted.

"No," Ben said as he moved toward a slope down to the ice.

Ezekiel stood there somewhat dumbfounded, rubbing his face and beard with his great big hands.

By the time we were across, there was no more than an hour of daylight left, although it was hard to call it light since for the last week the daylight seemed a gray fog, never getting any lighter or darker but always the same shade of gray. We made camp and were soon asleep.

Morning came quickly and we were up and moving just as the daylight began. There were a few small patches of blue between the gray clouds, and it promised to be a fine day. My aunt Charity always said that the clouds would give way to sunny skies if the patches of blue were big enough to make a pair of breeches.

All day we trudged through the snow on the rackets, not minding the aches and pains of the constant slogging, lifting your legs up high to step perhaps a foot. By this time, we were not aware of the exertion needed to make this trip. As the light began to fade, we made it close enough to the town to see the great high cliffs fronting the river.

We were tired and hungry, so we stopped at an inn just up from the river. Before we went in, I looked around and saw that most of the buildings were made of stone and the streets were paved with it. At the end of the street, the cliffs rose up 300 feet, commanding over the lower town.

The inn was on the first floor of a three-story stone building. It was snug and warm and smelled of roasting meat. We ate and stayed the night, sleeping on the floor in the downstairs room because all the beds were full. It took a little time to get used to since none of us had slept under a solid wooden roof since leaving Albany almost three months before.

Even though we cleaned as best we could at Sorel, we still smelled and looked ragged. The innkeeper had a pretty girl, who Ezekiel watched constantly, and she put a kettle on the hearth to heat water so she could wash our clothes. Ezekiel noticed that many of the townspeople were dressed in heavy wool clothes with fur hats and jackets. He declined having his clothes washed, leaving in mid-afternoon to look around. I didn't trust him to stay out of trouble because even if he didn't find it, it somehow found him.

He returned a while later with an armful of wool clothes. He had new breeches, jerkins, a type of coat for Ben, Stephen, and me, and a large fur coat and hat for himself.

Ben was suspicious. "Where did you get these?"

"I traded for them," Ezekiel boomed, looking offended. "I didn't steal them if that's what you are asking."

"That is what I am asking," Ben replied. "What did you trade? You had almost nothing when you left here."

"Well, I did have a few things the people here think are valuable. Like a long knife I found."

"Where did you find the knife?" I asked.

"Outside, down the street. It was sticking out of the snow. I didn't want to leave it there so I took it. An old woman had some extra clothes she didn't need so I traded her the knife for them."

My concern was that Ezekiel picked up a few more than things than he said he did and traded the stolen goods for the clothes. Ben called Stephen and me over to the hearth.

"Jack, I know he's a friend of yours, and I think his heart is in the right place, but I won't put up with thieving. It will only get us into trouble and that's the one thing we do not need now."

Stephen nodded in agreement.

"He can't do anything that might jeopardize our chances of getting our families back. We've come too far to have his antics ruin our efforts."

I realized that they were right and that I needed to speak to Ezekiel. I took him to the far end of the main room, across from the fireplace.

"You need to stop it now," I told him.

He opened his mouth to answer but closed it again.

"We need to ransom everyone and your stealing things and possibly upsetting the people here won't help our chances."

"Now Jack— "

"Now nothing. Did you steal these clothes?"

"No, I didn't."

"Did you steal whatever you traded for them?"

He hesitated to answer.

"Never mind," I said. "Just stay out of trouble."

The innkeeper knew a military officer and arranged for us to meet with him the next morning. He told us that Quebec was made up of two towns, the lower and upper villages. The governor's house was in the upper town.

Gaston Hotard was a captain and reported to Governor Frontenac, the military commander for all of Canada. When we explained our situation and the ordeal we had been through, he promised to do all he could to have the governor meet with us as soon as possible and sent word late that afternoon that the governor would meet with us the next morning.

After a good breakfast, the innkeeper was kind enough to take us through the lower town, which was made up of many inns, shops, and warehouses, to a large arched stone gate. He explained in broken English that the upper town was beyond the gate and that the governor's house was at the end of the long street on the right. We made our way, receiving stares from the inhabitants.

The governor's mansion, or chateau as they call it in French, was at the top of the cliff. It was a huge building, three stories high and over 100 feet long. Each floor had sixteen windows on the front side alone. There were well over 100 windows in the building. I counted eight chimneys from where I stood and I was sure there were more to see from the rear. As I looked closer, I could see that it was in need of repair. A small part of the roof looked as if it crumbled, two of the windows on the top floor of the west side were broken, the small porch enclosing the front entryway tilted back against the building, a sure sign that it was poorly built.

A servant admitted us, and Captain Hotard met us in the front room of the mansion. The room was large, twice the size of my home, with golden chandeliers hanging from the ceilings and thick rugs on the brilliantly polished floor. The captain led us to another room, as nice as the first, at the end of a long hallway of wide planked wood polished to the point where it reflected everything above it. The room was a light blue with large windows, each as tall as a man, looking out over the river. The chateau, built on the highest point in the upper town, gave a view of the mountains to the left, the wide frozen river in the front, and on the right, the snow covered land across the river, sweeping back toward Sorel. The view went for fifty miles in every direction.

We walked around the room looking at the brilliant lamps made of glass with gold stems. I definitely felt out of place, never having been in a building so richly appointed. I was afraid to get too close to anything for fear that I would break it. Ezekiel stood in the middle of the room, not seeing a chair large enough to accommodate his frame. Stephen wandered back and forth, looking at the room a few times, examining the small statues and ornaments on the tables scattered around the room. Only Ben seemed unfazed by the splendor. He sat in a chair by the windows, watching us marvel at the luxury and wealth.

After a while the door opened and a tall man with graying hair and beard, dressed in a rich, dark red coat and breeches, and black shoes with gold buckles, walked in accompanied by Captain Hotard.

"May I introduce you to the Count de Frontenac, Governor and Lieutenant General for His Majesty in Canada, Acadia, Newfoundland and other territories of New France. Governor General Frontenac," the captain said, "is the military commander of all New France."

Frontenac smiled at us and nodded, indicating that we should sit.

Ezekiel fumbled around and decided it was better not to accept the invitation to sit than to try to fit himself into a gold and cloth chair he knew he would break.

"I told the governor of your situation and need of assistance," Hatord said, "and before he can offer any help, he must know more of your troubles and has questions for you."

Hatord talked to the governor in French and us in English, going back and forth, as we answered the governor's many questions. After a long while, the governor understood our present dilemma and agreed to arrange for a ransom. Ben presented him with the letter from Governor Leverett promising payment of 200 pounds. Frontenac spoke for a few moments, telling us through Hatord, that he would be happy to arrange a meeting with the local sachems to enlist their help. He ended by telling us he intended to see our families reunited with us and safe from any harm very soon. He asked where we were staying and asked that we remain there until he could make arrangements for the captives to be freed. We thanked him several times before Hatord escorted us out. He said he would contact us within the next day or two with what he knew would be good news.

Two days later, one of the captain's men came to get us, telling us that Hatord wanted to see us right away.

When we got to the governor's mansion, he was waiting for us. "Good news, my friends. The governor has arranged for the release of your families and friends. He made arrangements with the local sachems and your people are waiting for you at

Sorel. Tomorrow, two traders will go with you to bring supplies, food, and clothing to your people. You will have to stay with the townspeople since, as you said, three women are with child and cannot travel far in the snow and cold."

At that, my thoughts turned to Becky. I had been without her for so long, the ache I felt inside made me numb, and it was as if I were in a strange dream, from which I would never wake. I needed to get back to her to see her, touch her, and kiss her. I needed to feel her next to me as I fell asleep and snuggled under my arm when I woke.

Stephen shook me out of my reverie with a slap on the back.

"Did you hear that Jack? They are free but we cannot start for home for another three months. Stuck here for the whole winter. Well, it must be for God's purpose that we will be here."

Ben nodded in agreement.

"The Lord has guided us to this place to redeem our families and neighbors. Through his wisdom and guidance, it was accomplished. Let us say a prayer for their deliverance."

We bowed our heads as Ben opened his little prayer book and began to read.

"Through Your intercession we succeeded in our efforts and we thank You for bringing praise to Your good name. The

Lord declared His salvation, His righteousness has He shown in the fight of the heathen. With His own right hand, and with His holy arm, has He gotten himself the victory. Lord, Thou knowest better than I know myself I am entirely dependent upon Thee for support, counsel, and consolation. Uphold me by Thy free Spirit, and may I not think it enough to be preserved from falling, but may I always go forward, always abounding in the work Thou givest me to do. Strengthen me by Thy Spirit in my inner self for every purpose of my Christian life. God be merciful unto us and bless us, and show us the light of Your countenance."

CHAPTER 20

We left for Sorel the next morning as a light snow began to fall. Our guides, loaded with packs of supplies as we were, told us it would take six days to reach the village. We were happy that we had ransomed our families and neighbors but the reality of what came next began to settle upon us. We knew there wasn't enough supplies of clothing, shoes, blankets, or food to last us until we left for home in April. We recognized that we would need to make this trip again, probably in mid-March, with two or three other men to get what we would need to get us back. We stopped once in the morning and again in the afternoon but only for a few minutes to rest, so anxious we were to see our families.

At our afternoon rest on the second day, Ben approached Ezekiel. "Ezekiel, I want to thank you for coming with us. It is not something you needed to do. You have no relations who were taken captive, yet you did all, and sometimes more, than we did. It is good of you to do this and I want you to know that I think highly of you."

Ezekiel sat there staring at the tall trees that surrounded our resting place, not saying a word, taking in all Ben said. He heaved himself up, went to Ben, and shook his hand. "I do have family who were taken," he said, cocking his thumb at me. "Jack's family. They may not be blood relation but they are family anyway. Since I don't have any real family, I took them as my own."

His words struck me, a smile coming to my face as I realized what started out as an accidental friendship had grown into something more. His words would haunt me two years later, but I was happy in his profession of friendship.

We reached Sorel on the afternoon of the sixth day, tired but very happy to be with our families. While we were gone, Ben's wife Martha gave birth to a little girl they named Canada.

My second son, Ephraim, named after Ephraim Curtis, my good friend and a man I will never forget, was born in a snug hut during a howling early February blizzard. Like many winter storms, it began as a light snow just after dawn, lazily drifting down, a slight northeastern wind swirling it as it made its way to the ground. As the morning went on, the wind picked up and the snow began to fall heavily. The house we lived in was quite crowded, with Stephen Jennings, his pregnant wife Hannah and their two children, the old man and wife who owned the house, and Ezekiel. The house was big enough for four or five people to sleep comfortably but with eleven of us, it was tight.

Becky began having pain at mid-morning and it increased as the day went on. By late afternoon, she began having severe pain. Ezekiel took Sam and went to one of the other houses, lumbering through the snow with Sam in his arms, looking like a giant carrying a doll. Hannah and the old woman took things in hand, shooing me to the other end of the room to sit next to the fire with the old man, who sat there smoking his pipe, content in the cozy warmth against the biting cold and falling snow.

Several times I went to Becky to hold her hand, to stroke her face, or to wipe the sweat off of her with a cloth, but there was nothing else I could do but sit and wait. She cried out several times, arching her back while biting on a piece of round, smooth wood. The blizzard began in earnest by late afternoon, the snow falling heavily as the wind whipped through the trees, slamming into the little house with a force that worried me. As the darkness began to descend, she cried out and shuddered as she gave birth to our little boy. He was a large baby with a full head of black hair. The old woman cleaned him up while Hannah waited on Becky. The old woman put Ephraim in Becky's arms. She held him tight as he yelled and cried. After he calmed down, getting used to being out in the world, he fell fast asleep. I took the mess of blood soaked cloths and afterbirth outside, burying them in the snow a few hundred feet from the house so animals would not come to get them.

When I came back, covered in snow and feeling the sting on my face from the wind driven snowflakes, I sat on the floor next to Becky, stroking her damp hair with my fingers. At that moment, one I will never forget, I loved her more than ever.

"Do you want to hold your son?" she asked me in a soft voice. I put my arms out and took him from her. He was so small, so delicate, I was afraid of holding him too tight for fear I would hurt him. Ezekiel went and got Sam, who came to me as soon as he was in the door.

"See your little brother?" I asked him. He looked at us, the curiosity lighting his eyes. He put a finger to touch Ephraim, and withdrew it quickly when his brother burped. Becky took Ephraim and, after feeding him, slept for a few hours until Ephraim woke us with his crying, needing to be fed again.

The next three months dragged on, each day grinding into the next. Snowstorms swept in every few days, the snow piling up and the constant wind blowing it into drifts twice the height of a man. Four weeks after Ephraim was born, Hannah Jennings gave birth to a little girl they named Captivity. Gradually, the snowstorms began to lessen, both in frequency and in intensity. The cold slipped away a bit each day until the snow began to melt. We were able to get out and begin preparations to leave, which was a good thing as being together in one small house for the better part of three months wore on everyone. When the ice on the river melted and it was open, we made another trip to Quebec for supplies, only this time we went in three large canoes. Governor Frontenac arranged for an escort of eleven soldiers under the command of Sieur de Lusigny to accompany us home. We started out on Monday, May 2.

It took three weeks to reach Albany, less time than we thought it would. Each of us wanted to be back so much that the miles we walked didn't seem that many. We traveled from sun up to sun down, making a good distance each day. Most of the days were clear and filled with sunshine, although there were three or four rainy days. By the time we got to Albany, we were a ragged, smelly, hungry lot. This did not appeal to the clean and orderly Dutch, who refused to help us, except for one family. We had no money or food, and our clothes were in tatters. They gave us as much food as they could and allowed us to clean ourselves and mend our clothes. Captain Salisbury learned of our arrival and, being no different than he was six months before, refused to help us. Three of his men rode out to tell us that news. It didn't surprise us and all we could do was shake our heads in bewilderment at such people.

We were tired and discouraged. Our families had been away for almost eight months and it seemed like six years instead of six months since Ben, Stephen, Ezekiel and I left Hatfield to rescue them. We needed to get word to those still in Hatfield to come to our aid. We talked about two or three of us going but Sieur de Lusigny told us he and some of his men would go to bring word to Springfield of our plight. Ben suggested they take a letter that he and I wrote on the morning after our arrival.

We didn't think it was much of a letter, more like an urgent plea for assistance, but it was read in meetinghouses all over New England.

Albany, May 23, 1678.

To my loving friends and kindred at Hatfield. These few lines are to let you understand that we have arrived at Albany now with the captives, and we now stand in need of assistance, for my burden is very great and heavy, and therefore any that have any love to our condition, let it move them to come and help us in this strait. Three of the captives have been murdered - old Goodman Plympton, Samuel Foote's daughter, and Samuel Russell. All the rest are alive and well and now at Albany, namely, Obadiah Dickenson and his child, Mary Foote and her infant child, Hannah Jennings and three children, Samuel

Kellogg, my wife and four children, Becky Parker and two sons, and Quintin Stockwell. We pray you come quickly, for it requires great haste. Do not stay for the Sabbath or to shoe the horses. We shall endeavor to meet you at Kinderhook; it may be at Housatonic. We must come very slowly because of our wives and children. I pray that you come quickly, do not stay for a night or day, for the matter requires great haste. Bring provisions with you for us.

At Albany, written from my own hand. As I have been affected to yours all that were fatherless, be affected to me now, and hasten the matter and stay not, and ease me of my burden. You shall not need to be afraid of any enemies.

Your loving kinsman,
Benjamin Wait

The day after the escort left, we began our trek to Kinderhook, twenty miles south of Albany, so we could be closer to the route home. Here we waited until, on the seventh day, our neighbors from Hatfield arrived in three carts filled with food, clothing, and shoes. We ate and burned our old lice ridden clothes, starting out the afternoon of the day after our townspeople arrived.

We made it to Springfield five days later to cheers and celebration throughout the Colony, and great thanks to God from all the people in New England.

A week after our return, Ben, Stephen, Ezekiel, and I wrote a short letter to all the congregations in the area asking for their prayers to God for our salvation, asking them to pray for His great goodness to us in preserving our life, and those of our loved ones and neighbors, through the dangerous campaign and preserving us from sickness and returning us safely to our friends.

For three months after our return, there was talk of what heroes we were, having bravely gone after the Indians who stole our families and neighbors. We heard the same thing, mostly from people we didn't know, and sometimes from people we did, that we were men of simple faith, resolute will, and indomitable courage, who overcame many obstacles and with undaunted hearts faced the perils of an untrodden wilderness on a trip of 1,500 miles, enduring the bitter cold of winter, suffering the cruel pangs of hunger and thirst. I was asked many times to talk about us, a group of poor farmers, meeting with the lordly Governor Frontenac. What it all came down to was that we wanted our families and neighbors back and we went and got them. I will endure any hardships and make any sacrifices to keep my family and friends safe from harm.

I do not consider myself a hero. I like to think I did only what any man would do for the wife and sons he loves. Not one of us thought of ourselves as heroes. A hero, in my mind at least, and I think Ben, Stephen, and Ezekiel would agree, is someone who does a tremendous, truly courageous act. A hero is someone who does something momentous that changes the course of history, perhaps or such other unequaled influence, something that is rarely accomplished by common men. We were just going about our business, our daily life, the same as we had for years.

CHAPTER 21

It was a long time since we had seen Hatfield. Coming home to anywhere is always special, but this time was something I will never forget. It was Saturday, June 4, and the trees were lush and green, flowers were growing in patches here and there, and the soft warm wind felt so good after the bone-chilling cold of our journey to Canada. While we all lost weight, I could have eaten six times day for a week and it would not have hurt me any, I felt sorry for Ezekiel. He lost more weight than anyone else, partly from not getting enough to eat and partly through his insistence that the women and children, then all men smaller than him, which was everyone, ate before he did. There were a couple of times when everyone told him they would not eat just so he could have a good meal. He did not say no those times.

It is difficult to express the range of emotions I felt when I got to our house. I was very happy to have my family around me, safe and sound and in good health after such a tremendous journey. I was also sad that Hatfield was different, being the place where we were attacked. A weariness fell upon me from the seemingly endless fighting. I was sick of it, plain and simple. I wanted to get on with farming my land, working hard so I was tired every night, get my hands dirty growing food for us, seeing the plants grow and ripen. I wanted to have several years of good daily routine, the kind that makes you smile with satisfaction, and makes you look forward to each new day.

Becky and Sam were thrilled to be home; they hadn't slept in their own beds for almost eight months. The first thing Becky did was clean the place so there wasn't a spot of dirt or dust anywhere to be found. Then she set up an area for Ephraim. She was almost in a fury, determined to make the house ready for a new beginning because that is really what it was. We were starting over again. Sam was cautious, inspecting everything methodically as if to make sure that no one had touched his things.

It took two days to get everything back to where it needed to be. I chopped wood, we got coals from our neighbors to start a new fire, and I went to Springfield to buy supplies but also to see Mr. Pynchon, for I missed him. It was odd that when we lived in Brookfield, twenty-five miles east of Springfield, I saw him more often than I did when we lived fifteen miles north of Springfield. I was glad when I found him at home.

Amy, his wife, opened the door when I knocked and was excited to see me, her hands going to her face in surprise. She called loudly to the back of the house. In a minute I heard Mr.

Pynchon's footsteps and saw him coming down the hallway. His face lit up when he saw me and I guess mine did too. I shook his hand, taking it in both of mine.

"Jack, it is so good to see you. We heard from the rider a few hours after you made it to Hatfield. We thought of you and the others every day, praying for you both here at home and at meeting on Sundays and Thursdays. It is good to see you," he said again, shaking my hand once more. "Come in, come in," he said as he put his arm around my shoulder.

"I came for supplies," I said, feeling very dejected at what we lost. "We have nothing and need everything."

"Don't worry," he told me. "We will work it out. Tell Smithson what you need and he will have it ready for you when you leave." Smithson was one of Mr. Pynchon's workers.

"Now, sit and tell me all about your journey to redeem your family and friends."

It took an hour, but I related our journey, answering all his questions as best I could. I would rather have forgotten the whole affair than tell it over and over to each new person that asked me about it. Knowing he was a busy man, I explained the incidents of our effort in a short while. As I told him the tale, I realized the extreme effort we made, although it did not seem like it at the time. You don't realize the degree of effort you put into something, focusing on the object at hand, until it is over and it becomes apparent of the pledge you made. I found it could be like that with several things in life.

As he was seeing me out the door, he brought up another proposal that I dismissed but that would later have another huge impact on the remainder of my life.

"One thing that will be needed, and that I want you to think about," he said, "is going back to Brookfield."

He saw the startled look on my face and, before I could object, raised a hand to stop me. "It will be re-settled at some time and, if our Lord, Jesus Christ, will once again look with favor on us by ending the attacks by the Indians, it should be sooner rather than later." He stopped for a moment, allowing me to absorb the thought. "It would be of great advantage if you were to be part of the re-settlement. Now, I know you have your farm and things will be well for you and us all if we continue to work to please our Savior, but I want you to think of it. I want to get people living there again. You know it is too good an area for farming to let sit unused. Think about it and we will talk again."

After I left Mr. Pynchon, I told Smithson what to get and added three large bottles of rum to the list, two for Ezekiel, and one for me. I then went to the tavern to see Jeremiah and Mary from whom I got a welcome as if I was the prodigal son returning home. It was good to see everyone but I couldn't dawdle any longer and had to get back to Hatfield. It was full dark when I got home. When I walked in the door it was a scene that made my heart happy. Becky was standing near the fireplace cooking a stew, while Sam played with the toys I made him just before they were taken, and Ephraim in the cradle I made for Sam, making infant noises, talking a mile a minute in a language only he could understand. I stood there taking it all in. Becky turned and jumped in surprise, not having heard me come in. She came to me and put her arms around me. I held her tight. Sam came running to me with his arms up, wanting me to hold him. I scooped him up and held him tight.

"Did you get everything?" Becky asked.

"I did and saw Mr. Pynchon and Amy. They are so happy we made it home." I kissed her softly on the forehead.

I went to the cart and brought all the supplies in. When I put the three bottles of rum on the sideboard, Becky gave me a questioning look.

"Two are for Ezekiel and one is for me," I told her, answering the question before it was asked.

"He mentioned that Brookfield will be re-settled someday, maybe soon, and he wants us to think about possibly going back."

She quickly turned from the hearth, spoon in hand, a look of surprise on her face. “What? He wants us to go back? After all the pain and suffering we went through there, he wants us to consider going back? No, I will not even consider it.”

That seemed to be her final word, but his comment planted a seed of thought for both of us. Though we didn’t speak of it much at first, the idea began to grow.

Just then, Ezekiel knocked on the door before coming in. “Well, I thought I would stop by to see how my good friends the Parkers are getting along.” He raised his nose in the air, sniffing at the stew.

“Come in,” Becky told him. “We were about to eat. Join us.”

“Well, I don’t know,” he said. “I’d be interrupting.”

“I got you two bottles of rum,” I told him.

He looked at me with a sudden gleam in his eye. “Then I’ll stay,” he boomed, rubbing his hands together and pouring rum into three mugs. “Thank you, Jack. It’s nice to know I was thought of.” He tossed the drink off and refilled his cup before I brought mine to my lips.

“Well, come on Becky. Take your mug before I drink it myself,” he said with a wide grin that made it all the way to his eyes.

It was a fine night.

Two weeks later, I was in the barn late one afternoon when Becky came in all flustered about something.

"What's the matter?" I asked.

"It's Ezekiel."

"What about him?"

"The Springfield constable is looking for him. He stole something, I don't know what, though." She stood there tapping her right foot. She always did that when she wanted something. "Do you know where he is?"

"No, I don't. I haven't seen him in three days. He could be anywhere. You know how he wanders."

I worried about him that night, wondering what he could have gotten into now. I didn't have to wait long for an answer because the next morning, bright and early, he strolled up and stood next to me as if we had seen each other a few minutes before.

"So," he said, putting his big foot on the chopping block.

"So," I said, standing there waiting for him to continue. "Where have you been?"

"Oh, here and there."

"The constable from Springfield is looking for you. I heard that you stole something, I don't know what, but I think you are in trouble."

He shrugged his huge shoulders. "Now Jack, I've been in trouble before, and it's never come to anything. Once they tell me what I stole, I'll give it back, same as I do most of the time. That is, if I still have whatever it is but I won't know until they ask."

I stood there shaking my head, thinking of the times when he pilfered something that he shouldn't have but did anyway. I told him that I knew it would catch up with him, but he shook his big shaggy head.

"No it won't," he said, "and if it does, no one will do anything about it. It would take several big strong men to put me in the jail."

I looked him up and down. "You're not so big that you can't be handled."

Becky came striding out the door into the yard, a long iron spoon in her hand. "Ezekiel Huff," she said, marching up to him, arm extended with the spoon pointing at him, "you are going to Springfield today to answer the charges, whatever they are, against you."

"No, I'm not," he said, standing to his full height.

Now I would say that Becky is an average-sized woman, a lot prettier than most, but no bigger or smaller than many other women. She looked tiny standing up to Ezekiel, the spoon in her outstretched hand pointing to his chin, a determined look in her eye, one that, from experience, I knew you did not want to cross.

"Yes, you are."

"Are you going to make me?" he asked staring down at her.

"Don't you talk back to me."

"I'll talk however I like," he said.

She brandished the iron spoon at him. "I will use this if I have to."

He shot me a sideways glance as if to ask if she would really use it on him.

I didn't respond but gave him a look that said she meant business.

"I am not going. Are you going to try to take me?" he said with a chuckle.

"I won't have to because you'll go now, on your own."

"You think I am going to go because you say so, little woman?" he asked with an edge in his voice.

"Yes, you are," she shot back. "Jack will take you now."

“What?” I said, surprised at being drawn into this. “Every man is accountable for his own actions,” I told her. “He can be a man and go alone.”

“You are taking him this morning,” she said turning around and walking back into the house.

Ezekiel looked at me, shaking his head. “Is she always like that?”

“No, I am not,” she answered from inside the house. “Now come in and have something to eat before you leave.”

I shrugged.

“I suppose it’s better than going to see the constable on an empty stomach.”

“All depends on how much you got to eat,” he said lumbering into the house. “I’m not a normal sized man and I have a big appetite.”

Becky tossed five bowls on the table and called Sam and Ephraim in to eat.

“Sit down and stop talking,” she told him. She spooned what looked like a couple of pounds of corn mush into his bowl. “Eat.” she said, dumping two big spoonfuls into my bowl. She filled her bowl and sat down with a thump.

After a few spoonfuls, she looked at me. “When we are done, you can get Bubs saddled while I talk to Ezekiel.”

I knew better than to say anything when she was in one of her determined moods. I learned at a young age that if you are not sure what to say, it is better to say nothing at all.

I had Bubs saddled in a short while. Ezekiel came out looking sheepish, his head hanging down with a thoughtful look on his face. I didn't hear what Becky told him, but I knew that it was the type of talk she would give to anyone she considered a troublemaker. We were off, me on Bubs and Ezekiel on a big draft horse, the only one large enough to carry him. Becky stood in the dooryard, her arms folded across her chest.

We rode the first few miles without talking. The only sound was the leather of the saddles squeaking underneath us. Ezekiel was caught up in his thoughts.

"You know Jack, this may not be as easy as you or Becky thinks it is. There is something else that might not look to good to people."

"And what's that?" I asked.

"Well, you know the Barnes girl from Hadley, Richard Barnes' oldest girl?"

"Yes I do. Why?"

"Well, I've been seeing her for a couple of months now and we've been laying together."

"Oh dear sweet Lord, Ezekiel, how do you get yourself into these messes?"

"I wonder the same thing," he answered. "It's not like I do anything wrong, at least it's not wrong when I do it, but a lot of times, it doesn't seem right later, you know what I mean?" He leaned down and touched me on the shoulder. "She's a good-looking woman and things went their natural way. You know how that is."

"Yes, I do know how that is." I rode on cursing to myself at the trouble he seemed always to get into. "Does anyone else know about this?"

"Besides her and me, no. Just you, at least as far as I know."

"What about her father or mother? I don't know them well so I don't know what kind of people they are."

"Her youngest brother is a snively little runt, always sneaking around, trying to catch us doing something but he never did as far as I know."

"So now, you may not only have to answer for thievery but also fornication. Do you know the penalties for those infractions?"

"No, but I'm sure they're not good."

"No, they are not. For thievery you could get your nose slit or be branded or whipped and sometimes both. For fornication you will definitely get whipped and have to pay a fine of probably fifteen pounds."

"Fifteen pounds?" he asked incredulously. "Where would I get fifteen pounds? I'd have to steal it or work for a long time, probably at something I would not like." He considered the situation for a minute. "What will happen to her?"

"Most likely, she will be whipped too. It's usually ten lashes."

We plodded along as he considered the implications of what I just told him. He shook himself and sat up straight in the saddle.

"Do you think they would let me take the whipping for both of us? I'd take thirty lashes to spare the poor girl."

I considered this for a moment.

"You wouldn't survive thirty lashes. For someone your size, they would be laid on heavy. If you are found out, it might be best for you to take your punishment and let her have her own. Besides, it would be up to Mr. Pynchon. As the magistrate, he determines the punishment."

"Talk to him, will you, Jack? I don't want her to get hurt. She's a good girl. I'll tell him it was all my doing."

"I have every intention of talking to him," I said.

We rode on quietly, each absorbed in our own thoughts.

It was early afternoon when we got to Springfield. We went directly to Mr. Pynchon's house and luckily he was home.

"You wait here," I told Ezekiel. "Don't go anywhere. He may want to talk to you."

He nodded.

After exchanging greetings with Mr. Pynchon, I came to the point. "I have Ezekiel Huff with me and he is prepared to answer the charges against him."

"Good," he replied. "Besides the charge of theft, there may be a complicating factor."

"Oh, what might that be?"

"Richard Barnes accused Huff of fornicating with his oldest daughter." He sat at the table, fingers pointed, almost as if in prayer, thumbs under his chin and index fingers just under his nose. He stood and walked to the window, looking out at Ezekiel standing next to the horses.

"I can't be lenient Jack. You understand that, don't you?"

I sighed and slumped into a chair.

"Yes, I know that. I just hoped that maybe you could see yourself to giving him a lesser punishment for my sake. He is a good friend who I shared much with, he went to Canada with Ben, Stephen, and me to get our families back. He almost never thinks of himself and is, in some ways, simple. I don't want to presume on our friendship, Sir, and would never ask you to do something that was against either your or my principles."

"I know Jack, I know, but he gets into trouble so easily. This is not the first theft reported to me about him. I cannot protect him, and you, any longer. He is thoughtless in many ways and does not seem to understand that what he does at times is wrong. Plus, he is an ungodly man, attending meeting only when he feels like it. That is what concerns me most. I may need you to post a bond for him. As for the Barnes girl, she deserves punishment too. It was not all Ezekiel's fault you know." He paced the room, holding a piece of paper in his right hand, staring at the floor then out the window at Ezekiel. He sat into his chair and looked at me. "What do you want me to consider?"

"That Ezekiel takes the whipping for both of them. He offered to do that on the way here."

"He should be branded as other thieves are. Maybe that and a whipping would get him to see reason. I think he will continue to steal and I can't have that."

I could tell that he did not like the situation but as the magistrate, he had no choice. “It may not be good to have him continue to live here Jack.”

This caught me by surprise. It was a practice for a person to be banished from a town or village if they caused repeated harm. He may be a minor thief, but I did not think he deserved that severe a punishment.

“Mr. Pynchon please don’t do that. I know he would take two whippings, branding, and pay a fine if he could stay here. Please don’t make him go away.”

He got up and began pacing again. After a few turns back and forth, he stopped and came toward me.

I stood as he approached.

“We have known each other for a long time Jack, and you have grown to be a good man. I respect your request to help your friend but I have to punish him in some way. I don’t see any way around it.” He sat on the edge of the table, tapping the fingers of his right hand on the wood, lost in thought.

An idea came to mind, one that I did not want to consider, but it was something Ezekiel mentioned and that might be the only way to help him.

“What if he went away on his own?” I asked.

He turned his head toward me, giving me a questioning look. "What do you mean?"

"Well, if he decided to go somewhere else and never return, would he escape punishment? I don't know if he would do it, but he might."

"From what you say, it seems like he would prefer the punishment to being banished."

"Maybe. Can I ask him what he would do?"

"The choice is not his."

"At least let me explain the situation to him."

"All right," he said tossing the piece of paper onto the table.

I went outside and found Ezekiel right where I left him. I motioned for him to follow me. We began to walk toward the river.

"So what did he say?" Ezekiel asked coming even with me.

"He said you will be whipped and possibly branded. He also said that Richard Barnes accused you of fornication with his daughter Ruth."

"Oh I was hoping that wouldn't happen. Well, what I did was wrong, so I will take the punishment." He stopped and considered what he just said. "It's only right isn't it?" He scratched his head with a meaty paw, as if he was not sure of the correct answer.

"Yes, it is only right. There is something he is considering that you may not like." He shot me a look that was questioning and cautious at the same time.

"What is that?"

"Banishment. There are other reports of you stealing things."

"You mean I'd have to leave here?"

I stopped walking and closed my eyes, thinking of how difficult it would be not having him here.

"Yes, that is what it means."

"For good? Never come back?"

"Yes, Ezekiel, you couldn't come back."

He suddenly had a sad look about him, the realization of what this punishment could mean. He hung his head, shaking it slightly back and forth.

"After all we've done together, I'd never see you, Becky, Sam, or Ephraim again."

When we got to the river, we stood there several minutes before he said anything. "Well, I was going to tell you this sometime soon, so I might as well do it now." He gave me a friendly, caring look. "I got the urge to wander. I want to smell the ocean. Did I tell you I was born on a ship? Don't know which one or where but I know that I was."

"You want to wander," I said, shaking my head. "Wasn't the trek to Canada enough for you?"

"Oh, Jack, that was nothing but a good stretch of the legs. I am getting restless and need to go somewhere else. This will all work out for the best. I promise you that I will be back probably sooner than later." He considered all this. His countenance brightened but became dark again as another thought crossed his mind. Sometimes it was like being outside on a windy day with white puffy clouds racing along. You can see the shadow they make on the ground, the earth alternates between dark and light. That's what it was like to see the emotions cross Ezekiel's face.

"What will happen to Ruth? Will she be whipped too?" He walked along the edge of the river for a bit before turning to me.

"Yes, she will be punished too. Mr. Pynchon didn't say what he was considering, but she will likely be whipped."

"I will take whatever punishment Mr. Pynchon thinks I should have. He can brand me, whip me, and make me pay whatever fine he wants but will not send me away. I will go on my own. I may not be as good as I should be, but I will not be banished."

"Ezekiel?" I asked, putting my hand on his arm, "Do you know if she is with child? Has she told you that?"

"Well, uh, no, she hasn't. We were together a lot if you understand what I mean. So, I am not sure if she is pregnant. I don't think so but I don't know."

"All right but let's make sure before you go offering yourself up." Luckily for Ezekiel, it turned out that she was not with child.

Mr. Pynchon had Ezekiel placed in the jail.

I rode home that night to tell Becky the news. She was upset when I related everything that happened.

"It is my fault," she said, her voice quivering with emotion. "I never thought he would have to go away. I thought Mr. Pynchon would fine him, maybe whip him or put him in jail for a few days, but not send him away." She sat at the table and put her head in her hands. "Does Mr. Pynchon understand he did not do this maliciously?"

"I think so, but am not sure." Sam came to the table and sidled up to Becky. He put his head on her leg. She put a hand on his back and held him to her. I reached down and picked him up.

"How is my boy today?" I asked with an enthusiasm I did not feel.

"Good," was all he said before sliding out of my arms and going back to his mother.

As luck would have it, Stephen Jennings told me he was about to go to Springfield. He said he would find out when Ezekiel would get his punishment. Everyone in the village knew about the situation.

When Stephen returned that afternoon, a Wednesday, everyone gathered at our house to hear the news that Ezekiel was to be whipped and banished on Friday morning.

Well before dawn, Stephen Jennings, Ben Wait, Hezekiah Dickenson, Samuel Kellogg, and Becky and I set off to make it to Springfield by mid-morning. When we arrived, there was a good deal of activity around the tavern. People milled about the meetinghouse, waiting for the court to begin.

We all took seats on the benches. Within a few minutes, Ezekiel and Ruth were led in. Mr. Pynchon, as magistrate, sat at the table in the front of the room. Ruth's father and mother were there on the first bench, the father angry with Ezekiel, the mother ashamed of her daughter.

"Ruth Barnes, you are accused of fornication with this man, Ezekiel Huff. You were brought before this court by your own father. Barnes," he said, "tell us how you learned of this terrible sin."

Barnes stood and bowed to Mr. Pynchon. He was a smallish man, with a grizzled look about him. "My youngest son told me, your Worshipfulness. He saw them."

Mr. Pynchon glared at Ruth. "Did you ever suspect something?" he asked Barnes.

"Not at the time. Huff seemed like a rough sort but a good man. Now I know he is not. But, your Worshipfulness, Ruth never got into any trouble at all and is a good girl."

"Do you have anything to say?" Mr. Pynchon asked Ruth.

She kept her eyes down and shook her head as she sobbed quietly.

"You are to receive ten lashes," he pronounced.

"Ezekiel Huff, you are accused of theft of several diverse items and of fornication with Ruth Barnes."

Ezekiel stood before Mr. Pynchon, hands in front of him, head down and bowed.

"Who did he steal from?" Two people got up and related the theft of their items. Although none of them saw Ezekiel actually take anything, they found it missing shortly after he visited, so it was presumed he made off with it.

"Mr. Pynchon, Sir," Ezekiel said in a quiet, humble voice, "I did take them things. I admit it. Ruth and I were together. I will take whatever punishment you give me, Sir, but I want you and everyone here to know that I am not a bad man. Jack," he said looking at me, "tell them about me."

All eyes turned to me. I rose, clearing my throat.

"Your Worshipfulness, what Ezekiel says is true. He is a good man. Yes, he gets into more trouble than anyone else I know, but he also gave of himself into going to Canada to redeem the captives when he did not have to."

Mr. Pynchon considered this for a moment then announced the punishment. "Ezekiel Huff, you are to receive fifteen lashes and are banished from Springfield."

Punishments were always handed out in front of the meetinghouse. There were a good number of people there waiting and watching. Josiah Leonard, the constable, led Ruth and Ezekiel out to the whipping post.

Leonard was in the militia and fought with us at the Great Falls fight. I had no respect for him after I saw him commit the atrocities he did that day for he seemed to have enjoyed it. He did not have a high opinion of me, either, and thought of me as a coward for not slaughtering the Indian children.

In front of the meetinghouse stood two large, wooden posts, about six feet apart. Two boards each with half circles cut in the top of the bottom one and the bottom of the top one formed the stocks, the top board able to be moved up and down by virtue of an opening in the middle of each post.

Ruth was taken up first, put in the manacles hanging from the top of the post, and stripped to the waist. I noticed the whip Leonard used was not the usual flagellation whip, but a small one. The flagellation whip has small metal bars imbedded in the leather that tears the skin. The whip the constable had was a two-foot long stick with two braided leather whips each three feet long. At the end of each whip were small leather tassels. While this whip would hurt, it was not nearly as bad as the flagellation whip.

When Leonard snapped the whip twice Ruth reacted as if hit.

"Ruth Barnes," he said, "you have been charged with fornication which you admit. Your punishment is ten lashes."

Everyone got quiet.

He snapped the whip again, her body tightened up and she whimpered. At the first stroke, she screamed. With each succeeding lash, her yelling became less. After the fifth lash, red marks were all over her back. By the eighth lash, she was bleeding. The whip had gone around her back, striking her in the breasts, which were bleeding in a few places. She sagged against the post, her body hanging down. Leonard gave one more hard lash, and then a soft lash that just rippled over her back. Two men approached and undid the manacles, covered her as best they could and helped her to her mother and father. I cannot imagine watching one of my children, especially a daughter, go through what Ruth had.

Ezekiel lumbered up to the post.

"Take off your shirt," Leonard told him. He stripped off his shirt, exposing his massive bulk. I noticed several men looking at him in surprise and some in wonder. He put his hands in the manacles at the top of the post. One of the men closed them about his wrists. They just barely made it around his thick wrists.

Mr. Pynchon stood off to the side by himself. He saw me and nodded. I nodded back at him. Becky caught his eye and he lowered his head so as not to have to look at her.

Leonard snapped the whip again.

"Ezekiel Huff, you have been charged with theft and fornication with Ruth Barnes. The punishment decreed by the magistrate is that you shall receive fifteen lashes of the whip, and be banished from Springfield."

Ezekiel spread his legs and leaned into the post, exposing his back. Leonard took the whip and hefted it in his hand, and snapped it once. Becky grabbed onto my arm, digging her nails into it. I pulled her to me and wrapped my arm around her shoulder.

"Oh Jack," she whispered. "This is all my fault."

"No, it isn't."

Ezekiel shifted his weight and leaned forward a bit more.

"Well, come on man, are you going to do it or not? I have to be leaving here soon," he hollered.

Many of the people laughed at his impropriety. The constable looked at Mr. Pynchon who nodded his head. Leonard drew his arm back and struck the first of fifteen blows. Ezekiel did not move. He stood there taking each blow without a sound. At the fifth lash, blood began to flow down his back. Leonard put all his might into the last lash, causing Ezekiel to grunt.

Leonard handed the whip to a boy and released Ezekiel from the manacles. Ezekiel rubbed his wrists and moved his shoulders around, picked up his shirt and put it on. He came over to us. We knew he was in pain but would not let us see it. He turned and looked around, and I could see the lines of blood on his shirt where the whip cut him. "I think I'll be going along."

I saw the sadness in his eyes, the hurt at being sent away from a place he called home, the only real home that he ever knew. It was difficult for Becky and me, as we knew he never had such a place his entire life. To him, it was clear he was not wanted and that hurt him deeply.

"Here is your basket," Becky told him, her eyes brimming with tears. I took two fathoms of wampum out of my possibles bag and gave it to him.

"No, Jack, I won't take your wampum. You don't have much more than me and I won't take it from you. I've gotten along with less than what I have now." Becky stepped up and gave him a hug. She could not reach all the way around him so he patted her on the back gently. He took my hand into one of his, covering it completely.

"I can't begin to thank you both for the friendship you've shown me. Not many people have ever done that in my life. Most thought me a freak because of my size but you didn't and it is a wonderful thing. Give Sam and Ephraim a kiss for me." He took the basket and began walking away.

After a few yards, he stopped and turned to us. "I'll go now to get the wandering urge out of me, but they can't keep me away. I'll be back." In spite of his pain, he winked, let out a small chuckle, and made his way up the road.

We stood there for a long time until he was out of site. As we turned to go to the tavern, I saw Mr. Pynchon still standing where he had been looking at us. He walked over to us, giving a deep sigh as he got close. He stood in front of us, looking at us intently.

"You shouldn't have banished him but made him pay a fine," Becky snapped at Mr. Pynchon. She turned and stomped away.

Both Mr. Pynchon and I stared at her for a few moments.

"I am sorry for that," I told him, barely able to conceal the shock of my wife talking in such a way to the man who had been our protector and friend. He waved his hand, dismissing her tirade. He turned and walked to his house.

I went to where Becky was standing, her mouth drawn tight, the anger still burning in her eyes.

"There was no need of that," I said. "Mr. Pynchon had a decision he had to make and he made it. Ezekiel knew he would be caught stealing at some point. I knew he would and he did too. I just never thought he would be caught fornicating."

She said nothing but stared at me, the hurt beginning to dissolve. Everyone else had gone and we were the last people there. I took her hand and, instead of going to the tavern, we went to the cart and headed home.

CHAPTER 22

It was in July 1679 when I got a letter from my aunt Charity telling me that my uncle Josiah died and she was leaving Ipswich to go back to Sandwich on Cape Cod to live with her sister. I remember that summer night. There was a warm, soft feel in the air, like running your hand over a fine cloth. The leaves of the cottonwoods and sycamores were hanging down while the crickets chirped and the grass on the ground smelled sweet.

It is difficult to see the older people passing away because that means that I am next in line to die, to leave this earth and be no more. I hope that what I leave behind is good enough to make the world a better place, to give those who come after me, a better life. I am not afraid for myself for I didn't know I was being born, so perhaps I won't know when I die, but somehow I think I will. I want my children to be good people, to live right, respect others, do good, help one another, help others, be strong, upright, and work hard.

Charity's letter said that Josiah left me their land in Brookfield and that Mr. Humfry, an esquire in Ipswich would handle the transaction. I confess that at that moment I felt a wealthy man, although I was not by any means, since I had forty acres of land in Brookfield and twenty in Hatfield. There were many men who owned a greater amount of land that I did, but it was more land than anyone in our family ever owned.

It was a shame that everything in Brookfield was gone, destroyed in a few hours while we watched everything we worked so hard for gone in what seemed like a moment. Forty acres of good land was something and I began to think of how to put it to use. The idea of going back there came and went in a second. I dismissed it because, while the war was over, being alone in such a place, with no other houses for miles in any direction, was foolhardy. Attacks could still happen, as we found out less than two years before. I considered selling it, possibly to Mr. Pynchon, but the idea of parting with the land for country pay bothered me. Since I did not know what to do, I did nothing.

Our daughter was born in March of the following year, but God proclaimed that, at the moment of her birth, she would not live long. Elizabeth died when she was six days old. I made her small coffin and we took her to the burial ground on a raw, misty day. A cloud of sorrow hung over us for two months as Becky and I went through the daily motions of life. Sam and Ephraim were affected in a small way, understanding the concept of death but not anything beyond that. Sensing our despondency, they didn't know how to act. Slowly, day by day, the cloud lifted and we began to get on with our life again. While you have no other choice but to go on, the memory of her stays with me every day. She was my little girl, the daughter I wanted so badly, that I could not have.

The summer weather was fine and the harvest was the best I had seen in years. Each of us in the village had enough to increase our holdings, buying livestock of some sort. I bought a young ox since one of ours was old and not able to work as hard as he once did, and I also bought two milk cows and six sheep.

One day, for some reason, all my work was done for the moment. Normally, we all worked from before sun up to after sundown, giving glory to God by our farms being well cared for and productive but today was different, for me at least. It was a fine late summer afternoon day, one of the finest I can remember. The sky was a clear blue with a few small white clouds drifting along on a soft breeze. I sat on the chopping block and watched all around me, seeing the village drowsing away the afternoon. The gate to the stockade was open and people were moving about. Some of the men gathered, talking, making points to each other with their hands. Women were standing outside the gate chatting and children were playing up and down the lane. Becky was in the house cooking. I could hear the pans when she clanged the sides with a spoon. Sam and Ephraim ran out the door, tearing past me, to go play with the other children. As I watched them go, I felt Becky's hand on my shoulder and I looked up into her face. She looked down at me and smiled, holding my gaze for an instant before thoughtfully patting my arm and going back into the house.

There are moments that stick in our memory though there is no great event associated with them and this is one such memory of mine. I can still see the people, feel the breeze, smell the growing things, hear the chatter of people talking, and the laughter of the children.

That day was a weather breeder and brought a tremendous storm the next day, the rain pelting down while the wind tore across the sky, bending trees half over, flattening some of the corn, and beating down the wheat. Following it was a stretch of five miserably hot days, each seeming worse than the previous one. Working at harvesting the wheat and corn was terrible, the sun and heat bearing down on us every moment we were in the fields. I never stopping sweating for the entire time. None of us did. We started early in the day, rested at mid-day and began again at mid-afternoon but even so, the sweat poured down my face, blinding me as I worked and I wiped my face with my wet sleeve so many times it did not help anymore.

CHAPTER 23

Time has a way of moving quickly and catching you unaware of the passing years. It seems just yesterday that I was young, newly married, and embarking on my life with Becky. Yet in a way, it seems like eons ago, and I wonder where the years went.

For the next several years the seasons marched on, one moving into the other. Fields were planted and harvests made, Sabbaths came and went, food was prepared and eaten, wood was cut and burned, the warmth followed the cold. For the most part, it was a good time, a happy time.

Our wish for another daughter came true in September of 1680, when Becky gave birth to a beautiful little girl we named Sarah. She was a good baby, always gurgling and giggling, rarely crying, and slept well right from the start. She was, and still is, happy most of the time. Sam was six years old and Ephraim four years old when she was born, so we had our hands full for a while but they behaved themselves, at least for the most part.

The boys grew faster than we thought possible, learning to do their chores, helping Becky with the garden and taking care of the animals. Even when she was three years old, Sarah wanted to best her brothers at whatever they were doing and let nothing stand in her way unless it was Becky and me. She had a stubborn streak that was obvious even then, wanting her way most of the time. She was a cute little girl, the cutest in the entire village.

I looked at the boys and wondered what my mother thought of me at that age and what her hopes and dreams for me were.

We lived well during that time, the fruits of our continuous labors providing plenty of food. We bought more livestock almost every year, adding some new to replace the old animals that I sold off to other farmers.

Things in Hatfield continued on with several interesting developments taking place. The whole town worked on building the fortifications at the north end of town, a labor of weeks because the trees had to be cut and hauled many miles, one large tree would make up to ten stakes. The palisade was ten feet high and covered the entire village, being 500 feet wide and 1,000 feet long. Military training took place every other month with sixty Hatfield men making up the militia. Each of us were required to keep guard, watching by night and warding by day. There were fines if we did not guard when supposed to or if we left our post. While the possibility of another major attack was much less than it had been, there was still a chance of a band of Indians from the north sweeping down on the village. On some of our training days, we would do highway work, repairing roads and fences as needed and time allowed.

In 1679, the town started a school, allowing boys between six and twelve years old and girls that were sent by their parents or masters. The teacher, Dr. Thomas Hastings, was provided with twenty pounds a year, provided he taught all the children in town that were capable. A rate of three shillings per child was declared. In 1681, the schoolmaster was allotted thirty pounds, a fourth in wheat, a fourth in peas, a fourth in corn and the remainder in pork. School was kept at Dr. Hastings house until we built a schoolhouse, a fine building that each man gave much time to build. Sam started school that year and was so happy and excited, it made our hearts happy. He would come home every day to tell us the wonderful things he learned.

The town agreed that there would be no firing of guns near the village except for alarm because of the 1677 attack. In 1681, we began looking for a bonesetter but were unsuccessful in securing a doctor. Lucky for us, Dr. Hastings, who had until this time, been in town only for that part of the year that school was in session, decided to settle in Hatfield in 1684 and traveled throughout the area, attending to many illnesses and broken bones. A new minister, Nathaniel Chauncey, settled in Hatfield in

1683, providing the religious ministry so needed. Samuel Partridge from Hadley across the river, a man of many talents who in some ways reminded me of Mr. Pynchon, settled in town in 1680.

In the spring of 1683, Thomas Hovey and John Younglove, both former neighbors from Brookfield who were living across the river in Hadley, approached me about the possibility of re-settling Brookfield. They made many arguments, which convinced them it was a wonderful idea while leaving me unsure that it was something that should be attempted, at least at that time.

I was never eager to participate in anything John Younglove proposed. He was the former minister at Brookfield, though he was not ordained, he was the best we had at the time. He did not fit well in that small village, being a disagreeable man, sometimes vindictive, taking each of us to County court for some minor occurrence that he took as a personal affront. Tom, on the other hand, was always reasonable and even-minded. His father, Daniel, known as Deacon to everyone in Ipswich, Brookfield, and Springfield, was the largest landowner in Brookfield, and Tom's brother Jim, was a good friend of my uncle Josiah, but never made it to the fortified house on the day of the ambush and his body was never found. His wife Priscilla always held out hope that he was alive, taken captive, but those of us who fought the enemy knew better. They told me that another man, John Scott, Sr., who I didn't know and was supposedly living in Brookfield, which I doubted, was to prepare a petition to the governor asking that a Prudential Committee be authorized to provide for the re-settlement. They asked that I be one of the petitioners. I told them I would think about it.

I will admit that the thought of going back did cross my mind from time to time but I never mentioned it to Becky because I knew she would be dead set against it. I told Tom and John that I would think about it but left it there, giving it no more thought until Mr. Pynchon brought it up again.

Becky and I talked about it a couple of times a few months apart over the course of a year, discussing the possibilities and known hardships we would face, and the best way of making the re-settlement a success.

We knew things would be much different there. There would only be a few families, probably not more than thirty people, and we would be entirely self-sufficient, something that appealed to both of us. We had the children to think of. We debated whether moving them to what would be a small frontier outpost would harm them in any way. Becky's concerns were that there was no school as there was in Hatfield and there was no minister. As we got older, and the children began to learn, we realized a formal religious upbringing was necessary.

Now, I may have told you but, although it was required for everyone to attend Sabbath each week and strongly suggested to go to lecture on Thursday evening, and those that did not were fined and ordered not to do it again, I was, like my father, never as influenced by the rigorous religious attitudes of the time. I told Becky that while both of those were good points, the children were easy about learning as I was and that we could teach them from the Bible.

The more I thought of it, the more appealing it became. Becky told me it was the same with her. It would give us a chance to start over, something that had been gnawing at us even though we did not realize it at the time. While we understood you could not go back in time, we could try to resurrect what we had and make it better. The Indian threat was gone for the time being. Many of the Indians were dead, sold into slavery, gone to the west, or to Canada. Those few that were in our area adopted our ways and religion.

I slowly came to understand that I no longer felt we belonged in Hatfield. We established a good farm, our children were growing, and we had good neighbors. What we realized is that we did not know everyone, and that people were coming in greater numbers, seemingly by the month. It was becoming crowded, at least to our way of thinking. We enjoyed our time in Brookfield since there were less than 100 people in the entire village. We realized we liked that and did not want to be near larger towns. The thought of rebuilding the farm in Brookfield, once as productive and better situated than in Hatfield, stayed in my mind for greater amounts of time each day. I realized that I too wanted to go back to start over again.

Another consideration was to sell our land and Josiah's in Brookfield and stay in Hatfield but without an ongoing settlement, the land in Brookfield was not worth much to anyone but us.

Becky and I talked about this a few times and, since we did not know what to do, we didn't do anything. A few weeks later, after the morning meal, we sat and talked about it.

"Jack, I want to go home."

I looked at her, puzzled. "What do you mean?"

"I want to go home."

"Home as in Ipswich?"

"No, Brookfield."

"You want to go back to Brookfield?" I smiled at her request.

“Hatfield is getting too crowded. There are too many people, new people that we don’t know.”

“This is a bit of a surprise,” I said.

“I’ve been thinking of it more and more. Hatfield doesn’t feel like home anymore. Do you know what I mean? It’s hard to explain.”

“I think I do.”

“Brookfield is where we were happiest even though we went through the attack and siege.”

“You can’t recapture what has already gone by,” I told her.

“I know that. I just do not think I want to live here anymore. Besides, we still have the farm there and you own Josiah’s. That’s forty acres, more than we have here. We could sell this place.”

I watched the animation come to her face, lighting up at the thought of starting over again. There was a joy to her that I could not deny. Until that moment, I didn’t realize I was feeling many of the things she mentioned. Hatfield was crowded with over eighty families, almost 400 people.

“Maybe it is something to consider,” I said. “Let’s think about it and talk tomorrow.”

I lay in bed that night as Becky slept beside me. I watched the rhythm of her breathing as I thought of the good and bad points of going back to Brookfield. It occurred to me that the fact I was thinking about it so much meant it was important to me and required a decision soon. I dreamt that night of my mother baking pies and breads at our house in Ipswich. I was no more than six or seven and I could smell the aromas as they wafted through the house. It was a good dream that gave me a warm, happy feeling and made me realize what home could be. When she woke, I told Becky we were going back to Brookfield.

When we told the children about it, they were not happy at first but the idea began to grow on them. I could see in Sam many of the same ways I felt when Charity and Josiah first told me about possibly moving to Quaboag Plantation. I was fourteen then, and can still remember the excitement I felt at starting out on a new adventure.

So, with some of the same excitement we experienced leaving our beloved village of Brookfield ten years ago to escape the war, we made our plans to leave Hatfield and return to where we began life as husband and wife.

Chapter 24

James Ford went to Brookfield in 1676 as part of garrison from Marlborough under Captain Samuel Wadsworth. A former soldier, Ford found the area appealing and wanted to settle it.

In March of 1686, Ford acted as the agent for Tom Hovey, John Younglove, Hezekiah Dickinson, James Scott, Sr. of Suffield who purchased Sam Kent's property, and me, and made a petition to Governor Bradstreet asking for encouragement and guidance in resettling the village, and that we be named as the Prudential Committee to manage the affairs for the plantation. It came as no surprise to me when I learned from Tom that the only reason he wanted Younglove on the petition was because he was a minister and it might give it a better chance of being approved.

To protect the property rights we held, that is those of us who lived at Brookfield at the time of the attack and siege in August 1675, the General Court decreed in May 1679 that anyone who intended to resettle any village deserted in the late war must apply to the governor and council, or County Court in which the village lay.

Our request was granted in November, but none of us was named to the Prudential Committee. It didn't bother me for I had plenty to keep me busy and did not need the aggravation of trying to come to what would be, for the most part, small decisions that some of the other committee members might spend an unnecessary amount of time arguing about. However, not being selected for the committee did bother Younglove because he thought he was the prime candidate for such a role. He never seemed to understand that people didn't like him for his abrasive manner. What he considered a further insult, and surprised the rest of us, was that the requirement that the village have a minister was not included in the reply, something required for every other settlement. It was obvious to all of us that the governor decided that the cost of maintaining a minister would be too much for a small hamlet such as we intended.

Governor Dudley named Mr. Pynchon, Joseph Hawley, Samuel Glover, Samuel Marshfield, Samuel Ely, and John Hitchcock, all from Springfield, to the committee.

Knowing from the past that a response could take many months, as it did, I decided we wouldn't wait since we owned forty acres and didn't need permission to live on the land, and began preparations to go to Brookfield and build our new home. We weren't the first new residents there, since Jim Ford was already living there with his wife, two sons and two daughters two miles east of the original settlement. He and his family had been there over a year.

I went ahead and began building, or rather re-building our house. I decided to use the original foundation since it was well constructed to begin with, as I did it myself, stone by stone. The building would be thirty-six feet long, eighteen feet deep and two stories high. We always wanted a big house and this would give us plenty of room for our family. While Becky took care of the farm in Hatfield, I cut a dozen chestnut trees and dragged them back to the site with Jim Ford's two oxen, squared them, and placed them next to the stone foundation.

Luckily for me, a small garrison was being built at the bottom of the hill in order to protect the frontier. There had been reports of a roving band of Indians from Canada moving through New York and north of the Bay Colony. I questioned the wisdom of such an undertaking because there were only six men and their success against a group of Indians set on their destruction was doubtful. Once the two-story building of thick logs was complete, the men, a ragged group, didn't have much to do so each of them was looking for something besides ward all day, watch all night, and do road work, clearing the trees to widen the Bay Path. When I explained to them that I could not pay them, at least at that time, they agreed to help provided I give them meat since they didn't have enough to eat. Deer were abundant, as were moose, beaver, turkey, and pigeons. I had seen three bears, so I knew it wouldn't be difficult. I kept the possibility of the Indians being around in mind as I began each hunt. I went out as the sun rose the next morning, moving to the places I remembered and that brought back many memories, mostly good and a few bad. It seemed like it was just a short time ago that I was hunting there for the first time. After a little while, I saw movement fifty yards to my right. As I waited, a fat bear came waddling into view. It came rambling toward me until it was finally no more than thirty yards away. When I moved it stopped and looked at me and I killed it. The gunshot seemed to echo for several moments and I was sure it could be heard for miles. Since it was only a mile to the garrison, I left the dead bear and went to get help moving it. Before mid-morning, the bear was butchered. One of the men, Bill Hutchinson, agreed to give me two days labor, provided the commander, Captain Nicholson, allowed him. Nicholson gave his permission and he spent a few days himself helping me.

With the help of two or three of them every day, it took three weeks to complete the house. One thing that was different about this house from the first was that it did not have glass windows. We were lucky in 1674 when I built our house to get two windows from Mr. Pynchon in return for several days' labor. Thick oiled paper would have to do this time.

My arms ached and my back hurt. I was not getting any younger, and I felt it. Building the house and barn, even with help from the soldiers at the fort, was difficult, more so than I remembered from building it the first time twelve years earlier.

I went to get Becky and the children and, early one fine June morning with the sun barely above the horizon, we loaded the cart and left Hatfield, riding to the east to begin our next adventure. Becky drove the cart with Ephraim and Sarah while Sam and I herded the livestock.

At last, we arrived, and as we stood there, surveying the scene before us, many memories came back to me. I never thought we would be here again, not watching our sons and daughter live where we were almost killed.

After we unloaded, we rested and watched the sunset. The last rays of the setting sun were golden, lighting the western sky with a beautiful color. The grass was deep and rich, blowing in the gentle breeze. From a treetop, a robin sang its evening song and the air was soft, warm, and full of promise.

Becky was upset at not having a settled minister since she wanted the children to continue the religious practices they had in Hatfield. When we lived in Brookfield before, we had Younglove and though no one liked him, he was better than nothing, at least as far as Becky was concerned. I found it a bit humorous that when we had a minister we didn't like him and now that we wanted one we didn't have one. There is no way such a small community of five families could support a settled minister. We'd have to make do with our own religious efforts but it did not bother me since, like my father, I held less rigid views than many of the people of that time, my wife included. Becky called me a hypocrite more than once for going to Sabbath meeting every week while being less than zealous about it. To be honest, I would rather have gone hunting, but that was not possible. It was not unknown for people to be brought up before the magistrate on charges of profaning the Lord's Day by travelling from one place to another regardless of the distance. Going from Brookfield to Springfield could result in a fine of five shillings or more.

The lack of a minister stirred something in Becky because she spent a great deal of her time instructing the children in the Bible. Her frustration continued for years, as we did not make an attempt to get a minister until 1692 when we petitioned the governor and Great Council for assistance in obtaining a settled minister. She said many times that we must remember that the Sabbath is not the same as any other day. Not having a minister is not the way she was raised and she vowed not to raise our children that way. She would get angry with me when I pointed out that we had no choice but to get along without a minister because one would not be interested in settling in such a small, poor hamlet as ours.

For almost a year, our family and Jim Ford's family were the only settlers in the area. John Woolcot, Jr. came to live in Brookfield in April of 1687 and he was very welcome. He received a grant of land, supposedly belonging to his father and brother previously, though no record of their deeds were known. I came to learn that John had been one of the soldiers who came to the rescue of Brookfield as part of a special cavalry troop under the good Captain Prentice. He liked the area and decided that someday he would return. John's brother Joseph also came to Brookfield at the same time as his brother. Hezekiah Dickinson bought a part of Will Pritchard's land in 1688 and built a small hut, his dwelling before building the tavern.

There are certain moments where time seems to stand still and give us deep memories, things that stay with us our whole lives. One of those moments was a cold, November day the year we came back to Brookfield.

I was coming out of the barn when I saw the first few snowflakes drifting down slowly, one here and another there, and then it began softly. The light was just beginning to fade a bit and the air was calm, no hint of wind. The clouds were low and a slate gray color and it smelled like snow. There is always silence before the first snow. There is no noise of any kind. Even the animals were quiet. No one else was outside, so I found myself alone to enjoy this wonderful moment. Since I was a child, the first few minutes of the first snowfall always took my breath away with wonder. It was no different now. I stood there looking at the sky as the snowflakes multiplied. It fell into my hair and onto my face and clothes. I took a breath and smiled like a little child, happy at being by myself and feeling like a little boy again.

The first snow is always magical and after standing there a few minutes, I wanted to share this with my family. I went to the door and as I opened it, I saw Becky by the brightly burning fire, the light reflecting off the walls and ceiling, casting a warm glow over the room. I opened it further and saw Sam and Ephraim sitting on the bench talking quietly. Sarah was sitting on the floor playing with a doll I made her. None of them saw me as I entered.

"It's snowing! Come outside and see it!" I said, my voice full of childlike wonder. We all went out and stood there watching the flakes fall. None of us said a word. Becky came to me and I put my arm around her and pulled here close. I turned and saw Sam and Ephraim, happy and smiling, their sister standing in front of them. We stayed there for a while being covered in the fluffy, silent snow enjoying the beauty and silence.

Two years later, in the late afternoon of a beautiful early fall day, as I was coming out of the barn, I saw a large man appear from behind the house heading towards Becky who was picking the last of the apples from the small orchard we had. Something about him seemed familiar. I stood puzzled for a bit until he stopped.

"So what do you have to eat?" he bellowed. As he came closer, he rubbed his face with his big hands, a gesture I had seen many times, and one that brought a smile to my face.

Becky swung around and almost dropped her basket. "Ezekiel! How did you find us?" she asked, as she gave him a big hug.

"I went to Hatfield looking for you. They told me you were here."

He was a bit heavier and his hair was shorter than last time we saw him, his clothes were newer and fit him well and were clean, something I had never seen with him before.

"Where did you come from?" Becky asked putting her basket down.

"I been lots of places since I seen you last," he said putting his hands on his hips.

"Hello old friend. Did you make it to the ocean?" I asked shaking his hand. Sarah came to the door, looking out at this huge man. Sam and Ephraim were coming back from the field where they spent the day haying. They stopped short too as they came over the hill staring at Ezekiel.

"I did. Spent three years doing shore whaling on Cape Cod, fighting the mighty beasts who thought they were a match for me. A piece of blubber right off the whale is a fine bit of food," he said.

Becky made a face, disgusted at even the thought of eating such a thing. "When I got tired of that, I went to Boston for a bit but I left because they were too hard to get along with and we didn't agree on most anything."

I wondered whether he really left on his own or was run out for any one of several possible reasons.

He patted his stomach. "Enough of this chatter. What do you have to eat?"

Becky served a simple meal of stew and bread baked fresh that morning. It was good to see that his appetite had not changed. Wiping his mouth with a linen napkin, he turned to the children.

"Now," he said pointing at Sam, "I haven't seen you since you were three years old. And you," he said looking at

Ephraim, "were just a newborn when I left Springfield. We came back from Canada together we did, though you don't remember that being so young and all."

"Ezekiel," Becky said, "he was six months old when we came back."

"Well, I was right then wasn't I? And you," he said, reaching out toward Sarah, "I never laid eyes on you until a few minutes ago. You are as pretty as your mother and you boys are a bit more handsome than your father." He gave a big laugh at his own lopsided joke.

Sam reached for the remaining crust of bread, all that was left after Ezekiel was done with it, and looked at it for a moment before popping in into his mouth. "You'll have to bake more bread, Mama." Then he turned and looked at Ezekiel. "Lots more bread."

Ezekiel laughed at that jest.

During the time he was with us, Sam, Ephraim, and Sarah came to adore him for he played with them whenever they were not at their chores. He helped out, too, although he got in Becky's way most of the time. He had advice for her on almost everything from washing clothes to adding more spice to her cooking to the way she dried apples and pumpkins. There were a few times when she told me she was ready to hit him she was so mad.

One morning about two weeks after he arrived, Becky and Sarah were making soap, an art in and of itself. It is too easy to do it wrong and difficult to make it come out right. Ezekiel watched for a bit as he helped me with a few things outside the barn.

After seeing how Becky was getting along, he shook his shaggy head and lumbered over to her. “You’re putting in too little ash,” he said. “The soap will be like water. You need lots of ash to make it solid like it should be.” He put his hands on his hips and looked at her, waiting for her to take his advice. Sarah stood between them watching one then the other.

Without responding, Becky turned and went into the house and came out with a big iron spoon, almost two feet long. “Do you remember this?” she asked him, shoving it towards him.

He just folded his arms and stood there.

“Well, do you?”

“And why should I remember a spoon?” He scratched his head trying to think of a reason she would be asking him about a spoon. “Did I eat with it once?”

“This is the same spoon,” she said the anger and frustration rising in her voice, “that I threatened you with ten years ago. I didn’t hit you with it then, but I should have.” She drew back her arm, brandishing the spoon like a tomahawk and began advancing on him.

He threw back his head and let out a long, loud laugh.

She stopped and looked around at us watching her.

"Now Becky," he said, "there's no need to get upset. I was only trying to help, you know. If you were doing it right, I wouldn't had to even mention it to you."

She cocked her arm again and he stepped to her and took the spoon out of her hand. "You would have given me a good sized bruise, but you wouldn't have hurt me," he said. He gently took her hand and looked down at her. "I am sorry," he said, "I didn't mean to upset you."

She grabbed the spoon and stormed back into the house.

He stayed with us a month, sleeping in the barn and eating us out of food before moving on. I only saw him once again, many years later.

CHAPTER 25

My trouble with Mr. Pynchon started when Sir Edward Randolph arrived from England in May of 1686. King James II revoked the Massachusetts charter and sent Randolph to set up a new government. I will admit that I never saw any of the men involved in this new government, except Mr. Pynchon, but heard much from the travelers and soldiers that came through our small village. They passed on every bit of news they had for we were always interested in what was going on in other places near and far.

Randolph selected a new President, Joseph Dudley of Roxbury, himself as Secretary, and an appointed council of which Mr. Pynchon was one of eight men. This new government replaced the one in which Mr. Pynchon played a large role since he was an assistant to the governor and General Council for years, being an advisor to the men in power.

The supposed purpose of this drastic change was that unifying the colonies for defense and administrative control was regarded in Britain to be a thoughtful move and not a punitive measure. We thought differently. To us, it was a strong-armed attempt to take away our entire government and subject us to the rule of men across the ocean, who knew nothing of our situation and needs. It angered me and most everyone else.

When I mentioned my opinion to a few men when in Springfield once, I didn't know Mr. Pynchon was within earshot. He came over to me and touched me on the arm. "Jack, you don't know what you are talking about so just leave it alone. It is the way it should be. Do not question it … or me." He turned and walked away, leaving me slightly dumbfounded for he had never spoken to me that way before.

Things got worse when Sir Edmund Andros was named the new President of the Dominion of New England in 1688. He forbade any local assembly, except for the annual meeting, laid heavy taxes on us without hearing from any of the towns' selectmen, or any other officials for that matter, taxes that we could not pay. In his attempt to end what he called smuggling, that is, ships from the colony not paying a duty on certain items, he raised a ruckus. One of the most important was molasses. This caused a lack of rum, something that did not sit well with anyone. He ruled with an iron fist, requiring every order to be obeyed immediately and without question.

One of the things that caused the greatest distress among us was his support of the Church of England, something many of those that came to the colony from England wanted to escape. He was a military man and allowed the soldiers in Boston to engage in loose activity, drinking to excess and harassing women.

It was a cold, blustery, mid-October day in 1688 when Mr. Pynchon summoned Hezekiah Dickinson and me to his house. We were in Springfield at his request and went to the tavern when we were told he was busy with Sir Edmund Andros. Mr. Pynchon was his host while he was in Springfield, I am sure discussing the potential Indian dangers, since there was an attack in August on Northfield where six townspeople were killed. When we returned to Mr. Pynchon's house, he was alone in his business room.

"You are aware," he said as we entered, "that Sir Edmund Andros is here inspecting the area as he makes his way back to Boston from New York."

We said we understood that was the case.

"Good. I want you to accompany Sir Edmund to Brookfield. He and his guard will stay the night and be on their way early tomorrow morning."

I stood there, not saying a word, my anger at Sir Edmund building. Mr. Pynchon knew how I felt but was requiring me to escort the man I despised.

"Where will he stay?" I asked, having every intention to have as little to do with him as possible. "There is no tavern."

"He will stay with Hezekiah."

Hezekiah looked up in surprise. "With me, Sir?"

"Yes, I think it is best. Some of the soldiers will be staying with you and the rest will stay with Jack. Remember," he said, pointing his finger at us, "he represents the King." He put his hands together in front of his chest. "Now, you will leave in a short while. His horse is in the stable. See that it is ready for him."

I started out the of the room, a bit miffed at Mr. Pynchon's dismissive attitude toward me and many others. Over the past few years, he changed into a hard man, giving harsh orders for everything.

Hezekiah hesitated. "Your Worshipful, might we be paid for our services?"

Mr. Pynchon looked at Hezekiah, then at me, and nodded. "I will pay you seven shillings for your services. Now go."

During the ride to Brookfield that took the last part of the morning, all afternoon and sometime just after dusk, I came to learn what type of man Sir Edmund Andros really was. I took an instant disliking to the man. The feeling grew as we made our journey to Brookfield. I met many men in my life and there are only a few that I did not like; Sir Andros was one of them, on the same level as Gurdon Goodfield, the man to whom I was apprenticed when a boy.

He talked down to us the entire time, talking of his importance, meetings with the King, how he came to set things right since it was obvious to him that we in the Massachusetts Bay Colony and the other colonies around New England could not govern ourselves. He didn't stop speaking the entire trip, boring me with details of places and events that I did not care to hear about. When we were almost back to Brookfield, I began to feel sorry for Hezekiah for he would have to put up with this man's arrogance and demanding ways for the rest of the night.

Andros was not a good looking man by any means, his thin lips pressed tight, his long pointed nose always wrinkled as if he smelled something foul, his eyes a little too far apart and mean, able to stare down anyone with a haughty look. Even his nasally voice was bad, grating on you every time he spoke, which unfortunately was often. I think he talked to impress himself because I couldn't think of another reason he would talk so much.

When I got home, Becky and the children were waiting for me. They were surprised with the news of Sir Edmund being with us and more surprised when six soldiers came in. Becky made a large pot of mush in addition to the stew she had on the hearth. The soldiers were polite but drank most of our cider. They left very early the next morning.

The next two years were tumultuous with Sir Edmund's domination of the politics of the New England colonies causing rebellion. It led to a strong difference of opinion between Mr. Pynchon and me although I was careful not to be too forceful in expressing my opinion to him for while I may have earned his affection and good will over the years, I did not want to throw that away because it would mean a possible permanent rift in our friendship. He was my superior in all ways, in wealth, power, and influence. The man had corresponded with the King at times. The King did not know or care that I, a poor farmer, existed. Even though I thought the King was wrong in ordering the changes to our form of government and that Mr. Pynchon was wrong in supporting Andros, I kept my tongue in my head and shared my views only with Becky and few others.

When Andros forbade town meetings except for annual elections, there was something close to outright revolt from most people in the various colonies. Mr. Pynchon did not understand our reaction to this. He saw it that Andros was carrying out the King's orders and we did not have the right to question that. He believed that we should understand and accept Andros' mission.

While he was still a very important person in the colony, he was in the minority on this issue.

Sir Edmund's rule came to an abrupt end on April 18, 1689 when, as a result of his dictatorial rule, he was arrested by the men of Boston, put in chains, and carted off to prison. Governor Bradstreet was restored to his office. As far as I was concerned, it was a glorious day for all of New England.

CHAPTER 26

It was a mild spring day with a warm wind coming from the southwest. The final patches of snow had melted a week before. I was chopping wood behind the house when I stopped to wipe the sweat off my brow with my sleeve. I looked up and saw a man two hundred yards away walking towards me. I recognized something about him, the way he carried himself and his overall figure. The recognition stirred a memory from years ago when I had just come to Brookfield, then called Quaboag. Three Indians, two men and a boy, came through the small village within an hour of our arrival, Conkganasco and his son Ahanu, and Muttawmp. As he got closer, I realized it was Ahanu. I leaned my ax against the woodpile and wiped my face again as I watched him approach, coming at a pace that showed he was seeing memories of those days in his mind too. When he was ten feet away, he stopped. I found myself smiling. We stood looking at each other for a moment before shaking hands.

"Ahanu," I said.

"Jack," he replied.

"It is good to see you," I told him.

"It is good to see you too." He looked around and pointed to a spot a few hundred feet to our left, down the old town road. "Do you remember?" he asked.

"I do. That is where we first met the day I came to Quaboag eighteen years ago. You were with your father and Muttawmp. Much has happened in those years."

He had wrinkles on his face and hands, and he looked old and beaten, a man who's world came crashing down around him and never got any better.

Ahanu looked toward the house. I turned to see Becky step outside with Sarah following her. Becky was looking for me, and gave a start when she saw me standing with an Indian. She started toward us, wiping her hands on her apron, and put her hand on Sarah's shoulder as if protecting her from an unknown threat. As she got closer, I could see the recognition grow followed by a stern look with a clenched jaw and a spark in her eye replaced with a softer, more amiable look. Sarah came up and stood next to me, looking Ahanu up and down, inspecting every inch of him.

"It's Ahanu," I told Becky in case she did not recognize him.

"What are you doing here?" she asked him.

“I have been away from my home for too long and wanted to see it again. While I am here, I want to visit you. It has been a long time since we have seen each other. Not since the fight at the Peskeompscut.”

I nodded, understanding what would make a man come back to the place he knew as a young man when he knew he might not see it again.

Becky was unmoved. “I don’t see how your coming back is any good for you or us,” she said with a vehement tone.

Ahanu bowed his head, contemplating the meaning of her words. “Yes, I fought against you ten years ago. I was a young man then and thought that it was best for my people. Now I am older and have gained some wisdom and realize that it is better to talk than to fight.”

“I understand,” I told him. “I’ve had the same thoughts over the years.”

He gave a weak smile. I could tell from her face that Becky wavered in her opinion of him. She took her hands from Sarah’s shoulders and dropped them to her side. Sarah walked to Ahanu and looked up at him.

“Are you a good Indian?” she asked. “You know my father?”

Ahanu took a step forward and squatted down so that he was at eye level with her. "When your father first came to this village, he and I were friends. We would hunt and sometimes fish together. He and everyone here were friends with my people. We lived well together. Then trouble started and we fought against each other because we believed different things. It was a terrible war. Your father is a good man. Do not ever forget that. He saved several Indian children who were your age at a battle when others were killing them. I was there too, fighting against him. He sent me those children to protect them from harm, something no one else would have done." He stood and looked me in the eye. "That is only one of the reasons he is a good man."

"What children?" Sarah asked. "What did he do?"

"Your father," Ahanu began, "saved little boys and girls, some no older than you." He nodded at Sarah. "Those children are alive today and grew to be good people, all because of your father's courage on that horrible day."

Becky wrapped her arm inside mine and pulled me closer. She softened and invited him to stay with us for a while. He accepted and we sat in the sun on a bench outside the door, drinking cider.

"I heard of your escape from the Mohawk," Ahanu told me. "It was a brave but foolish thing to do. If they caught you, they would have tortured you for days before they killed you."

The memory of John Stuart being tortured and his screaming all night came back to me, shaking me, sending a shiver down my back. "But I wasn't caught," I told him, "and am here with my family."

"We all heard, as everyone in New England did, of your going to Canada and rescuing Becky and the others. That was a brave thing. The English do not know how to travel through the forest in winter, especially such a long way, but you did."

When we finished our cider, he and I walked down the road toward the brook, talking about how we changed over the years. I realized that it was good to see him and his visit made me think of things and people I had not thought of in a long time. Some memories jumped out to me. The day my aunt, uncle, and I came to Quaboag, the time he and I killed three wolves one day, the time he visited with the Wekapauge when I was down there to see Oota-dabun, one of the prettiest woman I ever knew who I was in love with before I knew what love really was. My thoughts were tinged with small fond memories and other larger painful ones. My thoughts were interrupted when I saw Sam and Ephraim coming toward us. Sam was big for his age and looked like my father. Ephraim was slender with a mischievous gleam in his eye. He looked like Becky's mother Elizabeth. I introduced them and we stood talking for a short time when Ahanu said he must go.

"Will we ever see each other again?" I asked.

He looked around at the fields and woods, seeing the past in his mind's eye.

"No, this is the last time we will ever see each other."

We stood without speaking. I looked at him closely, taking in his features. There was not much of the boy I knew in the man who stood before me. He looked around once more.

"Ohwakanoeenay netomp" he said, which means, "Goodbye, my friend" in the Nipmuck language.

"Ohwakanoeenay netomp," I replied.

I watched him walk away, heading toward the abandoned village on the lake where he grew up.

Becky and the children joined me. Ahanu looked back once but did not wave. Sarah lifted her little hand to him, waving her farewell. We stood in silence watching him go, Becky and I knowing that a part of our life was over.

"Goodbye!" Sarah called to him in a voice loud enough to carry through the stillness.

I found out the next year that Ahanu had been killed in Sudbury. No one knows why or by whom. His body was found near the river; he had been stabbed to death. He was a good man in his heart, a man who might have led the New England Indians, if things had gone differently. I mourned for him.

CHAPTER 27

We had been in Brookfield four years and since we still didn't have a minister, Becky insisted we on beginning to hold Sabbath services at Hezekiah's tavern. There were only eighteen of us and not everyone was able to attend each week. Some saw this as blasphemy but I understood, as did some of the others, that there are things that need to be done every day, and cannot be left undone. Becky shamed any of the men who did not attend by telling them they were not setting a good example for the children. Hezekiah always told her that they were not his children.

We took turns leading the service though Hezekiah never did, being a temperamental man, and wanting nothing to do with leading a service. He attended only because he thought he should. Jim Ford, John Woolcot, and I led most of the services. The children seemed somewhat interested but mostly indifferent as they did not have a minister's presence and influence over them as Becky and I did when we were their age. In a large prosperous village, the service would be all day with a time in the middle to eat. In Brookfield, it was not possible to keep those few people together for an entire day. Since we had no minister or constable to force us to go, we faced no repercussions, besides the sharp tongue of my wife berating those that did not go.

Food became a problem because the weather was difficult that year, with too much cold in the spring, too much heat in the summer, and too much rain in the fall. My crops of wheat and corn did not do well and made me worry that I would not be able to provide enough food for my family and animals. My worries grew as the corn began to wilt, the edges of the leaves turning brown and drooping toward the ground. The ground was dry and dust rose when you walked between the rows. The sky was clear, day after day, with not a cloud in sight. As July turned to August, I knew we would have a difficult winter and spring. The Indians always called late spring the starving time because it was when the food you stored for the winter was gone and there was very little you could take from the woods, especially if the snow was deep and did not allow you to hunt.

Becky and I walked through her garden looking at the beans, peas, and squash plants that were stunted and saw how small the vegetables were.

"We'll have trouble Jack. We need more food if we will make it through the winter."

I rubbed my neck with my hand and looked at the ground, the frustration growing inside me.

"I can hunt more so we can dry the meat. Sam and Ephraim can fish, we can smoke those. You and Sarah can pick berries and nuts later on. Or, I can go to Mr. Pynchon and get bags of beans, peas, and corn meal."

"Maybe we need to do all of that," she said a weary look on her face.

Her look reflected my feelings.

"I knew we would have some difficult times but I never thought we might not be able to feed ourselves, at least with the crops we grew. This isn't what I wanted for us."

"I know that," she said, putting her hand on my arm. "We will get through it like we've gotten through everything else."

I nodded and watched her walk away. I thought she was right, although there was a gnawing worry deep inside me that grew by the day, a fear that we would have to go back to Hatfield. The only good thing was that our neighbors were in the same situation. All of us shared with the other families when we had enough, which was not often.

The year turned even worse when Northfield was attacked two weeks later. A rider, Tom Powell, rode into our yard, his horse frothing at the mouth. I ran from the barn at hearing the pounding hooves.

"Indians attacked Northfield yesterday," he told us. "Killed six people. Pynchon said to be ready in case they attack here. Savages from up north, Canada, is what I heard."

Becky and Sarah came out of the house. Ephraim and Sam were down at the river fishing.

"What's wrong?" Becky asked.

"Northfield was attacked," I told her. "Six dead. They might come here."

The color drained from her face.

"No … please, my dear Lord no," she said. "Get in the house and stay there," she told Sarah, the urgency in her voice something I had not heard for a long time.

I turned to the rider. "Go tell the others and have them come here with their guns," I told him.

He sat there for a minute as if trying to understand what I had just told him.

"Go! Now!" I yelled.

Becky came to me, shaking from fear. "From Canada. He said they were from Canada … not again Jack, not like the last time. It won't happen again will it?"

I didn't know what to tell her. It was a factor in my thinking when deciding to move back to Brookfield, although a minor one since the Indians were defeated. I never considered that Indians from Canada might attack us.

"We can't worry about that now," I told her. "It doesn't matter where they are from but only that they might attack here. I'll get the boys." I dashed off to the river. When I returned Jim Ford, Joe and John Woolcot, and Hezekiah were waiting, along with the rider.

"How much powder and ball do each of you have?" I asked. From their answers, we realized we had only enough for a dozen shots for each man, not enough to defend ourselves.

"Tell Mr. Pynchon that we need men and ball and powder as soon as possible. Did you see Captain Nicholson at the fort?" I asked, wondering if he came straight to us.

"No, I came to warn you."

"Stop at the fort and let the captain know what happened and that we will all be there soon."

He jumped on his horse and looked at each of us. "I'll be in Springfield tonight. I'll tell him to hurry," he said before heading to the fort, then back to Springfield. His horse was tired from the ride out and would not be able to make good time on the way back.

"We'll be lucky if he gets there by tomorrow morning," Hezekiah said. "His horse is worn out. It can't go any faster than a trot and then not for long."

We all agreed and discussed our defenses.

"What should we do Jack? You've been through this more times than we have," Joe said.

"Everyone goes to the fort. It is the biggest, most fortified house. Bring food, buckets, all the powder and ball you have, and hurry."

"Why buckets?" John asked.

"For water," I said, "in case they try to burn us out."

With that, they ran back to their houses to gather their families and things.

I was glad the fort was there because if we had to go to Hezekiah's, it being the strongest house and easiest to defend, the thought of having to fight another battle against Indians wishing us dead, in the same spot as we did years ago, sent a shiver down my spine. I thought of Sam Prichard, who was caught by Matchitehew, an evil man if there ever was one, and beheaded with a tomahawk. They put his head on a pole in front of the tavern where we were trapped and left his body where he fell, in front of his parents' house, right where Hezekiah's tavern now stood. While I killed many Indians and took no pleasure in it, I admit that when I shot and killed Matchitehew, it gave me a sense of great satisfaction.

When we got to the fort, Captain Nicholson, commander of the six men at the fort, took charge of the situation, ensuring everyone was safe. He discussed the situation with us, and let us know that he asked Mr. Pynchon for supplies as they were running low. This is not what I wanted to hear because we had little also, and if there were twenty-eight people to feed, it would require us to hunt, which is something I did not want to do, especially with the possibility of Indians roaming nearby.

Two days later, six men with Tom Powell as their leader, arrived to strengthen our numbers. The Woolcots and Fords were planning to leave for Springfield, not willing to be caught in a deadly attack. The men brought us two pounds of powder and six pounds of ball. He also brought orders from Mr. Pynchon, the commander of all militia in the western colony, that we had to remain, except for any women or children that wished to leave. Joe began to fume at Mr. Pynchon's orders.

"Let *him* stay here," he said. "He's not facing a bunch of roaming savages, not when he is safe in his house in Springfield instead of out here with just a few men."

With the arrival of Powell's men, there were seventeen of us to defend the small fort, a number I was comfortable with. In

1675, there were only twelve of us against 400 Indians for three days. I liked our chances now a lot better than they were back then.

"Northfield is the only place that has been attacked," I told him. "That may be all they do. For all we know, they could be headed back north." I didn't really believe what I it was saying.

"For all we know, they are headed here now!" he shot back at me.

I couldn't argue with him.

We all gathered together in the small fort. Tom repeated Mr. Pynchon's orders and asked which women and children would be leaving. I looked at Becky and saw the indecision on her face.

"If you want to go, you can probably stay with Jeremiah and Mary," I told her.

"We are not going," she said vehemently. "I am not leaving you here. If there is trouble we will be together. I do not want to go to Springfield and find out something awful happened to you. You know what those savages would do if they caught you," she said, choking back a sob at the thought.

I knew all too well what would happen to me if I were captured by the Indians. Ben, Stephen, and I received frontier fame because of our exploits. If any of us were captured, we would be tortured, perhaps for days, before being killed in what would be a most horrible way. It was something I did not want to think about.

CHAPTER 28

Until July 27, the summer of 1693 was beautiful, the weather warm with enough rain to make the crops grow well but not oppressive. At mid-day the peace and prosperity of that fine summer was shattered as forty Indians descended on the eastern part of the settlement, killing six people and taking three captive. With the garrison manned by six soldiers and fifteen able-bodied men to protect the town, we felt secure as we could be. Attacks had happened in other places but none near us, not for a couple of years.

Joe Woolcot stopped as he came up to Sam, Ephraim and me working in the field near the road. He was out of out of breath and holding his four-year old crying daughter.

"Attacked! They attacked!"

"Indians?" Sam asked.

"Yes!" he started off toward the garrison. "They got my wife and children, they killed them."

"Who else?" I asked, turning toward the house.

"My brother and Mason. They had Mason's wife and little baby, and Dan, too, dragging them off…"

“Go!” I yelled. He ran at a gallop toward the garrison. They boys and I ran as fast as we could to the house. Becky and Sarah were making bread. We charged into the house, grabbed our guns and pouches filled with powder and ball. Ephraim slammed into the table, knocking it over, covering Sarah with flour.

“Indians attacked Woolcots,” I said. “We need to get to the garrison.”

Becky dropped the pan of bread she was about to put into the oven, grabbed Sarah and ran out the door.

The boys and I loaded our guns. “Go with them,” I told Ephraim. “Sam, you stay with me.”

Ephraim took off after Becky and Sarah, running down the road, his gun at the ready, prepared to protect his mother and sister.

“Grab those two buckets, fill them with the bag of peas and cornmeal … take the dried apples, too.” I flew up to the second floor, grabbed two large pieces of smoked meat, and came charging down the stairs. I grabbed a cotton bag from the table, dropped the meat into it, tossed the bag into a large bucket, picked up my gun and the bucket, and ran out the door. “Let’s go!” I yelled at Sam. We ran to the garrison as fast as we could.

When we got there, all was in turmoil. Sam Owen and John Lawrence, Joe and Tom's brother, came running when they heard the commotion. Joe was bent over trying to catch his breath, sucking in air, with his hands on his knees and his daughter at his feet.

"What happened?" Sam asked.

"They were attacked," I told them. "Joe said they got his wife and children, Mason and Tom, too. Took Mason's wife and baby, and Tom's son, too."

By this time, Joe was barely able to speak. "There were two or three Indians after my wife, so I snatched up Annie," he said, giving a quick nod to his daughter, "and started to run. I only went a few yards when bullets began whizzing by my head. I turned into the swamp on the other side of the stream and hid from them. They didn't look for me but took off, running north." Becky went and picked up Annie, holding her in her arms, motioning for Sarah to take the things they carried and follow her. They headed into the house.

"I'm going to see what happened," John said.

"You've no gun," Sam Owen said.

I thought of taking a gun from one of the soldiers but there were only five men stationed at the fort, a pitiful number which could not stand up to a strong attack. "We'll go with you," I told John, putting my hand on Sam's shoulder, giving him a gentle push out of the stockade. "Tell your mother we've gone with John," I said to Ephraim.

We were at John's house, not far from Woolcot's and Mason's, in short while. A few hundred yards before we got there, John walked faster, almost running up the slight hill. I hurried to him and pushed him down.

"Stay low," I told him, "we don't know if they are still around."

"Joe said there were at least forty," Sam said.

John did not respond but stayed still. After staying there for a few minutes and hearing no noise or seeing any of the attackers, we made our way toward John's house. When we were about halfway, we came upon Tom Lawrence, face down, the back of his head smashed in, his scalp missing, blood congealing on his neck, hundreds of flies crawling on his body. John stood there, looking at his younger brother. He turned away for a moment, looking up at the sky and shaking his head in disbelief.

"Let's see who else there is," I said.

We moved along, looking in all directions for signs of a struggle but found none. We came upon Joe Mason and his young son, William. The boy had been tomahawked in the throat and

Mason had been shot with half a dozen arrows, before being bludgeoned with a war club. A little further on, we came to Joe's house but saw no sign of his wife, his eight-year old boy or his seven-year old daughter. I went around the back of the house as Sam and John looked around the other side and front. I heard Sam retching and knew he found the bodies. As I came around the side of the house, I saw him on his knees throwing up. John's face was white and he was sweating, turning in a circle, looking everywhere except where the bodies lay. I went and looked at them. The little girl, a sweet-faced child, showed no sign of injury. I bent and turned her over, feeling the blood on my hand. She had been slashed in the stomach with a tomahawk, her guts slipping out of the wound. The side of the little boy's head was bruised and pushed in at the temple, his vacant eyes staring at me. I closed them with my fingers and moved the few feet to where their mother lay on her side, her arms outstretched as if to protect her children from the danger upon them. She had been shot with arrows in the chest and left leg, clubbed, and scalped. I stood and took a deep breath, looking at the house and fields, listening to the quiet. It seemed so wrong to hear no sound except a bird chirping here and there, with the death all around me.

Sam was still retching and John stood, his head hung low, trying to deal with what he had seen. After all the death I had seen in my life, the sight of these poor people's bodies hurt in such a brutal manner, I just couldn't stand it. I felt horrible, and death still moved me the way it had eighteen years ago, when I first killed a man.

I caught a glimpse of something out of the corner of my eye and when I looked I saw two Indians, 200 feet away, moving slowly toward us.

"We need to go back now. There are two Indians coming toward us. One has a bow, the other a gun. Do not run. Just walk away. I will be behind you."

They did what I told them and I walked backwards a ways, keeping my gun at the ready. The Indians stopped as we began to go. I turned every few yards to see if they were following us but they did not.

By the time we got back to the garrison, it was mid-afternoon. Becky and Sarah got Annie to stop crying and she fell asleep after we left on our terrible chore. John left for Springfield right away to inform Mr. Pynchon of the attack. A man named Cooke was on his way from Springfield to Boston and stopped at the garrison in the late morning. He went on his way just after noon and came upon the Indians at Woolcot's. Up to that time, he told us, he had not heard or seen anything out of the ordinary. He was within a 100 yards of the house when he saw the Indians filling the entire yard. He turned his horse with the intention of sneaking back to the garrison but was spotted for bullets began flying around him. He made it back safe and stayed only a short while before he went back to Springfield, afraid of staying because there were so few men to defend it. He said he would tell Mr. Pynchon what he saw, which would add to what John would be able to tell Mr. Pynchon.

Joe came to me, upset as a man would be in his situation.

"We have to go get them. We can't leave them out there. We need to bury them."

"There's nothing we can do right now," I told him.

The others in the garrison began to gather around us.

"They are my wife and children, Mason, his boy and Tom, lying dead in the open. Animals will get to them. We need to bury them."

I felt my stomach tighten, knowing what needed to be done but not being able to do it.

"We can't Joe, not now. We don't know how many Indians there are, or where they are. John, Sam, and I may have been lucky that the two we saw didn't follow us. Maybe they are all that is left and the rest may be gone. We don't know and, with so few men, we can't risk more of us being killed or captured. Mr. Pynchon will send soldiers out tonight, I know he will. They will be here tomorrow morning then we will take care of them. If we went now it would be dark before we get the graves dug."

He stood motionless, staring at the ground, and realizing that I was right.

Sam Owen stood off to one side and I walked over to him.

"Ephraim and I brought food over, beer and cider too, so we have enough for all of us, at least for a while," he said.

"How long is a while?"

"Three, maybe four days. Enough to last until soldiers get here."

It was a long night, each and every one of us, except Sarah and Annie, awake the whole night through. From my experience, I knew that if the Indians were to attack, it would be before dawn, when most people were asleep. It was the best time to catch an enemy unaware. There was no moon and heavy clouds rolled in, blotting out the stars. The night was very dark, adding to the heightened nervousness we felt. Every noise was loud, each sounded like footsteps or voices. We wore ourselves out imagining the worst.

By the middle of the next afternoon, relief appeared with the arrival of Captain Thomas Colton and twenty-eight men. The captain immediately ordered sixteen of his men to stay at the garrison, and the rest to go to Woolcot's in search of Indians. Sam Owen, Henry Gilbert, and I went with the captain's men. We buried the dead in a small piece of ground behind Woolcot's. We made a short scout, seeing the trail made by the attackers, heading north, back to their hiding places. We knew where to begin our search the next morning. By the time we got back to the garrison, it was sundown. Another group of twenty soldiers from Hadley and Northampton, two of whom I knew, arrived at the garrison while we were on our sorrowful errand.

We weren't back more than an hour when one of the soldiers came pelting into the garrison with the news that he had seen six Indians on the hill behind the garrison. Several of us grabbed our guns and made our way on foot to the place where he saw them. The long grass was pushed aside where the Indian walked; it was an easy track to see and follow. From the look of it, there were several of them. I looked around but saw no one. There were trees at the back of the field and, with the light growing dusky, they would have been impossible to see. It was too dark to proceed and the captain decided not to attempt to pursue the Indians that night.

After everyone ate, several of us went to talk with the captain about his plans for finding those responsible for the deaths and capture of our neighbors and friends.

"We'll start out early with forty men to find signs of where the savages went and begin to track them down. I want to find them tomorrow. I don't care how far we have to travel, I don't want them to get far ahead of us. There have been too many captives taken to Canada and I don't want these to end up there."

You're Jack Parker," he said.

"I am."

"I've heard of your exploits. You've had quite a bit of experience in these matters and have been successful."

"I never thought of myself as having had exploits. To me, it was doing what needed to be done at the time. The last time I had any exploits was years ago."

"Will you come with us? I could use someone with your experience."

"Yes, I will."

Sam Owen and Henry Gilbert looked at each other, then at the captain and me.

"We need to figure out if we should stay here or leave," Henry said.

Sam Owens' wife Anna came in, followed by Becky. They looked troubled.

"That is what we want to talk about," Anna said.

"Do you think you should leave?" I asked.

"Me?" she asked. "I wonder if we should all leave, everyone but Captain Colton and his men."

We all looked at each other, the question hanging in the air.

"I think we should leave," Anna said. "We would be safer in Springfield than here."

"Yes, but we can't just leave everything we worked so hard for … the Indians could come back and burn it all," Henry replied.

"And what happens to the travelers when they come through? Where will they stay or eat? They can't go from Marlborough to Springfield in a day. If we abandon what little we have, it will affect more than just us."

"If we stay, we could get killed," Becky said.

"We should ask Mr. Pynchon what he thinks. He understands the situation better than we do," I said.

Everyone agreed.

"I will put it in my letter," the captain said. He looked at me. "Be ready to go before dawn." With that, he left to speak to his men, making sure they were prepared. Having been through this before, I knew that the next day or two would be very long.

Becky was not happy when I told her I was going.

"Why?" she asked. "Why do you have to go? There are almost sixty soldiers here now. Let them go. You've done enough. There's no need of you going."

"I want to. I want to find the savages who did this. Captain Colton asked that I go because I have more experience with this than he or any of his men."

She shot me an angry look.

"I'm going," I told her. "We leave before dawn. We should be back in two or three days."

"I want to go too," Sam said.

"No," Becky said as though hers was the final word.

"Why do you want to go?" I asked him.

"It doesn't matter why, he is not going," she said.

Sam gave me a pleading look.

"No, Sam, stay here. Your mother is right, it may be dangerous out there, and I do not want to come home and tell your mother that her oldest son is dead."

His head snapped up at that.

"Besides, you are needed here with your brother and the others to help guard the garrison."

He was disappointed but understood.

"Both of you," I said to Sam and Ephraim, "get your gun, powder, and ball and go see the captain. He will give you some work to do."

Sam came back a few minutes later with the news that the captain wanted him to take a message to Mr. Pynchon in the morning and asked if he could go. I told him yes he could, to be on his way when the rest of us left, to ride fast, and stay safe. By the look Becky gave me, I could tell she did not approve but I knew it was important for Sam to help in any way he could.

The next morning, a bleak and wet Saturday, Sam set off before the rest of us were ready to go, with most of the land still in semi-darkness, that time when there is no color to objects but just shades of gray. As I watched him leave, I thought of my own time riding as a messenger for Mr. Pynchon.

As we started to leave the garrison, it began pouring rain, so hard it was difficult to see more than 100 feet ahead. The captain decided to wait until the rain slowed before starting out. We left around mid-morning when the rain let up and the sky began to clear. We made our way to Woolcot's, picked up the trail and move along, two rows of twenty-five riders. The track was wide and easy to follow; they made no effort to conceal their number or direction. We were making good progress, thinking we were gaining on them but finding no evidence of their stopping or resting. Eventually, toward late afternoon, we found Mason's infant. It had been flung against the base of a tree. We made a halt and buried it a short distance from the tree in a small field. All of us were glum, the thought of a month-old baby being killed so ruthlessly and for no purpose, gnawing at us. We continued on, and after about ten miles as night began to fall, we came upon the remains of Henry Gilbert's horse that had been taken in the attack to carry their goods. It had been killed and a good part of it eaten, giving us an indication of the number of Indians we were chasing. We also found the drum taken from Joe Lawrence's house that was supposed to be used to sound an alarm in case of an attack.

The next morning we were on the march very early when there was just enough light to see. The weather became hot and humid and slowed our progress because of the sweat and flies on both the horses and us. We couldn't push the horses too far too fast and rested more than we wanted. Another ten miles on, we came to the shore of a large pond where we found the remains of another horse, one of Mason's, next to a still warm fire, tendrils of smoke rising like whispers in the humid air. Knowing we were getting closer, we pushed on hard, hoping to make up any distance. We ran into problems by mid-day with some of the horses going lame and the way choked with brush. No matter which way we went, the heavy brush surrounded us, closing in on each man as he passed through it. We continued making our way as best we could, getting slashed in the face and arms with branches. The blood drew mosquitoes, which swarmed on us. We were soon in a swamp that got deeper the further on we went. We turned to the east, hoping to get to a small hill we could see. Finally, we made it there by mid-afternoon. The ground became full of stones, large and small, some in layers and others in the open. It made going very slow and we couldn't stop since we were running out of sunlight.

It soon became clear that we would have to continue on foot. The captain arranged for some of the men to keep the horses and for the others who wouldn't be able to travel quickly on foot, owing to age or infirmity, to stay behind while the rest of us moved ahead. Those that didn't march with us would bring the horses along as best they could. We took off anything that would weight us down—coats and victuals among them—and made six or seven miles, dragging ourselves through shrubs and picker bushes, which scratched across our already cut faces and arms, drawing lines of blood, the cuts stinging as the sweat ran into them.

The falling darkness slowed our pace. After a short while, the captain called a halt so we could rest for a few hours.

I dozed on and off and after what seemed like only a few minutes, I saw a very faint glow of sunrise in the eastern sky.

It was a muggy Sunday morning as we pressed on faster, making the best use of the cover of low light as we could. Twenty-three of us tried to make as little noise as possible so that, if the Indians were near us, we would not alarm them.

After about two miles, we approached a small hill that was enclosed in more shrubs and heavy brush. As we got closer, we smelled the faint odor of smoke and knew we were near the enemy. Moving very slowly, not causing so much as a whisper of noise, we came upon their encampment not more than three rods ahead. The small hill ran around on three sides, with the middle lower than the sides, forming a cup shaped area. I spotted Mrs. Mason on the far side, sleeping between two Indians, and motioned to the captain. He nodded, indicating he had seen her too. We made our way around the rim, each man taking a spot from which to fire. Men were still coming up when the captain gave the order to fire.

The Indians sprang up and ran around in confusion, trying to grab their weapons and run away but were stopped for a moment as four of their number fell from our shots. One picked up a war club and intended to bring it down on the Lawrence boy. I fired, hitting him square in the chest, dropping him to the ground in an instant. The rest of the men came running up, firing as they reached the spot. One Indian was killed by a shot and another that was wounded was finished off by one of our men with a hatchet, and the rest, about twenty of them, some wounded and bleeding, tore off into the bushes so that they had no time to gather any of their belongings or weapons. The bushes were so thick that once the Indians were gone, we couldn't see or hear them. There was a lot of blood on several of the bushes indicating severe wounds. Knowing from past experience, those Indians went off somewhere to die.

We captured nine guns, twenty hatchets, four long knives, sixteen or eighteen horns of powder, and two small bark kegs full, about two pounds in each keg. There were other items: four bows, a few quivers of arrows, several war clubs, a cooking pot, and the like that we destroyed before we left.

The men with the horses were only two miles behind us, which was good because we were hungry, tired, and sore from our exertions. Dan Lawrence was amazed at our rescue of them, and tired from hunger, he said little until the afternoon. Mrs. Mason, a very intelligent woman, gave us a full account of what happened.

There were three that spoke good English, one of them the leader who called himself Captain John. He told her that most of them were from Canada and that others were from Pemaquid and planned to attack Lancaster but two of their scouts reported the village appeared to be well defended and people on alert. Being strangers to the area, they didn't know what to do but wandered a bit looking for a place to attack. They were on a high hill some miles away when one of them climbed a tall tree and saw a house in the distance that, from the description, must have been Lawrence's. They had been around Brookfield for six days, watching and waiting for an opportunity to strike.

She related that when they attacked, the Indians told Tom Lawrence they would spare his life if he told them how many men were at the garrison. He told them six. They knocked him down with a tomahawk blow, and when he tried to defend himself by raising his arms to fend off a blow, his hand was cut off from a tomahawk. As he lay there bleeding, blood gushing from his arm, one Indian knelt over him and scalped him. He lay there yelling for help, knowing he was about to die.

She said that when one of them came for her, she began to beat him with her hands and told them that if she had a weapon she would cut them to pieces. That cause them to disagree over whether to take her with them or not. She told us that if she had had a weapon she knew she could have escaped. They took the Lawrence boy to carry their burden but would kill him when they reached their canoes, which were two days from where we found them.

She said they would go on a great lake like the sea for five or six days and would soon be home to Canada. That description caused me to think back to the trek to Canada and the great lake we followed; it must be the same one. She said they boasted that they said they did not care if 200 English came after them, that they could defend themselves well.

We travelled as far as we could that day, no more than fifteen miles through the difficult terrain with many lame horses. We stopped before sunset and were up before dawn. We made it back to Brookfield by the middle of the next afternoon. We had been gone only four days but it felt like it was much longer.

All the women and children were gone. While we were away, Mr. Pynchon ordered that all the women and children be brought to Springfield. From what I heard, Becky put up quite a stink but went when the other women agreed to go for the sake of the children. Her stubbornness was short lived because they were back in Brookfield two days after we returned.

Mr. Pynchon arrived a week later to see the state of the village. He stayed for two days and I was on my way to Owens tavern when I saw him and his escort of four soldiers arrive. By the time I got there, he was already inside. As I walked into the dark room, I saw him talking to Sam Owen. As usual, he didn't wait to get down to the business at hand.

"So," he said, pulling out a chair, "people want to leave. Is that right Sam?"

Sam nodded and noticed me standing in the doorway. "Jack," he said, "his Worshipfulness was just asking about how people feel about staying or leaving."

"Jack," Mr. Pynchon said, "Captain Colton told me of your service to him, how valuable it was to have someone with your experience in fighting these savages."

I sat down heavily in a chair across from him.

"It was a long few days but we were able to get Mrs. Mason and Dan Lawrence back." Sam brought over mugs of cider for both of us and took one for himself. He settled himself next to me but didn't sit for long as other men began coming in after hearing of Mr. Pynchon's arrival.

John Lawrence was one of them. "Good afternoon, Your Worshipfulness."

After everyone else paid their respects to Mr. Pynchon, we gathered around his table.

"So," Mr. Pynchon began. "Do you want to leave or stay?"

Sam and I exchanged looks, having talked about this the previous afternoon.

John Lawrence looked around at the others before he began. "We are of two minds, Sir. If we stay, we run a great risk of being attacked again and everything could be destroyed, including all of us."

"But, on the other hand," Sam added, "there are still many travelers and if we leave, they will have no place to stay. We will be abandoning the whole area to the Indians. Will we all go to Springfield?"

"There is no other place between Marlborough and Springfield," Henry Gilbert pointed out, "and the trip cannot be made in one day. If we leave, it will affect the entire colony, not just us."

Mr. Pynchon listened to all of the others speak their minds, all offering similar opinions, and then he turned to me. "You have not said anything. What do you think we should do?"

I looked around at my fellow settlers.

"I think we have to stay. Leaving here would be the worst thing we could do. The only way to establish a village is to show that it is a permanent settlement, not something that will be abandoned at the first sign of major trouble. We can't do like we did eighteen years ago. If we do, we should give up our efforts to ever settle this place again."

He held my gaze for a moment before looking at the others.

"I will come and meet with each of you and the others who aren't here tomorrow and the next day."

By the end of the following day, Mr. Pynchon decided that, based on all he heard, it was best for us to stay. However, he also said if anyone wanted to leave, he would understand, but would rather we didn't.

CHAPTER 29

The next ten years passed quickly. The little village began to grow before our eyes. Stephen bought Hezekiah's land, intending to open a tavern, which he did, but not until 1696. Henry Gilbert was granted a license for a tavern. His was right across the road from Sam Owens and was needed because the number of people traveling on the Bay Path seemed to increase every week.

Sam and his wife Ann gave us our first grandchild, Thomas. He was born in a howling blizzard in December 1695. Ephraim and his wife Jane gave us our second grandchild, a beautiful little girl they named Elizabeth, followed by twin boys, John and Nathaniel, a year and a half later. Sam and Ann had two more children, both girls, Alice and Mary, within three years.

Sarah fell in love and married Henry Deacon, a soldier at the fort. Henry was originally from Suffield and we were afraid they would move there, but our fears were unfounded. Henry was granted land in the western portion of the village past the Great Field. In March of 1703 they had a boy, Jeremiah, a mischievous lad from the start.

By the end of 1703, we had seven grandchildren surrounding us, making life a bit easier for, and, while the village grew as more people came in, it was still a difficult existence.

There were continuing threats throughout New England from various bands of Indians who were being stirred up by the French. A peace treaty was signed with the Iroquois to keep them from allying with the French in the future.

A planked bridge with stone abutments over Coy Brook was built by Sam Owen and Henry Gilbert. It was something that had been talked about for years. Richard Coy attempted it but it was a narrow, rickety footbridge that was only wide enough for one person and would not support a horse.

The middle of May 1695 was a sad time for me. Bubs, my long-serving, wonderful horse died at the age of thirty. He was worn out after many years of being my faithful partner and friend. Bubs was the living thing I knew the longest other than my aunt Charity and uncle Josiah.

Bubs was my last connection to my father and to my home in Ipswich. I remember when my father got him. He took me through many years of fighting and served me well, never once letting me down. I rode him all over when I was a messenger for Mr. Pynchon, he carried me back to Brookfield after the Indian ambush in 1675 when we thought the village had been destroyed. I remember him flying over the ground, galloping so fast I thought his heart would burst, to get us back to our home. During the three-day siege, the Indians killed most of the animals, including horses. After the siege, I couldn't find Bubs and thought they had got him, but he came stumbling back from the woods after being gone almost a week, worse for the wear.

I buried him in a special spot on our land, a spot that faced north where you could see the hills a few miles away. It was a good view of the valley and I knew he would have liked it. In my mind and heart, I knew Bubs would stand looking proudly across the valley, ears up, shoulders straight, a young, strong horse full of life and vigor. While we know and understand that death is the last part of life, I will admit that I cried when he died and after I buried him. I did it alone and it took me all day but I felt that I needed to do it without anyone's help. Bubs was a member of our family and I would do no less for him than anyone else.

Many people thought I was crazy to be going through all the hard work to bury a horse, since many times farm animals were either butchered and eaten or dragged to a secluded spot and left for the wolves. I wouldn't even consider either of those ideas for Bubs.

Stephen and his family were startled by the news, right after they arrived, that their daughter Captivity, the same one born in Canada, was pregnant by Will Barnes, a young man from Brookfield. She had the baby several months later. This was a grievous situation because a bastard child had no legal rights and was a shame for both families. Will was a bit shiftless, always looking for a way to get out of whatever he was supposed to be doing. Rather than allowing Will to marry his daughter, since Will was not a man Stephen wanted in his family, he took Will to the court in Northampton to seek support. Will was fined fifteen pounds upon the admission of his fornication and ordered to give up all rights to the child. It was not the way Stephen wanted to begin his life in Brookfield.

Since the threat of Indian attacks came and went, the decision was made by the Prudential Committee that the garrison was to be maintained from June 1 to November under the impression that the Indians would not be searching for a place to attack unless there was good cover. This proved to be a false assumption a few years later, one with deadly consequences.

We were honored by the arrival of Judge Samuel Sewall, Associate Justice of the Superior Court of Judicature for the Province of Massachusetts. He rode into Brookfield in the pouring rain with an escort of ten soldiers, showing his importance in the affairs of the Province. He heard a case in Springfield of Sarah Smith, a woman of whom some of us knew, an unstable woman who suffered from the devil's influence. She murdered her fourteen year old illegitimate daughter, one of two she had by different men, by stabbing the girl as she slept. She confessed to her sin both times, promised to repent, and was given fifteen lashes. Both of the fathers left before it was known she was pregnant and she either did not know or refused to tell who they were. The crime was horrific and Judge Sewall sentenced her to death by hanging.

He was a short, pudgy man with stern features. Several of us went to Owen's tavern to see him and found him cordial and interested in the state of our little settlement. He asked question after question on everything from the state of Indian affairs to the poor crops we were suffering to the possibility of expanding the settlement with many additional families. His curiosity knew no end. He told us of his travels from Springfield to Northampton, talking at length about what a paradise the area was, and the opportunity it offered. After two hours with him, we left wishing him a safe and pleasant trip back to Boston.

Amy Pynchon, always a frail woman, died in January 1699 at the age of 74. She was a good woman, always pleasant and welcoming to Becky and me. She had bouts of ill health over the years, and Mr. Pynchon sought treatments from John Winthrop, Jr., governor of the Connecticut Colony, a long-time friend of his. The next time I was in Springfield I visited with Mr. Pynchon, expressing our sympathies for her death.

CHAPTER 30

On a cold, gray mid-January afternoon in 1703, a rider came to the house with the message that Mr. Pynchon was sick and his son John, Jr. wanted me to be notified. I knew in my heart that if I didn't go, I would regret it the rest of my days and if I went, that it would be the last time I saw Mr. Pynchon. I bundled up for the raw wind blowing while Ephraim saddled the horse. I gave Becky a kiss and we looked at each other, the acknowledgment of our own mortality passing between us. We understood that someday, hopefully later rather than sooner, we would be gone too. I wrapped my arms around her and pulled her tight. Sarah had been to the well and was just coming in the door as I was going out. I stopped and kissed her on the forehead. I took the horse from Ephraim and was on my way, hoping to get to Springfield before the snow, which had been coming down in fits and starts all day, began coming down hard.

As I rode on, I thought of the many other times I made this same trip, always with a lighter heart. The footing was not good and the wind picked up, blowing in gusts, both making me realize it was going to be a long, slow, cold trip.

When I finally got there, I was so cold I was shaking. I went into the tavern and stood near the fire, putting in a couple more logs to build it up. There was some stew in a pot on the hearth that smelled wonderful. Just as I thought about waking Jeremiah, he came out of their room, the same one in which Sam was born, a grease lamp in his hand.

"Who is it?" he asked squinting to see who was standing in the darkness.

"It's Jack," I said softly not wanting to disturb anyone else.

He sat at the table next to the fireplace and motioned for me to join him.

"You're cold," he said.

"Freezing is more like it. May I have some of that stew?"

"Of course you can," he said as began rummaging around for a trencher and spoon. "I was planning on serving it for breakfast but there will be plenty."

I finally stopped shivering and slowly began to warm up. I was heated from the outside by the fire and from the inside by the stew.

Jeremiah leaned forward, putting his elbows on the table. "You're here for Mr. Pynchon," he said more as a statement than a question.

"Yes," I said between spoonfuls. "A rider came through this afternoon. I left home right after he left for Marlborough."

He nodded slowly. "He's not been well for quite a while, being sick then getting better only to fall back worse than he was. He will be gone soon."

The matter-of-fact way he said this, while true, startled me. While I knew it was so, it was beginning to sink in that the man I had known for almost thirty-five years was about to be gone from my life.

"I have no bed to give you," Jeremiah said as he heaved himself up from the table.

"I'll sleep on the floor," I said. "As long as I'm warm, I don't care where I sleep."

He left me without a word.

As I lay there, I thought about Mr. Pynchon. Memories were running through my mind one after another: meeting him in Boston when I was a fourteen year old apprentice, being one of his messengers after Charity, Josiah and I came to Quaboag, him marrying Becky and me, his trying to ransom me from the Mohawk, our long discussion about going back to Brookfield, and the trouble Sir Andros brought about. We did not always see eye to eye, but we got along well. I remembered wondering in the first couple of years I knew him, why such an important and powerful man took such an interest in a lowly boy like me.

Before I knew it, I was being nudged awake by someone's boot. I looked up and saw Mary, her heavy body topped with a head of long gray hair tucked under a white cap.

"Get up Jack. I need to get at the fire. Go sleep on a bench if you want."

I dragged myself to a bench that was against the wall and dropped onto the seat, curling up for a bit more sleep. I was not to get it because, within a few minutes, a man came with word that Mr. Pynchon was failing. I rubbed my eyes, adjusted my clothes, and made my way quickly to his home. There were several other people in the large room to the left of the main door. I greeted those I knew.

Mr. Pynchon's oldest son John, a successful merchant in Boston who moved to Springfield to take over his father's work over the last couple of years, noticed my arrival. "Jack, I am glad you could come. My father asked about you yesterday."

"Will I be able to see him?"

"Yes, of course, in little while. Someone will come to get you."

John was a few years older than I was and I didn't know him well. He was in England for quite a few years before coming back to begin working with his father.

I walked to the window and saw a faint gray in the eastern sky, the sun making its way to the horizon. My stomach rumbled as I realized I had nothing to eat since yesterday noon except two bowls of stew. I made my way to the kitchen and asked one of the servants for some bread. As I finished it, another servant came hurrying toward me, telling me that I should go see Mr. Pynchon.

He was propped up in bed with pillows behind him and blankets on top of him. His skin was gray, his face unshaven, and his hair fell around his face. There was a dry, sour smell of death in the room. His head hung forward as if he were sleeping. I looked at Doctor Hastings standing behind me and he made a motion with his hand for me to approach Mr. Pynchon. I walked to the side of the bed, not sure what to do.

"Mr. Pynchon, Sir?" I said. He did not respond. "Mr. Pynchon?" I repeated a bit louder, "it's me, Jack Parker."

He slowly raised his head and looked at me with tired, weary eyes. He tried to sit up but was not able to so I knelt next to the bed. "I came to see you."

He gave the slightest hint of a smile.

"You were a boy when I first met you," he rasped in a voice just above a whisper. "Now you are a man with a fine family and farm. That's what you told me you wanted. The things you did showed everyone what a fine man you are. You give glory to God."

Such a statement was not expected, not by me from a man on his deathbed.

"You have been a protector and friend, and I could not have asked for more," I told him. "You do not know how much you changed my life over the last thirty-five years, all from that simple errand Goodfield sent me on all those years ago."

He nodded and his lips moved but no sound came out. I reached out and put my hand on his, a simple sign of affection. His eyes opened and he gave me a clear, knowing look. I felt a slight pressure from his hand. My heart began to hurt as the thoughts of all this man meant came to me. I squeezed his hand and let it go.

With tears in my eyes, I began to leave but before I went, I turned and looked upon this wonderful man who made the western Bay Colony what it was. A once vibrant, powerful man was now a weak shell of who he was, an old man now on the edge of death. I sighed, hung my head, wiped my eyes, and made my way back to the tavern where I sat alone at a table near the fire.

Without my asking, Mary brought me a mug of beer and a big hunk of bread and cheese. I ate without tasting it, without really knowing what I was doing. I was lost in thought. Several other men came in, all quiet and subdued, knowing that Mr. Pynchon would be gone soon, waiting for the news together.

The sun had been up for a while when a young man, one of those I had seen in the rooms at Pynchon's, came into the tavern. We all turned toward him. He stopped and looked around, his hands squeezing the hat he was holding.

"He's gone," was all he said before turning and walking out the door. The room was quiet, each of us lost in our own thoughts.

I stayed for a short time before making my way back home. I spent most of my time on the way back thinking about Mr. Pynchon. He was in public service for over fifty years, both to the colony and to those of us in the western bay. He managed the military and civilian affairs of the area, was an assistant to the Great and General Court, and a successful merchant and trader. I knew we would feel the effect of his death for a long time to come. I thought of all he meant to me and could only imagine what my life would have become had I not met Mr. John Pynchon.

Becky was upset when I told her, even though she knew it was the news I would bring home with me. I was very tired but we talked for a long time in front of the fire while she made candles and I carved hinges for the small door on the barn. We reminisced about Mr. Pynchon and the affect he had on us. By the time we were done talking, she was falling asleep and I was not far behind her. It had been a very long and difficult day but as you get older you realize death is just a part of life.

CHAPTER 31

There was a harsh nip in the air as the cold promised the first frost. The sweet scent of dying leaves floated on the breeze. I had taken corn to be milled in Springfield the day before and was on my way back. The road was rough from use and the ground was worn down to hard gray rock that bounced the cart every couple of rods, or at least it seemed like it, and heavy summer rains had washed away small parts of it. Even with the bad travelling, I made it home by late afternoon, having left at first light.

I pulled up in front of the house and was starting to take the bushels out of the cart when I heard the door open and saw a man standing there. Confused at first, since I couldn't understand why a strange man would be standing in the doorway of my house, until I heard his booming voice.

"Let me give you a hand with that," Ezekiel said.

When he came out into the yard, he looked like a different man than the one I knew. He lost weight and was as slim as he ever could be. His hair and beard were almost all gray, his shoulders drooped a bit, and he had a less mischievous air about him. He looked smaller than I remembered.

I shook his hand and couldn't help but smile. "It is always a pleasant surprise when you show up."

"Well, I got the urge to see you and Becky again. I've been thinking of the two of you lately and decided it was high time I came to visit."

"I am glad you did. It's been a few years since we saw you last."

"A few years?" he bellowed, his voice still as strong and powerful as ever. "It's been almost fourteen years, Jack! I didn't know if you were still alive. For all I know you might have been killed in all the Indian attacks."

I stood looking at him and realized he was a true friend. When he arrived, it felt like he never left. He would pick up right where he left off so it was as if he was gone for only a week, not so many years. As we brought the corn in, I told him all that had happened since his last visit.

"Stephen runs the tavern over there. Has been here seven years now."

"Stephen? Jennings? Our Stephen?"

I smiled at his use of "our" like we had Stephen all to ourselves. "Yes, our Stephen. He's doing well, too. We'll go see him after we eat."

When I went in I gave Becky a hug and kiss on the forehead. “I missed you. Even though we’ve been married for twenty-eight years now, I still miss you even when I am away just a night.”

She gave me a smile that to me was still as pretty as it once had been, even though she lost three teeth in the last year, something that affected all of us as we got older.

“He was waiting when I got back from Owen’s,” she said, giving Ezekiel a smile.

“I just got here,” he said. “If I had to wait, I would have gone to the tavern. Jack said Stephen owns it.”

“He does,” she said.

“Well let’s eat so I can go see him.”

I looked at Becky and smiled as we watched him take a seat and begin to spoon out beans onto his plate just like he was one of the family, which he was in many ways.

We got to the tavern just after dark and a few men were straggling their way there. I introduced Ezekiel to them as we made our way. When we walked in, Stephen was at the bar, a small enclosure at the back of the room.

The moment Ezekiel saw him he gave out a yell. “Stephen! It’s good to see you!”

I could tell from the squinting of his eyes, Stephen was not sure who was hollering at him.

"It's Ezekiel," I said, walking to the bar.

"Ezekiel Huff?" Stephen asked after a pause.

"Yes, it's me," Ezekiel said. "How many times do you have to be told?"

Stephen came out and looked Ezekiel up and down not recognizing the man before him as the same that traveled to Canada and back with us.

"I didn't recognize you," he said.

"Well?" Ezekiel asked.

"Well what?" Stephen answered.

"Can a man get a drink around here?"

The two men broke out in laughter and shook hands. "Of course you can. Let me get you something. Cider?"

"Cider is for the old men and women, or if it is a really hot day, which it isn't."

"Some rum then?" Stephen said with a glint in his eye.

"That's more like it." I said.

Ezekiel leaned towards Stephen.

"Will it help with the cost if I tell you I know the owner?" he asked breaking into a loud guffaw, amused at his own wit. “I don’t have a lot of coin on me. I had three pieces of eight last week but I spent it. Of course, I could work it off.”

Stephen looked at me and grinned.

“If I remember your thirst, there isn’t enough work around here for you to do to pay for your rum.”

Ezekiel slumped onto a bench and drank the mug of rum in one gulp.

“How have you been?” Stephen asked.

“I’ve been fine, traveling around, seeing and doing things that took my interest at the time. I got married.”

“You what?” I asked, stunned at the thought that he had gotten married. “To who? When?”

Ezekiel rubbed his face with his hands, a gesture I remembered well. “If I am going to tell you all this, I need another mug.”

After Stephen filled his mug, he looked at both of us. “You are lucky men, both of you,” he said. “I always thought so. You have families and sons and daughters, good wives, houses and land.”

As he spoke I could see a bit of sadness creep onto his face, a look I had never seen on him before. “Me, I don’t have any of that. I just wander around, doing nothing of any importance, just things here and there, things that don’t really mean anything in the scheme of life. Not like the things you've done. Why, you are important men and have done real good for the villages and towns you lived in."

Stephen filled my mug as I sat there listening to the heartfelt feelings of this man I thought I knew so well. I was so absorbed in what he was saying that I didn't realize I drained my mug. "I was shore whaling for a time and thought I might like to go to sea but the ships were too small for me. I couldn't have slept anywhere except on deck and that wouldn't do. I went down to New York for a while and met a woman, Abigail Coleman. Fine woman. Pleasant to look at, gentle but had a firm hand when she needed it." He dropped his head and stared at the floor, moving his foot back and forth. "She made me happy."

He didn't continue, so we sat in the silence. He took a few sips from his mug and stared into the fire.

"When did you get married?" I asked gently.

"Seven years ago," he said, breaking into a smile at the memory. "We didn't have any children, though it was something I always wanted. We were happy for three years but then she got sick. I took care of her as best I could, with help from the women in the town, sisters, friends, you know." He stopped again, rubbing his big hands together. "She died three years and eleven months ago."

I didn't know what to say. Even after almost four years, he was still grieving.

"I am sorry for you," Stephen said.

"It was the best three years of my life. I miss her every day. I never had anyone to say that about, never had anyone love me the way Becky does you or I am sure Hannah does you," he said nodding to Stephen. "Not until I met her."

We sat staring at the flames as they danced about, sending shadows against the stones. Stephen got up and put more logs on the fire and that broke the spell.

"Well…" Ezekiel said, clearing his throat.

"Yes, well," I replied with a sad smile on my face. I was very glad that he found someone special and sad that he lost her after such a short time.

Ezekiel stayed through the winter and spring helping Stephen, me, and several others doing chores. He was with me when we learned of another attack, the worst since the war.

CHAPTER 32

I will never forget the afternoon of February 29, 1704. Ezekiel, a few others, and I were at Jennings tavern late in the day when a rider came charging in with word of an attack by the French and Indians on Deerfield just before dawn.

"Every town and village is being alerted of the danger," he said. "Most of Deerfield was destroyed. There were over 300 attackers according to the survivors... there was killing and burning everywhere in the village. Most of it is gone now, burned to the ground. They killed forty-seven men, women, and children and took over 100 captive. More than half of the town's people are gone. Almost half the houses have been burned. There is almost nothing left."

While that news was terrible by itself, what I heard next was even worse.

"A young boy escaped and made it to Hatfield shortly after the attack began. There were twenty-five men from Hatfield and Hadley that went to Deerfield as soon as they could. They got there an hour after the boy came in," the rider said. "They were all killed just outside the village."

"Who were they?" Ezekiel asked.

"Ben Wait was one," the rider said. He hesitated for a moment. "After they killed him, they skinned him."

I shut my eyes trying to block the horrible images that leapt to my mind but I could not stop them. Visions of an Indian slicing the skin from Ben's naked and bloody body caused my stomach to retch and a strong shiver shot through me. When I opened my eyes, Stephen stood with his hands against the wall, head hung down, his eyes closed. When he turned around, he looked at me.

"If they capture you or me," he said, "they will do the same to us. You know that, don't you?"

"Yes, I do," I said.

"Savages," Ezekiel said with rising anger in his voice.

"How did it happen?" I asked the rider.

"Twenty soldiers came up from Boston the other day. Everyone living outside the palisade moved in with the families inside it. There was a watchman who fell asleep last night in a barn. No one heard them coming with all the snow. There were drifts that went up to the top of the palisade in three places … sounds like the Indians walked right over the wall." I shook my head at the tragedy and felt deep sorrow for Ben.

The rider took a mug of cider and was off again, on his way to Worcester, Marlborough, and Boston. We sat quiet for a minute, lost in our own thoughts and then went home to tell our families and get them to the garrison.

Although no other attacks happened that winter, we did not let down our guard, never going anywhere without our guns, ready to get to the garrison at a moment's notice, watchful at every minute of the day.

It was a fine April morning when Ezekiel told us he was going to be leaving us.

"It's time for me to move on," he said as he, Becky and I stood outside the barn enjoying the warm air and sunshine after what was a long, cold, bleak winter.

"Do you really have to go?" Becky asked. "You could stay here, in the village, get yourself a small grant of land, make Brookfield your home."

"It would be good for you to be here," I added.

"No, I have to go. While it would be good to stay, I wouldn't be happy. After another year or so, I would get itching to move on."

"When are you leaving?" Becky asked.

"Today."

Becky was surprised. "Today? Do you have to go today?"

"Staying any longer, even a week or a day, wouldn't change things, Becky."

"Where will you go?" I asked. "What will you do?"

"I don't know," he said, "I haven't thought it out yet but it never stopped me before."

"You're not a young man Ezekiel, you can't do all that you once did."

"Neither are you," he shot back with a small smile appearing on his face.

"No, I am not."

He went into the house and got his bag full of his few belongings. He stood next to us, unsure how to say goodbye. I looked at this man, who walked into my life many years before and realized this would be the last time we would ever see each other again. I could tell from the look on his face that he understood that, too.

"It has been good to see you," I said, "especially after so many years."

Becky went into the house and came out with the iron spoon.

"Take this," she said, holding it out to him.

"And what am I going to do with this?" he asked taking it from her, turning it in his hands like it was the first time he had ever seen it.

"Keep it to remind you of us. When you look at it, think of the times you were with us whether it was at the tavern in Springfield or in Hatfield or when you saw me for the first time in Canada to now." She reached out and put her hand around his as best she could since her hands were less than half the size of his. He looked down at her. She reached up and pulled his head down so she could kiss his cheek. She turned and stepped back to stand at my side. I didn't know how to say goodbye to him so I took his hand in mine. He shook it gently with a tear in his eye and then grabbed me in a hug. I got a little teary-eyed myself. Becky was sniffling.

"I am not sure what to say," I told him.

"Neither am I," he replied.

Becky reached out and put her hand on his arm. "Please take care of yourself, no matter where you go. And remember, we will think of you and wish you well."

"Thank you," he said.

"You have been a good friend, Ezekiel," I said "One I never expected to have. We have been through a lot together, you and I, and I will miss you." For all of his rough ways, I saw the traces of a simple honest heart.

"I will miss both of you, too," he said. "Goodbye."

"Goodbye," we said.

I slid my arm around Becky's waist and pulled her close. "He's a good man," I said.

"Yes he is."

We stood there watching him walk away and realizing as we did when Ahanu left, that another part of our life was gone.

Hostilities continued throughout the spring, French privateers based out of Port Royal in Acadia seized small coastal traders for their cargo, and tried to overtake larger ships out of Boston, Newburyport, Salem, and Plymouth. While they didn't do a great deal of damage, the constant harassment needed to come to an end and in July, 500 men from the coast sailed up to Port Royal and laid siege to the town. The siege was abandoned after three weeks because of a lack of food and progress made in taking the town. The ships sailed back to Boston without victory but there were only a few attacks by the French ships for the rest of the year.

Two years went by without any further trouble but that changed when the son of one of the settlers from Quaboag was killed, along with a middle-aged widow named Tosh, in a quick attack. Judah Trumble, Jr. was the son of Judah Trumble, a teamster who lived in the eastern portion of the first settlement, halfway between our land and the other settlers. I remembered his father but didn't know the son as well. Widow Tosh was surprised in her yard, killed by a blow from a war club. Judah was shot and left. The attack was so sudden that they were not even scalped. The attackers worried about being discovered and hurried away.

Two years later a more serious attack took place on the morning of October 13, 1708. The people at Jennings Garrison heard firing in the distance towards the eastern part of the village near Woolcot's and after grabbing their guns, set out to assist their neighbors. They hadn't gotten more than two rods before they were waylaid by the Indians, a dozen of the attackers appearing from nowhere, driving Stephen, and the others back to his house. John Woolcot, a lad of twelve or fourteen, was chased by the Indians though he was on horseback, trying to ride to Jennings, and was captured after a short distance. They killed his horse, took him prisoner, and carried him to Canada. An attempt was made to ransom him but he refused to come home, deciding to stay with his captors.

The following August, two travelers, Robert Granger and John Clary, on their way to Springfield from Boston, were attacked on the Bay Path in the eastern part of town, being fired upon as they made their way along a straight wooded stretch of the road. Granger was killed at the first shot but Clary attempted to escape, riding almost half a mile before being shot. We found his horse by the side of the road a few yards from Clary's body. Neither of them was scalped showing that once again it was a quick attack, the Indians not wanting to stay in the area for longer than it took to kill.

In 1710, on a hot and humid July morning, two groups of us set out to hay a large meadow down by the river. It was about 100 acres, on a long sloping hill with a fine view of the river. We hayed four times during the growing season and this would be our second time. We were to start out shortly after sunrise for the two-mile walk.

Well before the sun cleared the horizon, I was up and in the barn, keeping watch on our most productive cow as she gave birth. Something was wrong because it was taking far too long. She had been in labor since early the previous night. Ephraim was going out with the first group; I told him that I would be out as soon as I could. About mid-morning, the calf was born and the mother cleaned and began to feed it. I got my scythe and gun and headed to join the others.

When I got there, seven men including Ephraim were in the lower part of the meadow closest to the river. The others, whom I joined, were in the upper meadow within fifty rods of the Bay Path. I took up a spot, laid my gun down and began working, moving the scythe in long sweeping strokes, slicing the grass a few inches from the ground. We worked on with a little talk now and then between us. When we rested, I looked toward the other group but could not see them for they were at the bottom of the slope of the hill. Just as we were about to get back to haying, we heard two shots followed by three more. I dropped my scythe and ran back to get my gun. I had worked away from it and it took me some time to get to it. By the time I had it and began running to down the hill, I saw seven Indians moving up from the river toward us. Five men were lying on the ground, I presumed they were dead. John White was running to us, yelling although he was too far away to hear what he was saying. He held his right hip as he ran. Ephraim was behind John running fast so as to give John a hand to escape. We watched the Indians reload and take aim. As I ran I realized I would not get there in time to prevent them from shooting. I ran as fast as my legs would take me, watching those savages take aim at my second son and could do nothing about it. One of our men fell as he ran, his gun flying up in the air almost hitting me as he went down. Three Indians aimed at Ephraim and John. They fired and both men went down. I yelled at the top of my voice and doubled my efforts to get to my son. As I got within range I saw Ephraim get up and begin to run again, keeping low, his hand to his right shoulder. I stopped and brought my gun up and fired. At that range I couldn't do any lethal damage but to my surprise, an Indian dropped but was soon on his feet being dragged off by the other attackers. Our other men fired but to no avail. The Indians were now out of range and moving away as fast as they could toward the river.

When I got to Ephraim, I saw the blood coming from his shoulder. He was shot in the back of the shoulder, the ball coming out cleanly and not breaking any bone. I took off my shirt, ripped a sleeve off, and wrapped it around his wound as best I could. The others ran to the men on the ground. Six were killed in the space of those few moments; John White, his brother in law John Grosvenor, who was brother of our last minister, William Grosvenor; young Joe Kellogg from Hadley, only seventeen years old but already received a grant of twenty acres; Ebenezer Hayward, who was from Concord but stationed at the garrison until a year ago when he got a grant of land.

My grief became almost intolerable when I saw Stephen laying on the ground face down, blood soaking into his shirt. Only a few feet to his right lay his son Benjamin, just twenty years old, named after our friend Ben Wait. I was almost overcome as I stood there. I knelt and gently turned Stephen over. He was shot in the back, the ball coming out the middle of his chest. I looked down at my friend, the thoughts of our adventures going through my mind for a second.

"Everyone with a gun, follow me. We're going to get these savages!" I said, grabbing my gun and heading toward the river. Only three men came with me, the others having left their guns at home. We ran to where we last saw the Indians. Out of the corner of my eye, I saw something move. It was a boy, maybe fourteen years old, tall, and slender, holding a gun so old that it looked like it would barely shoot. Tom Gilbert fired, missing the boy but alerting them to our presence. I expected the Indians to fire at us but nothing happened. I ran towards the boy and saw he was lagging behind the other Indians, the weight of the gun slowing him down. I put my gun to my shoulder and aimed at his back. I had a clear shot but something stopped me from pulling the trigger. The way the boy stood, his build and long hair on the left side of his head, all reminded me of my old friend William. By the time I remembered what they did to Stephen and the others, the Indians were out of range. The boy disappeared with the rest.

When we got back to the dead, a cart was brought out, led by an old gray horse. It was a forlorn site, one that filled me with sorrow. I had enough of the killing. I'd seen too much in my life and wished with all my heart that it would end.

We loaded the bodies into the cart. Ephraim was sitting up, able to talk but was still losing blood. We put him in the back of the cart, sitting next to Ben's body, and made our way back to the village. When we got to the top of the hill near the tavern, people were coming toward us, alerted by the gunshots. Hannah, Stephen's wife, came running out of the house, looking for her men. She saw me and began yelling.

"Jack, where are they? Where are Stephen and Ben? Where are they?"

I told her as gently as I could.

Hannah was beside herself with grief. As I watched her sobs wrack her entire body, it occurred to me that this is the second time I saw a new widow standing in almost the same spot, after learning the news of her husband's death. Susannah Ayres was the first, breaking down when I told her that her husband John had been one of eight men killed in the ambush back in

1675. It was, in some ways, as if I was re-living that moment again, a moment I hoped to forget but knew I never could.

By this time, others from the village came to see what was happening. Becky and Ephraim's wife Jane came running; she knelt beside her husband. They got him to the tavern where Becky took over, cleaning and washing the wound before sewing it with a large needle and heavy thread. Jane held his hand.

All eyes were on me as I placed my gun in the corner by the door.

"What happened?" was the question everyone asked. I told them all that I knew and said that someone should ride to Springfield to let Colonel Pynchon know and raise the alarm. Three of the men offered to go together for safety and were off in a short time.

There were six funerals in two days in our little village. Coffins were built in the early morning hours of the day after the attack. Each of the men was laid out at home, being washed, and dressed by their wives. Stephen, Ben, John Grosvenor, and John Kellogg were buried in the old burial ground we began at the start of the first settlement in 1665. John White and Ebenezer Hayward were buried at their homes.

A pall settled over the village, each house filled with both sadness from the loss of our men, our friends, and growing anger at the Indians and despair as to what we could do to stop the attacks. Soldiers came in the day after the attack and did what they always do, chase after Indians that are long since gone and will most likely never be found. Though the custom was for a small feast at the deceased's house, it was as if, by unspoken agreement, no gathering took place.

The deaths took the life out of me, pushing me down into a dark hole. I couldn't get the thought out of my mind that I too could have been killed if they attacked the group I was with instead of Stephen's.

Ephraim recovered well, though he had some trouble using his right arm, especially when bad weather came on.

No other attacks ever happened again in Brookfield.

CHAPTER 33

Time goes faster the older you get, until your life seems to have gone by in an instant. Becky and I watched the world change around us faster than we ever thought possible.

Her health began failing slowly, with pain in her knees and hands and terrible colds, each lasting longer than the preceding one. There were times when I would sit by the fire and watch her, much as I did on our early days together. It was difficult for me to accept that the beautiful woman I cherished and loved for so many years was now getting weaker by the month. Her hands were swollen to the point where she could do almost no work. The grandchildren helped us quite a bit and Sarah came to live with us. Her husband, a good man he was, got kicked in the head by a horse, and couldn't work after that. He was sick off and on for a few months before he died at thirty-one, leaving Sarah a young widow.

Becky got worse, most days not being able to get out of bed, and at times confused and not recognizing me or anyone else. Other times her mind was good, though she knew she could not remember things. At those times when she was aware of all that was going on around her, she would look at me with questioning eyes. That was the hardest part, seeing her like that, knowing there was nothing I could do to stop it.

Three months went by with her getting worse. Ephraim and Sam would come by each day to see their mother. The grandchildren would come to see her, hoping she was awake and could talk to them for when she could not they were nervous, unsure of what to do, never having seen anyone in this condition before.

It was a beautiful late October morning. The sky was a brilliant blue, with the sunshine and a soft breeze gently turning the yellow, red and gold leaves on the stem, causing them to float gently to the ground. It was just like the day years ago when Becky and I were young on the beach in Ipswich when we had our first kiss.

I sat by her bed, gently holding her hand in mine. We were alone in the house, as Sarah had gone to one of the neighbors.

Becky struggled to open her eyes. There was a terrible sadness in her face. “Am I going to die?”

“Yes.” I said. There was no other way to respond.

“I don’t want to leave you,” she said softly.

“You won’t leave me and I won’t leave you. I’ll always be with you.”

She sighed and gave me a weak, sad smile. “I love you, Jack,” she said, putting her other hand on mine.

“I love you, too. Thank you for sharing such a wonderful life with me.”

She looked at me with her soft green eyes, and asked me to hold her one more time. I held her for a long time, cradled her in my arms. I kissed her softly just like our first kiss on the dunes in Ipswich and held it, my lips touching hers for a sweet, wonderful moment.

I held her in my arms for a long time remembering all of the wonderful moments we shared … until I felt her take her last breath. I didn’t let go. I just sat holding her, not believing that she was gone, crying my tears of sorrow, of loss, of pain. My heart ached as it never did before as I relived those moments from our life together. I placed her gently on the bed and folded her hands together, kissed her on the forehead, and went out to tell the children.

I made her coffin, not wanting anyone else to help in what I considered a solemn right of the bereaved. I did

not think of my doing this to bury my wife but just as something that had to be done, possibly because I did not wish to face the reality that my love was gone and no more would I be able to look upon her face as she cooked, or feel her touch, or the warmth of her body in bed next to me or when I put my arms around her as I did so many times.

When her coffin was complete, I went into the house. Jane, Anne, and Hannah had washed her. I asked them to leave and wait outside until I called for them. I went and sat next to the bed, looking at her face, the face I realized I would never see again after this day, the woman who I met as a little girl sixty years before. The memories flooded back as my tears flowed, thinking of all the moments in our life together, missing her the times I went to Boston to that horrible merchant as an apprentice, to coming to this very village and leaving her in Ipswich, to her family coming here, to the birth of Sam and the rest of our children, the long, hard journey to Canada to rescue her, our son, and the others, the difficult years after we returned to Brookfield, and the last couple of years as we grew even closer, knowing our time together was coming to an end.

My life would never be the same from the moment she died. With these thoughts racking my heart, I took her hand in mine.

"Becky, my love. You have been my best friend since we were children and I love you more than any man can possibly love a woman. You were everything to me and I will miss you terribly every moment of every day until I join you."

I cried for another bit of time, how long I do not know, but I heard a soft knock on the door and turned to see Sam, poking his head in the door. His eyes were red from crying.

"Are you ready?" he asked.

I sat without answering him until he closed the door. I stayed for another bit just looking at my wife, trying to imagine my life without her and not being able to. I kissed her on the lips one last time, ran my fingers across her cheek, smoothed her hair, and kissed her on the forehead. I went to the door and called Sam and Ephraim. I saw that her coffin was in the cart and I told them to bring it in. I gently lifted her into my arms and put her into the coffin. We were all crying now, the boys having difficulty saying good-bye to their mother. I turned away to let the boys say goodbye, and then we gently lifted the coffin out the door and onto the cart.

I do not remember going from the house to the burial ground. I was too overcome to notice anything. Next I knew we were standing at the grave. I did not know who dug it because I had not asked anyone to, the thought never occurring to me. A memory of standing next to my mother's grave when I was just fourteen came back to me now. I shook it off and looked at the coffin on the cart next to me. Without a word, we lifted the coffin off the cart. Within a moment it was resting in the cold earth. I stood there unaware of the others as the flood of sorrow swept through me.

The new minister, Reverend Thomas Cheney, came to Brookfield a month before, being ordained a little more than a week before Becky's death. This was his first funeral oration.

"You always knew that your loved ones and friends must die; to grieve that they were mortal, is but to grieve that they were but men.

"If your friends are in heaven, how unsuitable is it, for you to be overmuch mourning for them, when they are rapt into the highest joys with Christ; and love should teach you to rejoice with them that rejoice, and not to mourn as those that have no hope.

"For your Godly loved ones and friends you must mourn for the sake of yourselves and others, because God has removed such as were blessings to those about them. For old, tired Christians your sorrow should be least, and your joy and thanks for their happiness should be greatest.

"Remember how quickly you must be with them again. The expectation of living on yourselves is the cause of your excessive grief for the death of loved ones and friends. If you looked yourselves to die tomorrow, or within a few weeks, you would less grieve that your friends are gone before you. Remember also that the world is not for one generation only; others must have our places when we are gone; God will be served by successive generations, and not only by one.

"Death is a comfort to us all whether poor or rich for one hour of death will make all alike. You grow old like others, then you shall fall sick like others, then you shall die like others, then you shall be buried like others, then you shall be consumed like others, then you shall be judged like others." He looked at me and bowed his head.

I wiped my eyes with my sleeve, took the shovel, and gently placed dirt onto the coffin. I handed the shovel to Sam, our first-born, and he handed it to Ephraim. He gave it back to me and I, as her husband, filled in the grave. The others left me there, my hands folded, silent tears running down my face, my thoughts swirling of the events of our life together. After what must have been a long time, for I realized the breeze turned into a wind, shaking me out of my state, I saw the sun had moved westward in the sky. I knelt on the ground and took a handful of the dirt covering my wife's grave in my hand.

"You will never be far from me Becky. I will hold you in my heart forever. When I wake in the morning my first thought will be of you. When I lay in bed at night my last thought of the day will be of you. I will never forget the life we had together," I said, the tears pouring from my eyes, my hands shaking. I stood and, wiping my eyes with my hand, walked away knowing I could never forget the woman of my dreams.

CHAPTER 34

It was just yesterday that I was a young man with a new wife starting out on our life together.

It is good to have many people in such a prosperous place as Brookfield, but it is difficult too, for I still see it in my mind's eye as it was when I first came here as an eighteen year old man. Some of the beauty had been taken away by the houses and mills. As I went by various houses, I remembered the fields that were there years ago, where I would see William and Oota, my young Indian friends. One of those places was where I kissed Oota, something that I probably should not have done but I am now too old for regrets. My life happened the way that it did based on the decisions I made in the circumstances I found myself.

I feel lost and useless, taking no part in the active goings on around me. I watched them build the meetinghouse, doddering around like an old fool, seeing the young men roll their eyes when I make a suggestion or give some word of advice. They don't realize that I know my condition and don't need to be reminded of it by some wise young men who were not yet born when I was in Canada.

I spend a lot of time now remembering how things were since I am more comfortable in my memories than I am with life today. I see what the world will be like years from now, long after I am gone. I see it in my grandchildren's eyes and hear it in their voices.

I am content to know that I was a good son, nephew, soldier, husband, father, and grandfather. I did what I believed was right although there were times when I was not.

Now my body has constant aches and pains that it never did before. I am not able to do all that I could in the past. Over the last couple of years, I have had to slow down and accept that I just cannot do everything like I used to do. My eyesight is failing; I have trouble seeing things at a distance and sometimes close up. My hands are sore all the time and shake now and then, not much but enough for people to notice and to remind me of my age.
My hand shakes so the quill scratches the page and doesn't let me get my thoughts down as well as I want.

It is a humbling feeling, the realization of your age. I sleep now at times I never did before, usually in the late afternoon. I was dozing before I wrote this. That is when I dream of days gone by, times from my youth. They are now all good dreams, happy dreams. I get to relive some wonderful times, feeling the same feelings I did when they first happened to me fifty years ago. When I wake from my afternoon dreams, it sometimes takes me a minute to realize where I am but it is only a momentary confusion.

I dream of Tinker often. He was my first dog, the best of dogs, better than any of the dogs I've met since. He was a black dog, heavy and wide, but with a sly, happy look in his brown eyes. He loved to run, play, and hunt. I can still feel the cool October air as we walked to the marshes to hunt ducks and smell the crisp, clean air in the early November mornings when we would hunt for turkeys. I remember the time he flushed a dozen large turkeys, who seemed riled at his intrusion into their peaceful world, which landed on a large tree branch fifty feet from me. They did not move as I shot six of them. We feasted for two weeks until we were all sick of turkey.

I dream of Bubs, the horse that carried me so many miles on so many adventures. We rode for Mr. Pynchon all over the Bay Colony, fought in seven military battles that almost ended both our lives more than once. I remember seeing him when I was a boy, nuzzling his head into my father's shoulder, keeping it there for a minute, my father patting his neck and talking to him in low tones, just as I did after my father died, before he was saddled or put to work. I cried, as did Becky, when Bubs died, what is it now? ten or fifteen years ago, although it seems much less time has passed than that.

I dream of Becky, oh how I dream of Becky. Sometimes the dreams are so sweet, so real, I wake up with silent tears running down my face. I wipe them away with my hand, feeling so alone, more alone than any other time in my life.

The sadness of being alone is overwhelming. It crushes my feelings to the point of numbness. My thoughts seem far away and everything is distant. Seeing other people's joy and happiness brings no feelings to me, I could care less if they are happy or sad. I do not care about anything; I just do not want to be alone anymore. To know that I cannot not be with her is almost too much to bear, that she is somewhere I cannot be hurts like very few things have in my life. I have been injured in many ways many times in my life, but none of that pain comes close to the hurt I am feeling.

I am lost without Becky and miss her so much, more than I can say in words. Our time together went too quickly. It seems like just yesterday we were young and in love. Now she is gone and I am old and alone. I expect to die soon too because none of us live forever. I want to be with her again so badly. I do not fear death any more than I feared being born. I think of her many times each day, when I wake up and before I go to sleep and many times in between. I go to tell her something or think of something she would find funny and realize she is gone. My world turns dark at those moments when it all comes back to me in a black sorrow that crowds my heart. I wish it were otherwise but it is not and, like many things in life, you must accept what you are given and make the very best of it.

We traveled through many a time and place, you and me, and now I am at the end of my story. I have nothing more to tell you.

May God bless all that go after me, both family and friends, keep them safe from all harm, and give them happiness and prosperity throughout their life.

Postscript:

July 15, 1721

I found my father's journal in a small wooden chest my mother gave him soon after they married.

This will be the last entry.

My father, Jack Parker, died last month at the age of 67. He was a good man, well respected by all, and loved by many.

We will miss him.

Ephraim Parker

Writing this book is not something I could do by myself.

Special thanks to:

My editor extraordinaire Cristy Bertini for a wonderful job of making this story the best it can be.

My readers Bill Jankins, Van Leichter, Jeff Fiske, Cynthia Kennison, Ralmon Black, and Carrie Feliciano, who provided invaluable suggestions, comments, and criticisms.

My wonderful wife Barbara, who was always there to provide much needed encouragement and support.

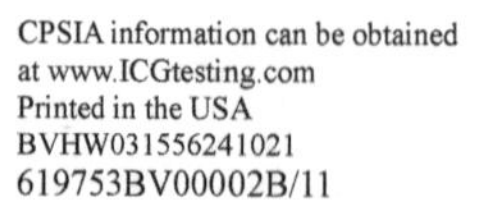

CPSIA information can be obtained
at www.ICGtesting.com
Printed in the USA
BVHW031556241021
619753BV00002B/11